to Manse and Jane Brackney

Contents

Anybody not a scientific illiterate knew it was impossible to get power from the atomic nucleus. Then uranium fission came along.

It was easy to show that energy projectors—the 'ray guns' of popular fiction—must necessarily be hotter at the source than at the target, and thus were altogether impractical. Then someone invented the laser.

Obviously spaceships must expel mass to gain velocity, and their crews must undergo acceleration pressure at all times when they were not in free fall, and must never demean themselves with daydreams about manoeuvres akin to those of a water boat or an aircraft. Then people were iconoclastic enough to discover how to generate artificial positive and negative gravity fields.

The stars were plainly out of reach, unless one was willing to plod along slower than light. Einstein's equations proved it beyond the ghost of a doubt. Then the quantum hyperjump was found, and suddenly faster-than-light ships were swarming across this arm of the galaxy.

One after another, the demonstrated impossibilities have evaporated, the most basic laws of nature have turned out to possess clauses in fine print, the prison bars of our capabilities have gone down before irreverent hacksaws. He would be rash indeed who claimed that there is any absolutely certain knowledge or any forever unattainable goal.

I am just that kind of fool. I hereby state, flatly and unequivocally, that some facts of life are eternal. They are human facts, to be sure. *Mutatis mutandis*, they probably apply to each intelligent race on each inhabited planet in the universe; but I do not insist on that point. What I do declare is that man, the child of Earth, lives by certain principles which are immutable.

They include:

(1) Parkinson's Laws:

(First) Work increases to occupy all organization available to do it.

(Second) Expenditures rise with income.

(2) Sturgeon's Revelation: Ninety per cent of *everything* is crud.

(3) Murphy's Law: Anything that can go wrong, will.

(4) The Fourth Law of Thermodynamics: Everything takes longer and costs more.

My assertion is not so unguarded as may appear, because characteristics like these form part of my definition of man.

—Vance Hall, *Commentaries on the Philosophy of Noah Arkwright*

The Three-cornered Wheel

'No!'

Rebo Legnor's-Child, Marchwarden of Gilrigor, sprang back from the picture as if it had come alive. 'What are you thinking of?' he gasped. 'Burn that thing! Now!' One hand lifted shakily towards the fire in the great brazier, whose flames relieved a little the gloom of the audience chamber. 'Over there. I saw nothing and you showed me nothing. Do you understand?'

David Falkayn let fall the sheet of paper on which he had made the sketch. It fluttered to the table, slowly through an air pressure a fourth again as great as Earth's. 'What——' His voice broke in a foolish squeak. Annoyance at that crowded out fear. He braced his shoulders and regarded the Ivanhoan squarely. 'What is the matter?' he asked. 'It is just a drawing.'

'Of the *malkino*.' Rebo shuddered. 'And you not even belonging to our kind, let alone a Consecrate.'

Falkayn stared at him, as if anyone of Terrestrial descent could read expressions on that unhuman face. Seen by the dull red sunlight slanting through narrow windows, Rebo looked more like a lion than a man, and not very much like either. The body was only roughly anthropoid : bipedal, two-armed, but short and thick in the torso, long and thick in the limbs, with a forward-leaning posture that reduced a sheer two metres of height to approximately Falkayn's level. The three fingers had one more joint than a man's, and narrow black nails; the thumbs were on the opposite side of the hands from those of Genus Homo; the feet were digitigrade. Mahogany fur covered the entire skin, but each hair bore tiny barbs, so that the effect was of rough plumage. The head was blocky and round-eared, the face flat, noseless, with breathing apertures below the angle of the great jaws and enormous green eyes above an astonishingly sensitive, almost womanlike mouth. But whatever impression that conveyed was overwhelmed by the tawny leonine mane which framed the countenance and spilled down the muscular back, and by the tufted tail that lashed the ankles. A pair of short scaly trousers and a leather baldric, from which hung a wicked-looking axe, enhanced the wild effect.

Nevertheless, Falkayn knew, inside that big skull was a brain as good as his own. The trouble was, it had not evolved on Earth. And when, in addition to every inborn strangeness, the mind was shaped by a culture that no man really understood ... how much communication was possible?

The boy wet his lips. The dry cold air of Ivanhoe had chapped them. He didn't lay a hand on his blaster, but he became acutely aware of its comforting drag at his hip. Somehow he found words:

'I beg your pardon if I have given offence. You will understand that foreigners may often transgress through ignorance. Can you tell me what is wrong?'

Rebo's taut crouch eased a trifle. His eyes, seeing further into the red end of the spectrum than Falkayn's, probed corners which were shadows to the visitor. No one else stood on the floor or behind the grotesquely carved stone pillars. Only the yellow flames acrackle in the brazier, the acridity of smoke from unearthly wood, stirred in the long room. Outside—it seemed suddenly very far away—Falkayn heard the endless wind of the Gilrigor uplands go booming.

'Yes,' the Marchwarden said, 'I realize you acted unwittingly. And you, for your part, should not doubt that I remain friendly to you—not just because you are my guest at this moment, but because of the fresh breath you have brought to this stagnant land of ours.'

'That we have perhaps brought,' Falkayn corrected. 'The future depends on whether we live or die, remember. And that in turn depends on your help.' *Well put!* he congratulated himself. *Schuster ought to have heard that. Maybe then he'd stop droning at me about how I'll never make merchant status if I don't learn to handle words.*

'I will not be able to help you if they flay me,' Rebo answered sharply. 'Burn that thing, I say.'

Falkayn squinted through the murk at his drawing. It showed a large flatbed wagon with eight wheels, to be drawn by a team of twenty fastigas. All the way from the spaceship to this castle, he had been aglow with visions of how awed and delighted the noble would be. He had seen himself, no longer Davy-this-and-Davy-that, hey-boy-c'mere, apprentice and unpaid personal servant to Master Polesotechnician Martin Schuster: but Falkayn of Hermes, a Prometheus come to Larsum with the gift of the wheel. *What's gone wrong?* he thought wildly; and then, with the bitterness common at his seventeen years: *Why does everything always go wrong?*

Nevertheless he crossed the floor of inland shells and cast the paper into the brazier. It flared up and crumbled to ash.

Turning, he saw that Rebo had relaxed. The Marchwarden poured himself a cupful of wine from a carafe on the table and tossed it off at a gulp. 'Good,' he rumbled. 'I wish you could partake with me. It is distressful not to offer refreshment to a guest.'

'You know that your foods would poison my race,' Falkayn said. 'That is one reason why we must transport the work-maker from Gilrigor to our ship, and soon. Will you tell me what is bad about the device I have illustrated? It can be easily built. Its kind—*wagons*, we call them—were among the most important things my people ever invented. They had much to do with our becoming more than——'

He checked himself just before he said 'savages' or 'bar-barians'. Rebo's hereditary job was to keep such tribes on their proper side of the Kasunian Mountains. Larsum was a civilized country, with agriculture, metallurgy, towns, roads, trade, a literate class.

But no wheels. Burdens went on the backs of citizens or their animals, by boat, by travois, by sledge in winter—never on wheels. Now that he thought about it, Falkayn remembered that not even rollers were employed.

'The idea is that round objects turn,' he floundered.

Rebo traced a sign in the air. 'Best not to speak of it.' He changed his mind with soldierly briskness. 'However, we must. Very well, then. The fact is that the *malkino* is too holy to be put to base use. The penalty for transgressing this law is death by flaying, lest God's wrath fall on the entire land.'

Falkayn struggled with the language. The educator tapes aboard the *What Cheer* had given him fluency, but could not convey a better idea of semantic subtleties than the first ex-pedition to Ivanhoe had got; and those men hadn't stayed many weeks. The word he mentally translated as 'holy' implied more than dedication to spiritual purposes. There were over-tones of potency, mana, and general ineffability. Never mind.

13

'What does *malkino* mean?'

'A ... a roundedness. I may not draw it for you, only a Consecrate may do that. But it is something perfectly round.'

'Ah, I see. A *circle*, we would call it, or a *sphere* if solid. A wheel is circular. Well, I suppose we could make our wheels slightly imperfect.'

'No.' The maned head shook. 'Until the imperfection became so gross that the wheels would not work anyway, the thing is impossible. Even if the Consecrates would allow it—and I know quite well they will not, as much from hostility to you as from dogma—the peasants would rise in horror and butcher you.' Rebo's eyes glowed in the direction of Falkayn's gun. 'Yes, I realize you have powerful, fire-throwing weapons. But there are only four of you. What avail against thousands of warriors, shooting from the cover of hills and woods?'

Falkayn harked back to what he had see in Aesca, on his westward ride along the Sun's Way, and now in this stronghold. Architecture was based on sharp-cornered polygons. Furniture and utensils were square or oblong. The most ceremonial objects, like Rebo's golden wine goblet, went no further than to employ elliptical cross-sections, or mere arcs of true circles.

He felt ill with dismay. 'Why?' he choked. 'What makes a ... a figure ... so holy?'

'Well——' Rebo lowered himself uncomfortably to a chair, draping his tail over the rest across the back. He fiddled with his octagonal axe haft and didn't look at the other. 'Well, ancient usage. I can read, of course, but I am no scholar. The Consecrates can tell you more. Still ... the circle and the sphere are the signs of God. In a way, they are God. You see them in the sky. The sun and the moons are spheres. So is the world, however imperfect; and the Consecrates say that the planets have the same shape, and the stars are set inside the great ball of the universe. All the heavenly bodies move in circles. And, well, circle and sphere are the perfect shapes. Are they not? Everything perfect is a direct manifestation of God.'

Remembering a little about Classical Greek philosophy—even if the human colony on Hermes had broken away from Earth and established itself as a grand duchy, it remained proud of its heritage and taught ancient history in the schools—Falkayn could follow that logic. His impulse was to blurt: 'You're wrong! No planet or star is a true globe, and orbits are ellipses, and your damned little red dwarf sun isn't the centre of the cosmos anyway. I've been out there and I know!' but Schuster had drilled enough caution into him that he checked himself. He'd accomplish nothing but to stiffen the enmity of the priests, and perhaps add the enmity of Rebo, who still wanted to be his friend.

How could he prove a claim that went against three or four thousand years of tradition? Larsum was a single country, cut off by mountain, desert, ocean, and howling savages from the rest of the world. It had no more than the vaguest rumours of what went on beyond its borders. From Rebo's standpoint, the only reasonable supposition was that the furless aliens with the beaks above their mouths had flown here from some distant continent. Reviewing the first expedition's reports of how upset and indignant the Consecrates at Aesca had got when told that its ship came from the stars, how hotly they had denied the possibility, Schuster had cautioned his fellows to avoid that topic. The only thing which mattered was to get the hell off this planet before they starved to death.

Falkayn's shoulders slumped. 'My people have found in their travels that it does not pay to dispute the religious beliefs of others,' he said. 'Very well, I grant you wheels are forbidden. But then what can we do?'

Rebo looked up again with his disconcertingly intelligent gaze. He was no ham-headed medieval baron, Falkayn realized. His civilization was old, and the rough edges had been worn off its warrior class, off peasants and artisans and traders, as well as the priest-scribe-poet-artist-engineer-scientist Consecrates. Rebo Legnor's-Child might be likened to an ancient samurai, if any parallels to human history were possible. He'd grasped the principle of the wheel at once, and——

'Understand, I, and many of my breed, feel more than simply benevolent towards your kind,' he said low. 'When the first ship came, several years ago, a lightning flash went through the land. Many of us hoped it meant the end of ... of certain irksome restrictions. Dealing with civilized outlanders should bring new knowledge, new powers, new ways of life, into this realm where nothing has changed for better than two millennia. I want most sincerely to help you, for my own gain as well as yours.'

Besides the need for tact, Falkayn hadn't the heart to answer that the Polesotechnic League had no interest in trading with Larsum, or with any other part of Ivanhoe. There was nothing here that other worlds didn't produce better and cheaper. The first expedition had simply come in search of a place to establish an emergency repair depot, and this planet was simply the least unsalubrious one in this stellar neighbourhood. The expedition had observed from orbit that Larsum possessed the most advanced culture. They landed, made contact, learned the language and a little bit of the folklore, then asked permission to erect a large building which none but visitors like themselves would be able to enter.

The request was grudgingly granted, less because of the metals offered in payment than because the Consecrates feared trouble if they refused. Even so, they demanded that the construction be well away from the capital; evidently they wanted to minimize the number of Larsans who might be contaminated by foreign ideas. Having completed the job and bestowed an arbitrary name on the planet, the expedition departed. Their data, with appropriate educator tapes, were issued to all ships that might take the Pleiades route. Everybody hoped that it would never be necessary to use the information. But luck had run out for the *What Cheer*.

Falkayn said only: 'I do not see how you can help. What other way can that thing be moved, than on a wagon?'

'Could it not be taken apart, moved piece by piece, and put back together at your ship? I can supply a labour force.'

'No.' Damn! How do you explain the construction of a unitized thermonuclear generator to somebody who's never seen a water-wheel? You don't. 'Except for minor attachments, it cannot be disassembled, at least not without tools which we do not carry.'

'Are you certain that it weighs too much to be transported on skids?'

'Over roads like yours, yes, I think it does. If this were winter, perhaps a sledge would suffice. But we will be dead before snow falls again. Likewise, a barge would do, but no navigable streams run anywhere near, and we would not survive the time necessary to dig a canal.'

Not for the first time Falkayn cursed the depot builders that they hadn't included a gravity sled with the other stored equipment. But then, every ship carried one or more gravity sleds. Who could have foreseen that the *What Cheer's* would be out of commission? Or that she couldn't at least hop over to the building herself? Or, if anybody thought of such possibilities, they must have reasoned that a wagon could be made; the xenologists had noted that wheels were unknown, and never thought to ask if that was because of a law. A portable crane had certainly been provided, to load and unload whatever was needed for spaceship repair. In fact, so well stocked was the depot that it did not include food, because any crew who could limp here at all should be able to fix their craft in a few days.

'And I daresay no other vessel belonging to your nation will arrive in time to save you,' Rebo said.

'No. The ... the distances we cover in our travels are great beyond comprehension. We were bound for a remote frontier world—country, if you prefer—to open certain negotiations about trade rights. To avoid competition, we left secretly. Nobody at our destination has any idea that we are coming, and our superiors at home do not expect us back for several months. By the time they begin to worry and start a search— and it will take weeks to visit every place where we might have landed—our food stocks will long have been exhausted. We carried minimal supplies, you see, in order to be heavily laden with valuables for—uh——'

'For bribes.' Rebo made a sound that might correspond to a chuckle. 'Yes. Well, then, we must think of something else. I repeat, I will do anything I can to help you. The building was erected here, rather than in some other marchland, because I insisted; and that was precisely because I hoped to see more of your voyagers.' His hand went back to his axe. Falkayn had noticed before that the heads of implements were heat-shrunk to the handles. Now the reason came to him: rivets would be sacrilegious. The fingers closed with a snap and Rebo said harshly:

'I am as pious as the next person, but I cannot believe God meant the Consecrates to freeze every life in Larsum into an eternal pattern. There was an age of heroes once, before Ourato brought Uplands and Lowlands together beneath him. Such an age can come again, if the grip upon us is broken.'

He seemed to realize he had said too much and added in

haste, 'Let us not speak of such high matters, though. The important thing is to get that workmaker to your wounded ship. If you and I can think of no lawful means, perhaps your comrades can. So take them back the word—the Marchwarden of Gilrigor cannot allow them to make a, a wagon; but he remains their well-wisher.'

'Thank you,' Falkayn mumbled. Abruptly the darkness of the room became stifling. 'I had best start back tomorrow.'.

'So soon? You had a hard trip here, and a short and unhappy conversation. Aesca is so far off that a day or two of rest cannot make any difference.'

Falkayn shook his head. 'The sooner I return, the better. We have not much time to lose, you know.'

II

A fresh fastiga—slightly larger than a horse, long-eared, long-snouted, feathery-furred, with a loud bray and a piny smell—waited in the cruciform courtyard. A remount and pack animal were strung behind. A guardsman held the leader's bridle. He wore a breast-plate of reinforced leather, a helmeting network of iron-studded straps woven into his mane, and a broad-bladed spear across his back. Beyond him, lesser folk moved across the cobblestones: servants in livery of black and yellow shorts, drably clad peasants, a maneless female in a loose tunic. Around them bulked the four squat stone buildings that sheltered the household, linked by outer walls in which were the gates. At each corner of the square, a watchtower lifted its battlements in to the deep greenish sky.

'Are you certain you do not wish an escort?' Rebo asked.

'There is no danger in riding alone, is there?' Falkayn replied.

'Gr-rm ... no, I suppose not. I keep this region well patrolled. God speed you, then.'

Falkayn shook hands, a Larsan custom, too. The Marchwarden's three long fingers and oppositely placed thumb fitted awkwardly into a human grasp. For a moment more they looked at each other.

The bulky garments Falkayn wore against the chill disguised his youthful slenderness. He was towheaded and blue-eyed, with a round face and a freckled snub nose that cost him much secret anguish. A baron's son from Hermes should look lean and dashing. To be sure, he was a younger son, and one who had got himself expelled from the ducal militechnic academy. The reason was harmless enough, a prank which had been traced to him by merest chance; but his father decided he had better seek his fortune elsewhere. So he had gone to Earth, and Martin Schuster of the Polesotechnic League had taken him on as an apprentice and instead of the glamour and adventure which interstellar merchants were supposed to enjoy, there had been hard work and harder study. He had given a whoop when his master told him to ride here alone and arrange for local help. It was vastly disappointing that he couldn't stay awhile.

'Thank you for everything,' he said. He swung himself into the saddle with less grace than he'd hoped, under a gravity fifteen per cent greater than Earth's. The guard let go the bridle and he rode out the eastern gate.

A village nestled below the castle walls, cottages of dove-tailed timber with sod roofs. Beyond them that highroad called the Sun's Way plunged downhill towards the distant Trammina Valley. It wasn't much of a road. The dirt surface was rough, weed-tufted, bestrewn with rocks which melting snows had carried down year after year from the upper slopes. Not far ahead, the path snaked around a tor and climbed again, steeply.

Falkayn glanced southward. The depot gleamed white on a ridge, like Heaven's gate before Lucifer. Otherwise he himself was the only sign of humankind. Coarse grey grass and thorny trees stretched over the hills, with here and there a flock of grazing beasts watched by a mounted herder. At his back, the Kasunian Mountains rose in harsh snow peaks, a wall across the world. One great moon hung ghostly above them. The ember-coloured sun had just cleared the horizon towards which he rode.

Wind roared hollowly, thrusting at his face. He shivered. Ivanhoe was not terribly cold, in this springtime of the middle northern latitudes; the dense atmosphere gave considerable greenhouse effect. But the bloody light made him feel forever chilled. And the fastiga's cloven hooves beat the stones with a desolate sound.

Forgetting that he was Falkayn of Hermes, merchant prince, he pulled the radio transceiver from his pocket and thumbed the switch. Hundreds of kilometres away, an intercom buzzed. 'Hullo,' he said rather thinly. 'Hullo, *What Cheer*. Anybody there?'

'*Sí*.' Engineer Romulo Pasqual's voice came from the box. 'Is that you. Davy *muchacho*?'

Falkayn was so glad of this little company that for once he didn't resent being patronized. 'Yes. How's everything?'

'As before. Krish is brooding. Martin has gone to the temple again. He said it would probably be no use trying to talk them out of their prohibition on the wheel that you called us about last night. I?' Falkayn could almost see the Italian shrug. 'I sit here and try to figure how we can move a couple of tons of generator without wheels. A sort of giant stoneboat, *quizá*?'

'No. I thought of that, too, and discussed the notion with Rebo, when we spent a lot of the dark period hunting for ideas. Not over a road like this.'

'Are you certain? If we hitch enough peasants and animals to the thing——'

'We can't get them. Rebo himself, if he drafted all the people and critters he can spare—remember, this is the planting season in a subsistence economy, and he also has to mount guard against the barbarians—doubts if there'd be enough power to haul such a load over some of these upgrades.'

'You said that quite a few of the *caballero* class were disgruntled with the priests. If they contributed, too——'

'It'd take a long time to arrange that, probably too long. Besides, Rebo thinks very few would dare go as far as he will to help us. They may not like being tied hand and foot to Consecrate policy, when there's a whole world for them to spend their energies on. But quite apart from religious reverence, they're physically dependent on the Consecrates, who supply a good many technical and administrative services ... and who can rouse the commoners against the Wardens, if it ever came to an open break between the castes.'

'So. Yes, Martin seemed to think much the same. We also

were thrashing this matter last night.... However, Davy, we should have at least a few score natives and a couple of hundred fastigas at our disposal, if Rebo is willing to help within the letter of the damned law. I swear they could move a stoneboat over any route. They might have to use winches——'

'Winches are a form of wheel,' Falkayn reminded him.

'Ay *de mí*, so they are. Well, levers and dikes, then. The Mayans raised big pyramids without wheels. The task would not be as large, to skid the generator from the Gilrigor to Aesca.'

'Oh, sure, it could be done. But how long would it take? Come have a look at this so-called road. We'd be many months dead before the job was finished.' Falkayn gulped. 'How much food have we got if we ration ourselves? A hundred days' worth?'

'Something like that. Of course, we could live without eating for another month or two, I believe.'

'Still not time enough to get your stoneboat across that distance. I swear it isn't.'

'Well ... no doubt you are right. You have inspected the terrain. It was only a rather desperate idea.'

'Wagon transport is bad enough,' Falkayn said. 'I don't think that would make more than twenty kilometres per Earth-day in this area. Faster, of course, once we reached the lowlands, but I'd still estimate a month altogether.'

'So slow? Well, yes, I suppose you are right. A rider needs more than a week. But this adds to our trouble. Martin is afraid that even if we can arrange something not forbidden by their law, the priests may have time to think of some new excuse for stopping us.'

Falkayn's mouth tightened. 'I wouldn't be surprised.' His fright broke from him in a wail: 'Why do they hate us so?'

'You should know that. Martin often talked to you while you rode westward.'

'Yes. B-but I was sent off just a couple of days after we landed. You three fellows have been on the scene, had a chance to speak with the natives, observe them——' Falkayn got his self-pity under control barely in time to avoid blubbering.

'The reason is plain,' Pasquel said. 'The Consecrates are the top crust of this petrified civilization. Change could only bring them down, however much it might improve the lot of the other classes. Then, besides self-interest, there is natural conservatism. Martin tells me theocracies are always hidebound. The Consecrates are smart enough to see that we newcomers represent a threat to them. Our goods, our ideas will upset the balance of society. So they will do everything they can to discourage more outworlders from coming.'

'Can't you threaten revenge? Tell 'em a battleship will come and blow 'em to hell if they let us die.'

'The first expedition told them a little too much of the true situation, I fear. Still, Martin may try such a bluff today. I do not know what he intends. But he has got ... well, at least not very *un*friendly with some of the younger Consecrates, in the days since you left. Has he told you of his lectures to them? Do not surrender yet, *muchacho*.'

Falkayn flushed indignantly. 'I haven't,' he snapped. 'Don't you either.'

Pasqual made matters worse by laughing. Falkayn signed off.

Anger faded before loneliness as the hours wore on. He hadn't minded the trip to Gilrigor Castle. That had been full of hope and riding on animals purchased with gold from a wealthy Aescan, through an excitingly exotic land, was just what a merchant adventurer ought to do. But Rebo had smashed the hope, and now the countryside looked only dreary and sinister. Falkayn's mind whirled with plan after plan, each less practical than the last—recharging the accumulators by a hand-powered generator, airlifting with a balloon, making so many guns that four men could stand off a million Larsans. . . . Whenever he rejected a scheme, his father's mansion and his mother's face rose up to make his eyes sting and he clutched frantically after another idea.

There must be *some* way to move a big load without wheels! What had he gone to school for? Physics, chemistry, biology, math, sociotechnics ... damn everything, here he was, child of a civilization that burned atoms and travelled between the stars, and one stupid taboo was about to kill him! But that was impossible. He was David Falkayn, with his whole life yet to live. Death didn't happen to David Falkayn.

The red sun climbed slowly up the sky. Ivanhoe had a rotation period of nearly sixty hours. He stopped at midday to eat and sleep awhile, and again shortly before sunset. The landscape had grown still more bleak: nothing was to be seen now but hills, ravines, an occasional brawling stream, wild pastures spotted with copses of scrubby fringe-leaved trees, no trace of habitation.

He woke after some hours, crawled shivering from his sleeping bag, started a campfire, and opened a packet of food. The smoke stung his nostrils. Antiallergen protected him against such slight contact with proteins made deadly alien by several billion years of separate evolution. He could even drink the local water. But nothing could save him if he ate anything native. After swallowing his rations, he readied the fastigas for travel. Because he was still cold, he left the lead animal tethered and huddled over the fire to store a little warmth in his body.

His eyes wandered upward. Earth and Hermes lay out there —more than four hundred light-years away.

The second moon was rising, a mottled coppery disc above the eastern scarps. Even without that help, one could travel by night. For the stars swarmed and glittered, the seven giant Sisters so brilliant in their nebular hazes that they cast shadows, the lesser members of the cluster and the more distant suns of the galaxy filling the sky with their wintry hordes. A grey twilight overlay the world. Off in the west, the Kasunian snows seemed phosphorescent.

Hard to believe there could be danger in so much beauty. And in fact there seldom was. Nonetheless, when a spaceship ran on hyperdrive through a region where the interstellar medium was thicker than usual, there was a small, but finite probability that one of her micro-jumps would terminate just where a bit of solid matter happened to be. If the difference in intrinsic velocities was great, it could do considerable damage. If, in addition, the lump was picked up in the space occupied by the nuclear fusion unit—well, that was what had happened to the *What Cheer*.

I suppose I'm lucky at that, Falkayn thought with a shudder. *The pebble could have ripped right through Me.* Of course, then the others would have been all right, with no more than a job of hull patching to do. But at his age Falkayn didn't think that was preferable.

He had to admire the way Captain Mukerji had got them here. By commandeering every charged accumulator aboard ship, he'd kept the engines going as far as Ivanhoe. Landing on the last gasp of energy, by guess, God, and aerodynamics, took uncommon skill. Naturally, the sensible thing had been to make for Aesca, the capital, rather than directly for Gilrigor. One did not normally bypass local authorities, who might take offence and cause trouble. Who could have known that the trouble was already waiting there?

But now the spaceship sat, without enough ergs left in her power packs to lift a single gravity sled. The accumulators in the depot were insufficient for transportation; besides, they were needed for the repair tools. The spare atomic generator couldn't recharge anything until it had been installed in the ship, for it functioned integrally with engines and controls. And a thousand wheelless kilometres separated the two....

Something stirred. One of the fastigas brayed. Falkayn's heart jumped into his gullet. He sprang erect with a hand on his blaster.

A native male trod into the little circle of firelight. His fur was fluffed out against the night cold and the breath steamed from below his jaws. Falkayn saw that he carried a rapier and—yes, by Judas, there was a circle emblazoned on his breastplate! The flames turned his great eyes into pools of restless red.

'What do you want?' Falkayn squeaked. Furiously, he reminded himself that the Ivanhoan's hands were extended empty in token of peace.

'God give you good evening,' the deep voice answered. 'I saw your camp from afar. I did not expect to find an outlander.'

'N-n-nor I a Sanctuary guard.'

'My corps travels widely on missions for the Consecrates, I hight Velodo Pario's-Child.'

'I, I ... David, uh, David Falkayn's-Child.'

'You have been on a visit to the Marchwarden, have you not?'

'Yes. As if you did not know!' Falkayn spat. *No, wait watch your manners. We may still have a chance of talking the Consecrates into giving us a special dispensation about wheels.* 'Will you join me?'

Vedolo hunkered, wrapping his tail about his feet. When Falkayn sat down again, the autochthon loomed over him on the other side of the flames, mane like a forested mountain against the Milky Way. 'Yes,' Vedolo admitted, 'everyone in Aesca knew you were bound hither, to see if that which your fellows laid in the sealed building was still intact. I trust it was?'

Falkayn nodded. Nobody in the early Iron Age could break into an inertium-plated shed with a Nakamura lock. 'And Marchwarden Rebo was most kind,' he said.

'That is not surprising, from what we know of him. As I understand the matter, you must get certain spare parts from the building to repair your ship. Will Rebo, then, help you transport them to Aesca?'

'He would if he could. But the main thing we need is too heavy for any conveyance available to him.'

'My Consecrate masters have wondered somewhat about that,' Vedolo said. 'They were shown around your vessel, at their own request, and the damaged section looked quite large.'

That must have been after I left, Falkayn thought. *Probably Schuster was trying to ingratiate us with them. And I'll bet it misfired badly when they saw the circular shapes of things like meter dials—stiffened their hostility to us, even if they didn't say anything to him at the time.*

But how can this character know that, unless he followed me here? And why would he do so? What is this mission of his?

'Your shipmates explained that they had means of transport,' Vedolo continued. 'That makes me wonder why you returned this quickly, and alone.'

'Well ... we did have a device in mind, but there appear to be certain difficulties——'

Vedolo shrugged. 'I have no doubt that folk as learned as you can overcome any problems. You have powers that we thought belonged only to angels—or to Anti-God——' He broke off and extended a hand. 'Your flame weapons, for instance, which the earlier visitors demonstrated. I was not present in Aesca at the time, and have always been most curious about them. Is that a weapon at your belt? Might I see it?'

Falkayn went rigid. He could not interpret every nuance in the Larsan voices, so strangely unresonant for lack of a nasal chamber. But—— 'No!' he snapped.

The delicate lips curled back over sharp teeth. 'You are less than courteous to a servant of God,' Vedolo said.

'I . . . uh . . . the thing is dangerous. You might get hurt.'

Vedolo raised an arm in the air and lowered it again. 'Look at me,' he said. 'Listen carefully. There is much you do not understand, you bumptious invaders. I have something to tell you——'

In Ivanhoe's thick air, a human heard preternaturally well. Or perhaps it was only that Falkayn was strung wire taut, trembling and sweating with the sense of aloneness before implacable enmity. He heard the rustle out in the brush and flung himself aside as the bowstring sang. The arrow buried its eight-sided shaft in the earth where he had been.

Vedolo sprang up, sword flashing free. Falkayn rolled over. A thornbush raked his cheek. 'Kill him!' Vedolo bawled and lunged at the human. Falkayn bounced erect. The rapier blade snagged his coat as he dodged. He got his blaster out and fired point blank.

Light flared hellishly for an instant. Vedolo went over in smoke, with a horrible squelch. After-images flew in rags before Falkayn's eyes. He stumbled towards his animals, which plunged and brayed in their panic. Through the dark he heard someone cry, 'I cannot see, I cannot see, I am blinded!' The flash would have been more dazzling to Ivanhoans than to him. But they'd recover in a minute, and then they'd have much better night vision than he did.

'Kill his fastigas!' cried another voice.

Falkayn fired several bolts. That should make their aim poor for a while longer, he thought in chaos. His lead animal reared and struck at him. Its eyeballs rolled, crimson against shadow-black in the streaming flame light. Falkayn side-stepped the hooves, got one hand on the bridle, and clubbed the long nose with his gun barrel. 'Hold *still*, you brute,' he sobbed. 'It's your life, too.'

Feet blundered through the brush. A lion head came into view. As he saw the human, the warrior yelled and threw a spear. It gleamed past, flattened shaft and iron head, Falkayn was too busy mounting to retaliate.

Somehow he got into the saddle. The remount shrieked as two arrows smote home in its belly. Falkayn cut it loose with a blaster shot.

'Get going!' he screamed. He struck heels into the sides of his beast. The fastiga broke into a rocking gallop, the pack animal behind at the end of its reins.

An axe hewed and missed. An arrow buzzed over his shoulder. Then he was beyond the assassins, back on the Sun's Way, westward bound again.

How many are there? it whirled in him. *Half a dozen? They must have left their own fastigas at a distance, so they could sneak up on me. I've got that much head start. But no remount anymore, and they certainly do.*

They were sent to waylay me, that's clear, to cause delay that might prove fatal while the others wondered what had happened and searched for me. They don't know about my radio. Not that that makes any difference now. They've got to catch me, before I get to Rebo's protection.

I wonder if I can beat them there.

With hysterical sardonicism: *Anyhow, I guess we can forget about that special dispensation.*

III

The *What Cheer* sat in a field a kilometre north of Aesca. By now thousands of local feet had tramped a path across it; the Ivanhoans were entirely humanlike in coming to gape at a novelty. But Captain Krishna Mukerji always rode into town.

'Really, Martin, you should too,' he said nervously. 'Especially when the situation has all at once become so delicate. They don't consider it dignified for anyone of rank to arrive at the, er, the Sanctuary on foot.'

'Dignity, schmignity,' said Master Polesotechnician Schuster. 'I should wear out my heart and my rump on one of those evil-minded animated derricks? I rode a horse once on Earth. I never repeat my mistakes.' He waved a negligent hand. 'Besides, I've already told the Consecrates, and anyone else who asked, the reason I go places on foot, and don't bother with ceremony, and talk friendly with low-life commoners, is that

I've progressed beyond the need for outward show. That's a new idea here, simplicity as a virtue. It's got the younger Consecrates quite excited.'

'Yes, I daresay this culture is most vulnerable to new ideas,' Mukerji said. 'There have been none for so long that the Larsans have no antibodies against them, so to speak, and can easily get feverish. . . . But the heads of the Sanctuary appear to realize this. If you cause too much disturbance with your comments and questions, they may not wait for us to starve. They may whip up an outright attack, casualties and the fear of a punitive expedition be damned.'

'Don't worry,' Schuster said. Another man in his position might have been offended; a first-year Polesotechnic cadet was taught not to clash head-on with the basics of an alien culture, and he had been a Master for two decades. But his face, broad and sabre-nosed under sleek black hair, remained blandly smiling. 'In all my conversations with these people, feeling them out, I've never yet challenged any of their beliefs. I don't intend to start now. In fact, I'm simply going to continue my seminar over there, as if we hadn't a care in the universe. To be sure, if I can steer the talk in a helpful direction——' He gathered a sheaf of papers and left the cabin: a short tubby man in vest and ruffled shirt, culottes and hose, as elegant as if he were bound for a reception on Earth.

Emerging from the air lock and heading down the gangway, he drew his mantle about him with a shiver. To avoid eardrum popping, the hull was kept at Ivanhoan air pressure, but not temperature. *Br-r-r*, he thought. *I don't presume to criticize the good Lord, but why did He make the majority of stars type M?*

The afternoon landscape reached sombre, to his eyes, as far as he could see down the valley. Grainfields were turning bluish with the first young shoots of the years. Peasants, male, female, and young, hoed a toilsome way down those multitudinous rows. The square mud huts in which they lived stood at no great separation, for every farm was absurdly small. Nevertheless, families did not outgrow the capacity of the land; disease and periodic famines kept the population stable. *To hell with any sentimental guff about cultural autonomy,* Schuster reflected. *This is one society that ought to be kicked apart.*

He reached the highroad and started towards the city. There was considerable traffic, food, and raw materials coming from the hinterlands, handmade goods going back. Professional porters trotted under loads too heavy for Schuster even to think about. Fastigas dragged travois with vast bumping and clatter. A provincial Warden and his bodyguard galloped through, horns hooting, and the commoners jumped aside for their lives. Schuster waved to the troop as amiably as he did to everyone else who hailed him. No use standing on ceremony. In the couple of Earth-weeks since the ship landed, the Aescans had lost awe of the strangers. Humans were no weirder to them than the many kinds of angel and hobgoblin in which they believed, and seemed to be a good deal more mortal. True, they had remarkable powers; but then, so did any village wizard, and the Consecrates were in direct touch with God.

Not having been threatened by war in historical times, the city was unwalled. But its area was pretty sharply defined just the same, huts, tenements, and the mansions of the wealthy, jammed close together along the contorted trails that passed for streets. Crowds moved by bazaars where shopkeepers' wives sang songs about their husbands' wares. Trousers and tunics, manes and fur, glowed where the red light slanted through shadows that were thick to Schuster's vision. The flat but deep Ivanhoan voices made a surf around him, overlaid by the shuffle of feet, clop of hooves, clangour from a smithy. Acrid stenches roiled in his nostrils.

It was a relief to arrive at one of the Three Bridges. When the Sanctuary guards had let him by, he walked alone. Only those who had business with the Consecrates passed here.

The Trammina River cut straight through town, oily with the refuse of a hundred thousand inhabitants. The bridges were arcs of a circle, soaring in stone to the island in the middle of the water. (Falkayn had relayed from Rebo the information that you were allowed to use up to one third of the sacred figure for an important purpose.) That island was entirely covered by the enormous step-sided pyramid of the Sanctuary. Buildings clustered on the lower terraces, graceful white structures with colonnaded porticos, where the Consecrates lived and worked. The upper pyramid held only staircases, leading to the top. There the Eternal Fire roared forth, vivid yellow tossing against the dusky-green sky. Obviously natural gas was being piped from some nearby well; but the citadel was impressive in every respect.

Except for what it cost those poor devils of peasants in forced labour and taxes, Schuster thought, *and what it's still costing them in liberty.* The fact that thousands of diverse barbarian cultures existed elsewhere on the planet proved that Pharaonism didn't come any more naturally to the Ivanhoans than it did to men.

White-robed Consecrates, most of their manes grey with age, and their blue-clad acolytes walked about the pyramid on their business, aloof in pride. Schuster's cheery greetings earned him little but frigid stares. He didn't let it bother him but bustled on to the fourth-step House of the Astrologers.

In a spacious room within, a score or so of the younger Consecrates sat around a table. 'Good day, good day,' Schuster beamed. 'I trust I am not late?'

'No,' said Herktaskor. A lean, intense-eyed being, he carried himself with something of the martial air of his Warden father. 'Save that we have been eagerly awaiting the revelation you promised us this morning, when you borrowed that copy of the *Book of Stars.*'

'Well, then,' Schuster said, 'let us get on with it.' He went to the head of the table and spread out his papers. 'I trust you have mastered those principles of mathematics that I explained to you in the past several days?'

A number of them looked unsure, but other shaggy heads nodded, 'Indeed,' said Herktaskor. His voice sank. 'Oh, glorious!'

Schuster took out a fat cigar and got it going while he squinted at them. He had to hope they were telling the truth; for suddenly his little project, which had begun as a pastime, and in the vague hope of winning friends and sneaking some new concepts into this frozen society, had grown most terribly urgent. Last night Davy Falkayn radioed that shattering news about wheels being taboo, and now——

He thought, though, that Herktaskor was neither lying nor kidding himself. The Consecrate was brilliant in his way. And certainly there was a good foundation on which to build. Mathematics and observational astronomy were still live enterprises in Larsum. They had to be, when religion claimed that astrology was the means of learning God's will. Algebra and geometry had long been well developed. The step from them to basic calculus was really not large. Even dour Sketulo, the Chief of Sanctuary, had not objected to Schuster's organizing a course of lectures, as long as he stayed within the bounds of dogma. Quite apart from intellectual curiosity, it would be useful for the learned class to be able to calculate such things as the volumes and areas of unusual solids; it would make still tighter their grip on Larsum's economy.

'I planned to go on with the development of those principles,' Schuster said. 'But then I got to wondering if you might not be more interested in certain astrological implications. You see, by means of the calculus it is possible to predict where the moons and planets will be, far more accurately than hitherto.'

Breath sucked in sharply between teeth. Even through the robes, the man could see how bodies tensed around the table.

'The *Book of Stars* gave me your tabulated observations, accumulated over many centuries,' he went on. 'These noontide hours I have weighed them in my mind.' Actually, he had fed them to the ship's computer. 'Here are the results of my calculations.'

He drew a long breath of tobacco smoke. The muscles tightened in his belly. Every word must now be chosen with the most finicking care, for a wrong one could put a sword between his guts.

'I have hesitated to show you this,' he said, 'because at first glance it seems to contradict the Word of God as you have explained it to me. However, after pondering the question and studying the stars for an answer, I felt sure that you are intelligent enough to see the deeper truth behind deceptive appearances.'

He paused. 'Go on,' Herktaskor urged.

'Let me approach the subject gradually. It is often a necessity of thought to assume something which one knows is not true. For example, the Consecrates as a whole possess large estates, manufactories, and other property. Title is vested in the Sanctuary. Now you know very well that the Sanctuary is neither a person nor a family. Yet for purposes of ownership, you act as if it were. Similarly, in surveying a piece of land, you employ plane trigonometry, though you know the world is actually round. . . .' He went on for some time, until he felt reasonably sure that everybody present understood the concept of a legal or mathematical fiction.

'What has this to do with astrology?' asked someone impatiently.

'I am coming to that,' Schuster said. 'What is the true purpose of your calculations? Is it not twofold? First, you wish to predict where the heavenly bodies will be in respect to each other at some given date, since this indicates what God desires you to do at that time. Second, you wish to uncover the grand plan of the heavens, since by studying God's works you may hope to learn more of His nature.

'Now as observations accumulated, your ancestors found it was not enough to assume that all the worlds, including this one, move in circles about the sun, and the moons in circles about this world, while the heavenly globe rotates around the whole. No, you had to picture these circles as having epicycles; and later it turned out that there must be epi-epicycles; and so on, until now for centuries the picture has been so complicated that the astrologers have given up hope of further progress.'

'True,' said one of them. 'A hundred years ago, on just this account, Kurro the Wise suggested that God does not want us to understand the ultimate design of things too fully.'

'Perhaps,' Schuster said. 'On the other hand, maybe God only wants you to use a different approach. A savage, trying to lift a heavy stone, might conclude that he is divinely forbidden to do so. But you lift it with a lever. In the same way, my people have discovered a sort of intellectual lever, by which we can pry more deeply into the motions of the heavenly bodies than we ever could by directly computing circles upon circles upon circles.

'The point is, however, that this requires us to employ a fiction. That is why I ask you not to be outraged when I lay that fiction before you. Granted, all motions in the sky are circular, since the circle is the token of God. But is it not permissible to assume, for purposes of calculation only, that they are not circular ... and inquire into the consequences of that assumption?'

He started to blow a smoke ring but decided against it. 'I must have a plain answer to that question,' he said. 'If such an approach is not permissible, then of course I shall speak no more.'

But of course it was. After some argument and logic-chopping. Herktaskor ruled that it was not illegal to entertain a false hypothesis. Whereupon Schuster exposed his class to Kepler's laws and Newtonian gravitation.

That took hours. Once or twice Herktaskor had to roar down a Consecrate who felt the discussion was getting obscene. But on the whole, the class listened with admirable concentration and asked highly intelligent questions. This was a gifted species. Schuster decided; perhaps, intrinsically, more gifted than man. At least, he didn't know if any human audience, anywhere in space or time, would have grasped so revolutionary a notion so fast.

In the end, leaning wearily on the table, he tapped the papers before him and said from a roughened throat: 'Let me summarize. I have shown you a fiction, that the heavenly bodies move in ellipses under an inverse square law of attraction. With the help of the calculus, I have proved that the elliptical paths are a direct consequence of that law. Now here, in these papers, is a summary of my calculations on the basis of our assumption, about the actual heavenly motions as recorded in the *Book of Stars*. If you check them for yourselves, you will find that the data are explained without recourse to any epicycles whatsoever.

'Mind you, I have never said that the paths *are* anything but circular. I have only said that they may be *assumed* to be, and that this assumption simplifies astrological computation so much that predictions of unprecedented accuracy can now be made. You will wish to verify my claims and consult your superiors about their theological significance. Far be it from me to broadcast anything blasphemous.

'I got troubles enough,' he added in Anglic.

There was no uproar when he left. His students were as wrung out as he. But later, when the implication began to sink in——

He returned to the ship. Pasqual met him in the wardroom. 'Where have you been so long?' the engineer asked. 'I was getting worried.'

'At the lodge.' Schuster threw himself into a chair with a sigh. 'Whoof! Sabotage is hard work.'

'Oh ... I was asleep when you came back here for noon, and so did not tell you. While you were out this morning, Davy called in. He is on his way back.'

'He might as well return, I suppose. We can't do anything until we get an okay from on high, and that'll take time.'

'Too much time, maybe.'

'And maybe not.' Schuster shrugged. 'Don't be like the nasty old man in a boat.'

'Eh?'

'Asked, "How do you know it will float?" Whereupon he said, "Boo!" to the terrified crew and retired to the cabin to gloat. Be a good unko and fetch me a drink, will you, and then I'm going to retire myself.'

'No supper?'

'A sandwich will do. We have to start rationing—remember?'

IV

The scanner alarm roused Schuster. He groaned out of his bunk and fumbled his way to the nearest viewscreen. What he saw brought him bolt awake.

A dozen Sanctuary guards sat mounted below the gangway. The light of moon and Pleiades glimmered on their spears. A pair of acolytes were helping a tall shape, gaunt in its robes, to dismount. Schuster would have known that white mane and disc-topped staff anywhere this side of the Coal Sack.

'*Oi, weh*,' he said. 'Get your clothes on, chumlets. The local Pope wants an audience with us.'

'Who?' Mukerji yawned.

'Sketulo, the Boss Consecrate, in person. Could be I've lit a bigger firecracker than I knew.' Schuster scuttled back aft and threw on his own garments.

He was ready to receive the guest by the time that one had climbed to the air lock. 'My master, you honour us beyond our worth,' he unctuated. 'Had we only known, we would have prepared a fitting——'

'Let us waste no time on hypocrisies,' said the Larsan curtly. 'I came so that we could talk in private, without fear of being overheard by underlings or fools.' He gestured at Pasqual to close the inner door. 'Dim your cursed lights.'

Mukerji obeyed. Sketulo's huge eyes opened wide and smouldered on Schuster. 'You being the captain here,' he said, 'I will see you alone.'

The merchant lifted his shoulders and spread his palms at his shipmates but obediently led the way—in Larsum the place of honour was behind—to that cabin which served as his office on happier occasions. When its door had also been shut, he faced the other and waited.

Sketulo sat stiffly down on the edge of a lounger that had been adjusted to accommodate Ivanhoe bodies. His staff remained upright in one hand, its golden circle ashimmer in the wan light. Schuster lowered himself to a chair, crossed his legs, and continued to wait.

The old voice finally clipped: 'When I gave you permission to instruct the young astrologers, I did not think even you would dare sow the seeds of heresy.'

'My master!' Schuster protested in what he hoped would be interpreted as a shocked tone. 'I did nothing of the sort.'

'Oh, you covered yourself shrewdly, by your chatter of a fiction. But I have seldom seen anyone so agitated as those several Consecrates who came to me after you had left.'

'Naturally the thought I presented was exciting——'

'Tell me.' Sketulo pursed his wrinkled lips. 'We will need considerable time to check your claims, of course; but does your hypothesis in truth work as well as you said?'

'Yes. Why should I discredit myself with boasts that can readily be disproven?'

'Thus I thought. Clever, clever . . .' The haggard head shook. 'Anti-God has many ways of luring souls astray.'

'But, my master, I distinctly told them this was a statement false to fact.'

'So you did. You are reported to have said that it might, at best, be mathematically true, but this does not make it philosophically true.' Sketulo leaned forward. Fiercely: 'You must have known, however, that the question would soon arise whether there can be two kinds of truth, and that in any such contest, those whose lives are spent with observations and

35

numbers will decide in the end that the mathematical truth is the only one.'

I certainly did, Schuster thought. *It's exactly the point that got Galileo into trouble with the Inquisition, way back when on Earth.* A chill went through him. *I didn't expect you to see it this fast, though, you old devil.*

'By undermining the Faith thus subtly, you have confirmed my opinion that your kind are the agents of Anti-God,' Sketulo declared. 'You must not remain here.'

Hope flared in Schuster. 'Believe me, my master, we have no wish to do so! The sooner we can get what we need from our warehouse and be off, the happier we will be.'

'Ah. But the others. When can we expect a third visit, a fourth, fleet after fleet?'

'Never, God willing. You were told by the first crew that arrived, we have no interest in trade——'

'So they said. And yet it was only a few short years before this vessel came. How do we know you tell the truth?'

You can't argue with a fanatic, Schuster thought, and kept silence. Sketulo surprised him again by changing the topic and asking in a nearly normal tone:

'How do you propose to move that great object hither?'

'Well, now, that is a good question, my master.' Schuster's forehead went wet. He mopped it with his sleeve. 'We have a way, but, eh, we have hesitated to suggest it——'

'I commanded that we be alone in order that we might both speak frankly.'

Schuster sucked in a lungful of air, reached for a pad and penstyl, and explained about wagons.

Sketulo didn't move a muscle. When at length he spoke, it was only to say: 'At certain most holy and secret rites, deep within the Sanctuary, there is that which is moved from one room to another by such means.'

'We need not shock the populace,' Schuster said. 'Look, we can have sideboards, or curtains hanging down, or something like that, to hide the wheels.'

Sketulo shook his head. 'No. Almost everyone, as an unwitting child, has played with a round stick or stone. The barbarians beyond the Kasunian Range employ rollers. No doubt some of our own peasants do, furtively, when a heavy load must be moved and no one is watching. You could not deceive the more intelligent observers about what was beneath those covers; and they would tell the rest.'

'But with official permission——'

'It may not be granted. God's law is plain. Even if you were given leave by the Sanctuary, most of the commoners would fear a curse. They would destroy you despite any injunctions of ours.'

Since that was what Falkayn had quoted Rebo as saying, Schuster felt that perhaps Sketulo was telling the truth. Not that it mattered if he wasn't; he was obviously determined not to allow this thing.

The merchant sighed. 'Well, then, my master, have you any other suggestion? Perhaps, if you would furnish enough labourers from the Consecrate estates, we could drag the workmaker here.'

'This is the planting and cultivating season. We cannot spare so many hands, lest we have a famine later.'

'Oh, now, my master, you and I have an identical interest: to get this ship off the ground. My associates at home can send you payment in metals, fabrics, and, yes, artificial food nourishing to your type of life.'

Sketulo stamped the deck with his staff so it rang. His tone became a snarl: 'We do not *want* your wares! We do not want you! The trouble you started today has snapped the last thread of my patience. If you perish here, despite the accursed rescue station, then God may well persuade your fellows that this is not a good place for such a station after all. At least, come what may, we will have done God's will here in Larsum ... by giving not a finger's length of help to the agents of Anti-God!'

He stood up. His breath rasped harshly in the narrow metal space. Schuster rose, too, regarded him with a self-astonishing steadiness, and asked low: 'Do I understand you rightly, then, my master, that you wish us to die?'

The unhuman head lifted stiffly over his. 'Yes.'

'Will your guard corps attack us, or would you rather stir mobs against us?'

Sketulo stood silent awhile. His eventual answer was reluctant: 'Neither, unless you force our hand. The situation is complex. You know how certain elements of the Warden and trader classes, not without influence, have been seduced into favouring somewhat your cause. Besides, although we could overcome you with sheer numbers, I am well aware that your weapons would cost us grievous losses—which might invite a barbarian invasion. So you may abide in peace awhile.'

'Until you think of a safe way to cut our thoats, hm?'

'Or until you starve. But from this moment you are forbidden to enter Aesca.'

'*Nu?* That would not be so good an idea anyway, with all those rooftops and alleys for an archer to snipe from. Well——' Schuster's words trailed off. He wondered, momentarily frantic, if this mess was his fault, going so boldly forward, fatally misjudging the situation.... No. He hadn't foreseen Sketulo's precise reaction, but it was better to have everything out in the open. Had he known before what he did now, he wouldn't have sent Davy off alone. *Got to warn the kid to look out for assassins....* He grinned one-sidedly. 'At least we understand each other. Thanks for that.'

For an instant more he toyed with the idea of taking the Larsan prisoner, a hostage. He dismissed it. That would be a sure way to provoke attack. Sketulo was quite willing to die for his faith. Schuster was equally willing to let him do so, but didn't want to be included in the deal. A wife and kids were waiting for him, very far away on Earth.

He led the old one to the air lock and watched him ride off. The sound of hooves fell hollow beneath the moon and the clustered stars.

V

It seemed to Falkayn that he had been riding through his whole life. Whatever might have happened before was a dream, a vapour somewhere in his emptied skull, unreal ... reality was the ache in every cell of him, saddle sores, hunger, tongue gone wooden with thirst and eyelids sandpapery with sleeplessness, the fear of death battered out of him and nothing left but a sort of stupid animal determination to reach Gilrigor Castle, he couldn't always remember why.

He had made stops during the night, of course. A fastiga was tougher than a mule and swifter than a horse, but it must rest occasionally. Falkayn himself hadn't dared sleep, though, and saddled up again as soon as possible. Now his beasts were lurching along the road like drunks.

He turned his head—the neckbones creaked—and looked behind. His pursuers had been in sight ever since the first pre-dawn paling of the sky made them visible. When was that—a century ago?—no, must be less than an hour, the sun wasn't aloft yet, though the blackness overhead had turned plum colour and the Sisters were sunken below Kasunia's wall. There were four or five of them—hard to be sure in this twilight—only two kilometres behind him and closing the gap. Their spears made points of brightness among the shadows.

So close?

The knowledge rammed home. Energy spurted from some ultimate source, cleared his mind and whetted his senses. He felt the dawn wind on his cheeks, heard it sough in the wiry brush along the roadside and around the staggering hoofbeats of his mount, saw how the snow peaks in the west were red-dening as they caught the first sunrays; he yanked the little receiver from his pocket and slapped the switch over. 'Hello!'

'Davy!' yelled Schuster's voice. 'What's happened? You okay?'

'So far,' Falkayn stammered. 'N-not for long, I'm afraid.'

'We been trying for hours to raise you.'

He'd called the ship while he fled, to relate the circumstances, and contact was maintained until—— 'Guess I, I got so tired I just put the box away for a minute and then forgot about it. My animals are about to keel over. And ... the Sanctuary boys are overhauling me.'

'Any chance you can reach the castle before they get in bowshot?'

Falkayn bit his lip. 'I doubt it. Can't be very far to go, a few kilometres, but—— What can I do? Try to make a run for it on foot?'

'No, you'd be ridden down, shot in the back. I'd say make a stand.'

'One of those bows, God, they've got almost the range of my gun, and they can attack me from every side at once. There's no cover here. Not even a clump of trees in sight.'

'I know an old frontier stunt. Shoot your animals and use them for barricades.'

'That won't protect me long.'

'It may not have to. If you're as near the castle as you say, Ivanhoan eyes ought to spot flashes in the air from your shots. Anyhow, it's the only thing I can suggest.'

'V-v-v——' Falkayn snapped his teeth together and held them that way for a second. 'Very well.'

Schuster's own voice turned uneven. 'I wish to God I could be there to help you, Davy.'

'I wouldn't mind if you were,' Falkayn surprised himself by answering. Now that was more like how a man facing terrible odds ought to talk! 'Uh, I'll have to pocket this radio again, but I'll leave the switch open. Maybe you can hear. Root for me, will you?'

He reined in and sprang to the ground. His fastigas stood passive, trembling in their exhaustion. Not without guilt feelings, he led the pack carrier around until it stood nose to tail with the mount. Quickly, then, he set his blaster to narrow beam and drilled their brains.

They collapsed awkwardly, like jointed dolls; a kind of sigh went from the loaded one, as if it were finally being allowed to sleep, but its eyes remained open and horribly fixed. Falkayn wrestled with the legs and necks, trying to make a wall that would completely surround him. Scant success ... Panting, he looked eastward. His enemies had seen what he was about and broken into a trot, scattering right and left across the downs before they stopped to tether their spare animals. Five of them, all right.

The sun's disc peered over the ridges. *Wait, the more contrast, the more visible an energy flash will be.* Falkayn fired several times straight upward.

An arrow thunked into fastiga flesh. The boy went on his stomach and shot back. He missed the retreating rider. Crouching, he glared around the horizon. Another Larsan was drawing a bow at him, less than half a kilometre distant. He sighted carefully and squeezed the trigger. The gun pointed a long blue-white finger. An instant later it said *crack!* and the Larsan

40

dropped his bow and clutched at his left arm. Two other arrows came nastily near. Falkayn shot back, without hitting, but it did force the archers out of their own range for a little while, which was something.

He hadn't many charges left in the magazine, though. If the Consecrates' hired blades kept up their present tactics, compelling him to expend his ammunition—— But did they know how little he had? No matter. They obviously were not going to quit before they finished their job. Unless he was lucky enough to drop them all, David Falkayn was probably done. He discovered he was accepting that fact soberly, not making much fuss about it one way or another, hoping mainly that he would be able to take some of them on hell road with him. *Rough on Mother and Dad, though*, he thought. *Rough on Marty Schuster, too. He'll have to tell them, if he lives.*

Two guards pounded down a grassy slope towards him, side by side. Their manes streamed in the air. When they were nearly in gunshot, they separated. Falkayn fired at one, who leaned so low simultaneously that the bolt missed. The other got off an arrow on a high trajectory. Falkayn shot at him, too, but he was already withdrawing on the gallop. The arrow smote, centimetres from Falkayn's right leg where he sprawled.

Nice dodge, he thought with the curious dispassion that had come upon him. *I wonder if they've met my kind of defensive manoeuvre before, or are just making a good response to something new? Wouldn't be surprised if that last was the case. They're brainy fellows, these Ivanhoans. While we, with our proud civilization, can't respond to so simple a thing as a local taboo on wheels.*

Shucks, it should be possible to analyze the problem——

Two others were galloping close from the right. Falkayn narrowed his blaster beam as far as he could, to get maximum range, and shot with great care. He struck first one fastiga, then another: minor wounds, but painful. Both animals reared. The riders got them under control again and wheeled away. Falkayn turned about in time to fire at the other two, but not in time to forestall their arrows. Misses on both sides.

—and figure out precisely what a wheel does, and then work out some other dodge that'll do the same thing.

Where was the fifth Larsan, the one who'd got winged? Wait . . . his fastiga stood riderless some distance off. But where was he? These bully boys weren't the type to call it a day just because of a disabled arm.

I got good grades in math and analytics. My discussants told me so. Now why can't I dredge something I learned back then, up into memory, and use it? I could solve the problem for an exam, I'll bet.

Most likely the wounded one was snaking through the taller bushes, trying to get so close that he could pounce and stab.

Of course, this isn't exactly an examination room. Analytical thinking doesn't come natural, most especially not when your life's involved, and it's very, very odd that I should begin on it at this precise moment. Maybe my subconscious smells an answer.

The four riders had got together for a conference. They looked like toys at this distance, near the top of a high ridge paralleling the road and sloping down to its edge. Falkayn couldn't hear anything but wind. The sun, fully risen now, made rippling shadows in the grey grass. The air was still cold; his breath smoked.

Let's see. A wheel is essentially a lever. But we've already decided that the other forms of lever aren't usable. Wait! A screw? No, how'd you apply it? If any such thing were practical for us, Romulo Pasqual would've thought of it by now.

How about cutting the wheel in slices, mounted separately? No, I remember suggesting that to Rebo, and he said it wouldn't do, because the whole ensemble viewed from the side would still have a circular outline.

The riders had evidently agreed on a plan. They unstrung their bows and fastened them carefully under the saddle girths. Then they started towards him, single file.

What else does a wheel do, besides supply mechanical advantage? Ideally, it touches the ground at only one point, and so minimises friction. Is there some other shape which'll do the same? Sure, any number of 'em. But what good is an elliptical wheel?

Hey, couldn't you have a trick mounting, like an eccentric arm on an axle that was also elliptical, so the load would ride steady? M-m-m, no, I doubt if it's feasible, especially over roads as dreadful as this one, and nothing but muscle power available for traction. The system would soon be jolted to pieces.

The leading Sanctuary guard broke into a headlong gallop.

Falkayn took aim and waited puzzledly for him to come in range of a beam wide enough to be surely lethal. The transceiver made muffled squawkings in Falkayn's pocket, but he hadn't the time for chatter.

Same objection, complexity, inefficiency, and fragility, applies to whatever else comes to mind, like say a treadmill-powered caterpillar system. Perhaps Romulo can flange something up. But there ought to be a foolproof, easy answer.

Crouched against the neck of his fastiga, the leading guard was nearly in range. Yes, now *in* range! Falkayn fired. The blast took the animal full in the chest. It cartwheeled several metres more downhill, under its own momentum, before falling. Its rider had left the saddle at the moment it was struck, before the beam could seek him out. He hit the ground with acrobatic agility, rolled over, and disappeared in the brush.

By the time Falkayn saw what was intended, he had already shot the second. It crashed into the barrier of the first. The third rushed near, frightened but under control.

'Oh, no, you don't,' the human rasped. 'I'm not going to build your wall for you!' He let the other two pound by. As they slewed about, exposing their riders to him, he had the bleak pleasure of killing an enemy. The fourth escaped out of range, jumped to earth, and ran towards the dead animals, leading his own but careful to stay on its far side.

Falkayn's bolts raked the slope, but he couldn't see his targets in the overgrowth and it was too moist in this spring season to catch fire. The third Larsan got to the barrier and slashed his fastiga's throat. It struggled, but hands reached from below to hold it there while it died.

So three warriors had made the course. Now they were ensconced behind a wall of their own, too thick for him to burn through, high enough for them to kneel behind and send arrows that would arch down on to him. Of course, their aim wouldn't be good——

The shafts began to rise. Falkayn made himself as small as possible and tried to burrow under one of his own slain fastigas.

Something which ... which rolls, and holds its load steady, but isn't circular——

The arrows fell. Their points went hard into dirt and inert flesh. After some time of barrage, a leonine head lifted above the other barrier to see what had happened. Falkayn, sensing a pause in the assault, rose to one knee and snapped a shot.

He ought to have hit, with a broad beam at such close range. But he didn't. The bolt struck the barricade and greasy smoke puffed outward. The Larsan dived for cover.

What made Falkayn's hand jerk was suddenly seeing the answer.

He snatched out the radio. 'Hello!' he yelped. 'Listen, I know what we can do!'

'Anything, Davy,' said Schuster like a prayer.

'Not for me. I mean to get you fellows out of here——'

The arrows hailed anew. Anguish ripped in Falkayn's left calf where he crouched. He stared at the shaft that skewered it, not really comprehending for a moment.

'Davy? You there?' Schuster cried across a thousand kilometres.

Falkayn swallowed hard. The wound didn't hurt too much, he decided. And the enemy had ceased fire again. They must be running low on ammo, too. The road was strewn with arrows.

'Listen carefully,' he said to the box. It had fallen to the ground, and blood from his leg was trickling towards it. A dim part of him was interested to note that human blood in this light didn't have its usual brilliance but looked blackish red. The rate of flow indicated that no major vessel had been cut. 'You know what a constant-width polygon is?' he asked.

A Larsan ventured another peek. When Falkayn didn't shoot, he rose to his feet for an instant and waved before dropping back to shelter. Falkayn was too busy to wonder what that meant.

'You hurt, Davy?' Schuster pleaded. 'You don't sound so good. They still after you?'

'Shut up,' Falkayn said. 'I haven't much time. Listen. A figure of constant width is one that if you put it between two parallel lines, so they're tangent to it on opposite sides, and then re- volve it, well, the lines stay tangent clear around the circum- ference. In other words, the width of the figure is the same along every line drawn from side to side through the middle. A circle is a member of that class, obviously. But——'

The Larsan whose left arm had been scorched to disability sprang from a clump of bushes along the road. There was a knife in his right hand. Falkayn caught the gleam in the corner of an eye, twisted about, and snatched for his blaster where it lay on the ground. The knife arm chopped through an arc. Falkayn shrieked as his own hand was pinned to earth.

'*Davy!*' Schuster cried.

Falkayn picked up the blaster with his left. The muzzle wavered back and forth. He shot and missed. The guard cleared the barrier at a jump, drawing his sword as he sprang. The blade swept around. Probably he had closed his eyes at the moment the gun went off, for he struck with accuracy. The weapon spun clear of Falkayn's lacerated grasp.

The human yanked out the knife that pinned him, surged to his feet, and attacked left-handed. His voice rose to a shout: 'A circle's not the only one! You take an equi——'

His rush had brought him under the Larsan's guard. He stabbed, but the point slithered off the breastplate. The native shoved. Falkayn lurched backwards. The guard poised his rapier.

'Equilateral triangle,' Falkayn sobbed. 'You draw arcs——'

A horn sounded. The guard recoiled with a snarl. On the hillside, an archer rose and sent a last arrow at Falkayn. But the human's hurt leg had given way. He went to his knees, and the shaft whirred where he had been.

Another arrow, from another direction, took the sword-wielder through the breast. He uttered a rather ghastly rattling cough and fell on top of a fastiga. The surviving Sanctuary agents pointed frantically at the circles on their cuirasses. But arrows stormed from the riders who galloped out of the west, and the episode was over.

Rebo Legnor's-Child drew rein at the head of his household warriors and sprang from the saddle in time for Falkayn to crumple into his arms.

Mukerji entered the wardroom to find Schuster alone, laying out a hand of solitaire. 'Where's Romulo?' he asked.

'Off in his own place, quietly going crazy,' Schuster said. 'He's trying to figure out what Davy was getting at just before——' He raised a face whose plumpness looked oddly pinched. 'Heard anything from the kid?'

'No. I shall let you know the minute I do, of course. His set must still be on, I hear natives speak and move about. But not a word from him, and everyone else is probably afraid to answer the talking box.'

'Oh, God. *I* sent him there.'

'You could not have known there was any danger.'

'I could know the ship was the safest place to be. I should have gone myself.' Schuster stared blindly at his cards. 'He was my apprentice.'

Mukerji laid a hand on the merchant's shoulder. 'You had no business on a routine mission like that. Fighting and all, it was routine. Your brains are needed here.'

'What brains?'

'You must have some plan. What were you talking to that peasant about, a few hours before sunrise?'

'I bribed him with a trade knife to carry a message for me to the Sanctuary. Telling Herktaskor he should come out for a private conference. Second in command of the astrology department, you may recall; a very bright fellow, and I think more friendly than otherwise to us. At least, he doesn't have Sketulo's fanatical resistance to innovation.' Schuster found he was laying a heart on a diamond, cursed, and scattered the cards with a sweep of his hand. 'Obviously Rebo showed up, having seen the gun flashes, and dealt with Sketulo's killers. But did he come in time? Is Davy still alive?'

The scanner hooted. Both men leaped to their feet and ran out of the door to the closest viewscreen. 'Speak of the devil,' Mukerji said. 'Take over, Martin. I shall go back and hunch above the radio.'

Schuster suppressed his inward turmoil and opened the air lock. A cold early-morning wind, laden with sharp odours, gusted at him. Herktaskor mounted the gangway and entered. His great form was muffled in a cloak, which he did not take off until the door had closed again. Beneath, he wore his robes. Evidently he hadn't wanted to be recognized on his way here.

'Greeting,' said Schuster in a dull tone. 'Thank you for coming.'

'Your message left me scant choice,' said the Consecrate. 'For the good of Larsum and the Faith, I am bound to listen if you claim to have an important matter to discuss.'

'Have you, ah, been forbidden to enter the ship?'

'No, but it is as well not to give the Chief the idea that he should forbid it.' Herktaskor squinted against an illumination which he found blindingly harsh, though it had been reduced well below normal to conserve the small amount of charge left in the accumulators. Schuster led the being to his own cabin, dimmed the lights further, and offered the lounger.

They sat down and regarded each other for a silent while. At length Herktaskor said, 'If you repeat this, I shall have to call you a liar. But having found you honourable'—that hurt a little; Schuster's plans were not precisely above board—'I think you should know that many Consecrates feel Sketulo was wrong in immediately banning your new mathematics and astrology. Could he show by Scripture, tradition, or reasoning that they contravened the Word of God, then naturally the whole Sanctuary would have joined him in rejecting your teachings. But he has made no attempt to show it, has merely issued a flat decree.'

'Are you permitted to argue with him about the matter?'

'Yes, the rule has always been that full-rank Consecrates may dispute freely within the bounds of doctrine. But we must obey the orders of our superiors as long as those are not themselves unlawful.'

'I thought so. Well——' Schuster reached for a cigar. 'Here is what I wanted to tell you. I wish the co-operation of the Sanctuary rather than its enmity. In order to win that co-operation, I would like to prove to you that we are no danger to the Faith, but may rather be the instruments of its further-ance. Then perhaps you can convince the others.'

Herktaskor waited, impassive. Yet his eyes narrowed and seemed to kindle.

Schuster started the cigar and puffed ragged clouds. 'The

purpose of your astrology is to learn God's will and the plan on which He has constructed the universe. To me, this implies that the larger purpose of the Consecrates is to search out the nature of God, insofar as it may be understood by mortals. Your theologians have reached conclusions in the past. But are those conclusions final? May there not be much more to deduce?'

Herktaskor bowed his lion head and traced a solemn circle in the air. 'There may. There must. Nothing of importance has been done in that field since the *Book of Domno* was written, but I myself have often speculated—— Go on, I pray you.'

'We newcomers are not initiates of your religion,' Schuster said. 'However, we, too, in our own fashion, have spent many centuries wondering about the divine. We, too, believe,' *well, some of us,* 'in a single God, immortal, omnipotent, omniscient ... perfect ... Who made all things. Now maybe our theology varies from yours at crucial points. But maybe not. May I compare views with you? If you can show me where my people have erred, I will be grateful and will, if I live, carry back the truth to them. If, on the other hand, I can show you, or merely suggest to you, points on which our thought has gone beyond yours, then you will understand, and can make your colleagues understand, that we outlanders are no menace, but rather a beneficial influence.'

'I doubt that Sketulo and certain other stiff-minded Consecrates will ever concede that,' Herktaskor said. His voice took on an edge. 'Yet if a new truth were indeed revealed, and anyone dared deny it——' His fists unclenched. 'I listen.'

Schuster was not surprised. Every religion in Earth's past, no matter how exclusive in theory, had had influential thinkers who were willing to borrow ideas from contemporary rivals. He made himself as comfortable as possible. This would take a while.

'The first question I wish to raise,' he said, 'is why God created the universe. Have you any answer to that?'

Herktaskor started. 'Why, no. The writings say only that He did. Dare we inquire into His reasons?'

'I believe so. See, if God is unbounded in every way, then He must have existed eternally before the world was. He is above everything finite. But thought and existence are themselves finite, are they not?'

'Well ... well ... yes. That sounds reasonable. Thought and existence as we know them, anyhow.'

'Just so. I daresay your philosophers have argued whether the sound of a stone falling in the desert, unheard by any ears, is a real phenomenon.' Herktaskor nodded. 'It is an old conundrum, found on countless planets. I mean in many countries. In like manner, a God alone in utter limitlessness could not be comprehended by thought nor described in words. No thinking, speaking creatures were there. Accordingly, in a certain manner of speaking, He did not exist. That is to say, His existence lacked an element of completion, the element of being observed and comprehended. But how can the existence of the perfect God be incomplete? Obviously it cannot. Therefore it was necessary for Him to bring forth the universe, that it might know Him. Do you follow me?'

Herktaskor's nod was tense. He had begun to breathe faster.

'Have I said anything thus far which contradicts your creed?' Schuster asked.

'No ... I do not believe you have. Though this is so new——Go on!'

'The act of creation,' Schuster said around his cigar, 'must logically involve the desire to create, thought about the thing to be created, the decision to create, and the work of creation. Otherwise God would be acting capriciously, which is absurd. Yet such properties—desire, thought, decision, and work—are limited. They are inevitably focused on one creation, out of the infinite possibilities, and involve one set of operations. Thus the act of creation implies a degree of finitude in God. But this is unthinkable, even temporarily. Thus we have the paradox that He must create and yet He cannot. How shall this be resolved?'

'How do you resolve it?' Herktaskor breathed, looking a little groggy.

'Why, by deciding that the actual creation must have been carried out by ten intelligences known as the *Sephiroth*——'

'Hold on!' The Consecrate half rose. 'There are no other gods, even lesser ones, and the *Book* does not credit the angels with making the world.'

'Of course. Those I speak of are not gods or angels, they are separate manifestations of the One God, somewhat as the facets of a jewel are manifestations of it without being themselves jewels. God no doubt has infinitely many manifestations, but the ten *Sephiroth* are all that we have found logically necessary to explain the fact of creation. To begin with the first of them, the wish and idea of creation must have been coexistent with God from eternity. Therefore it contains the nine others which are required as attributes of that which is to be created——'

Some hours later, Herktaskor said farewell. He walked like one in a daze. Schuster stood in the lock watching him go. He himself felt utterly exhausted.

If it turns out I've done this to him, to all of them, for nothing, may my own dear God forgive me.

Mukerji hurried from the wardroom. His feet clattered loudly on the deck. 'Martin!' he yelled. 'Davy's alive!'

Schuster spun on his heel. A wave of giddiness went through him, he leaned against the bulkhead and gasped weakly.

'His call came after you went off with that Brahmin,' Mukerji said. 'I didn't know if I would do harm by interrupting you, so—— Yes. He was wounded, hand and leg, nothing that won't heal, you know we need not worry about any local microbes. He fainted, and I imagine that he went directly from a swoon to a sleep. He could still only mumble when he called from Rebo's castle, said he would call back after he had got some more rest and explain his idea. Come, Romulo and I have already broken out a bottle to celebrate!'

'I could use that,' Schuster said, and followed him.

After a few long swallows, he felt more himself. He set down his glass and gave the others a shaky grin. 'Did you ever have anybody tell you you were not a murderer?' he asked. 'That's how I'm feeling.'

'Oh, come off it,' Pasqual snorted. 'You are not *that* responsible for your apprentices.'

'No, maybe not, except I sent him where I could have gone myself—— But he's okay, you say!'

'Without you here on the spot, that might make very little difference,' Pasqual said. 'Krish is just a spaceman and I just an engineer and Davy just a kid. We need somebody to scheme our way out of this hole. And you, *amigo mío*, are a schemer by trade.'

'Well, Davy seems to have thought of something. What, I don't know.' Schuster shrugged. 'Or maybe I do know—some item I learned in school and forgot. He's closer to his school days.'

'Assuming his idea is any good,' Pasqual said with a return of worry. 'I have not made any feasible plans myself, but believe me, I have thought of many harebrained ones.'

'We'll have to wait and see. Uh, do you have any more details on the situation in Gilrigor?'

'Yes, I spoke directly with Rebo, after Davy had shown him how the radio works,' Mukerji said. 'The assassins were killed in his attack. He said he ordered that because he suspected they were indeed Sanctuary guards. If he had taken any of them prisoner, he would have been bound to release them again, or else face an awkward clash of wills between himself and Sketulo. And they would promptly have taken word back here. As it is, he has avoided the dilemma, and can claim his action was perfectly justified. At arrow-shot distance, he could not see their insignia, and the natural assumption was that they were bandits—whom it is his duty to eradicate.'

'Excellent.' Schuster chuckled. 'Rebo's a smart gazzer. If he finds an excuse not to send a messenger here, as I'm sure he can, we'll have gained several days before Sketulo wonders what's happened and sends someone else out to inquire—who's then got to get there and back, taking still more time. In other words, by keeping our mouths shut about the whole business, we turn his own delaying tactics on him.' He looked around the table. 'And time is what we need right now, second only to haulage. Time for the Sanctuary to get so badly off balance, so embroiled internally, that no one can think up a new quasilegal gimmick for stopping us.'

'Be careful they are not driven to violence,' Mukerji said.

'That's not likely,' Schuster replied. 'The attempt on Davy was by stealth; I'm pretty sure Sketulo will disown his dead agents when the news breaks. Any decision to act with open illegality is tough for him, you see. It'd give people like Rebo much too good a talking point, or even an excuse to fight back. Besides, as I already remarked, time should now begin to work against the old devil.'

Pasqual cocked his head at the merchant. 'What have you been brewing?'

'Well——' Schuster reached for the bottle again. Liquor gurgled cheerily into his glass. 'First off, as you know, I introduced Newtonian astronomy. I disguised it as a fictional hypothesis, but that just makes it sneakier, not any less explosive. Nobody can fool himself forever with a pretence this is only a fairy tale to simplify his arithmetic. Sooner or later, he'll decide the planetary orbits really are elliptical. And that knocks a major prop out from under his belief in the sacredness of circles, which in turn will repercuss like crazy on the rest of the religion. Sketulo foresaw as much, and right away he forbade any use of my ideas. This simply delays the inevitable, though. He can't stop his astrologers from thinking, and some of them from resenting the prohibition. That'll make tension in the Sanctuary, which'll occupy a certain amount of his time and energy, which'll therefore be diverted from the problem of how to burke us.'

'Nice,' Mukerji frowned, 'but a little long range. The revolution might take fifty years to ripen.'

'Admitted. The trend helps our cause, but not enough by itself. So today I got Herktaskor here. We talked theology.'

'What? You can't upset a religion in an afternoon!'

'Oh, sure. I know that.' Schuster took a drink. His grin broadened. 'The *goyim* have been working on mine for two or three thousand years and got nowhere. I only pointed out certain logical implications of the local creed and suggested some of the answers to those implications which've been reached on Earth.'

'So?' Pasqual asked wonderingly.

'Well, you know I'm interested in the history of science and philosophy, like to read about it and so forth. Because of this, as well as some family traditions, I've got a knowledge of the Kabbalah.'

'¿Qué es?'

'The system of medieval Jewish theosophy. In one form or another, it had tremendous influence for centuries, even on Christian thought. But believe you me, it's the most fantastically complicated structure the human race ever built out of a few texts, a lot of clouds, and a logic that got the bit between its teeth. Jewish Orthodoxy never wanted any part of it—much too hairy, and among the Chasidim in particular it led to some wild emotional excesses.

'But it fits the Larsan system like a skin. For instance, in the Kabbalah there are ten subordinate emanations of God, who are the separate attributes of perfection. They're divided into three triads, each denoting one male and one female quality plus their union. There hasn't been much numerology here before now, but when I reminded Herktaskor that three points determine a circle, he gasped. Each of these triadic apices is identified with some part of the body of the archetypal man. One more *Sephirah* encircles the lot, which also accords nicely with Larsan symbolism, and the conjunction of them produced the universe. . . . Well, never mind details. It goes on to develop techniques of letter rearrangement by which the inner meaning of Scripture can be discovered, a doctrine of triple reincarnation, a whole series of demonologies and magical prescriptions, altogether magnificent, glittering nonsense that seduced some of the best minds Earth ever knew. I gave it to Herktaskor.'

'And——?' Mukerji asked very softly.

'Oh, not all. That'd take months. I just told him the bare outlines. He may or may not come back for more. That hardly matters. The damage has been done. Larsan philosophy is still rather primitive, not ready to deal with such strong meat. Religion is theoretically a pure monotheism, in practice tainted with the ghosties and ghoulies of popular superstition, and no one so far has given its premises a really thorough examination. Yet theology does exist as a respectable enterprise. So the Consecrates are cocked and primed to go off, in an explosion of reinterpretations, reformations, counter-reformations, revelations, new doctrines, fundamentalistic reactions, and every other kind of hooraw we humans have been through. As I've already said, the Kabbalah sure had that effect on Earth. In time, this should break up the Sanctuary and let some fresh air into Larsum.'

Schuster sighed. 'I'm afraid the process will be bloody,' he finished. 'If I didn't think it was for the long-range best, I wouldn't have done this thing, not even to save our lives.'

Pasqual looked bewildered. 'You are too subtle for me,' he complained. 'Will it?'

'If we can move that generator here within the next few weeks, I'm certain it will. Herktaskor is no fool, even if he is a natural-born theologian. After what happened about the calculus, he'll be discreet about who he picks to talk my ideas over with. But those are good brains in the Sanctuary, hungry to be used. If fact is denied them to work with, theory will serve. The notions will spread like a shock wave. Questions will soon be openly raised. Sketulo can't lawfully suppress discussion of that sort, and the others will be too heated up to obey an unlawful order. So he's going to have his hands full, that gazzer, for the rest of his life!'

VII

Rebo, Marchwarden of Gilrigor, reined in his fastiga on the crest of Ensum Hill. One hand, in an iron-knobbed gauntlet, pointed down the long slope. 'Aesca,' he said.

David Falkayn squinted through the day-gloom. To him the city was only a blot athwart the river's metal gleam. But a starpoint caught his eye, and his heart sprang within him. 'Our ship,' he breathed. 'We are there.'

Rebo peered across kilometres of fields and orchards. 'No armed forces are gathered,' he said. 'I think I see the townsfolk beginning to swarm out, but no guards. Yet undoubtedly the Sanctuary has had word about us. So it is plain they do not intend to resist.'

'Did you expect that—really?'

'I was not sure. That is why I brought so large a detachment of my own warriors.' The cuirassed figure straightened in the saddle. The tail switched. 'They would have been the ones breaking the law, had they tried to fight, so we would have had no compunctions. Not only the Wardens have chafed at the Consecrate bridle. My troop will be almost sorry not to bloody a blade this day.'

'Not I.' Falkayn shivered.

'Well,' Rebo said, 'peaceful or no, you have done more harm to them than I ever could. The world will not be the same again. So simple a thing as wagons—less toil, more goods moving faster, the age-old balance upset. And *I* will use some of that released power to overrun the Kasunians, which means I will be one to reckon with in the councils of the realm. Ever will your people be welcome in Gilrigor.'

Falkayn dropped his glance, guiltily. 'I cannot lie to you, my friend,' he stumbled. 'There may never be any more of us coming here.'

'I had heard that,' said Rebo, 'and ignored it. Perhaps I did not wish to believe. No matter now.' Pride rang in his tones. 'One day our ships will come to you.'

He raised his axe in signal. His riders deployed and the huge wagon lumbered over the ridge, drawn by twenty fastigas. The generator and crane lashed atop it glowed under the red sun.

The driver lowered his drag brake, a flat log, so the vehicle wouldn't get away from him on the downhill stretch. Groaning, squealing, banging, and rattling, the thing rocked onward.

It moved on eight rollers. They revolved between planks, the forward pair of which was adjustable by square pegs to permit turning. There were bumpers fore and aft to prevent their escape on an incline. As each roller emerged from the rear, two hooks caught two of the oblong metal eyes which ringed the grooves cut near either end of the log. These hooks were shrunk on to a pair of cross-braced, counterweighted arms mounted high on the wagon bed. The arms were held in place by leather straps within a frame that stopped sidewise motion and pivoted on shapeless leather pads atop their posts. A couple of workers hauled lustily. The arms swung high. At the limit of their permissible arc, the carefully shaped hooks slipped out of the eyes and the roller fell on to a wooden roof that slanted downward to the front. Two other natives, equipped with peavies, stood there to make certain of its alignment. It boomed quickly between its guideboards and dropped to the road behind the front bumper. The wagon passed over it, the arms dipped in time to catch the next log, and the cycle began anew.

Each roller had three curved sides.

Draw an equilateral triangle, ABC. Put the point of your compasses on A and draw the arc BC. Move to B and describe AC, then to C and describe AB. Round off the corners. The resulting figure has constant width. It will roll between two parallel lines tangent to it, maintaining that tangency for the whole revolution.

As a matter of fact, the class of constant-width polygons is infinite. The circle is merely a limiting case.

To be sure, Falkayn thought, the rollers on this Goldberg of his would wear down in time, approach the forbidden cross section and have to be replaced. Or would they? Someone like Rebo could argue that this proved the circle was actually the least perfect of all shapes, the degenerate product of a higher-order form. As if the poor old Consecrates didn't have theological problems enough!

He checked to his mount and rode on ahead of the wagon, towards his ship.

Before space flight it was often predicted that other planets would appeal strictly to the intellect. Even on Earthlike worlds, the course of biochemical evolution must be so different from the Terrestrial—since chance would determine which of many possible pathways was taken—that men could not live without special equipment. And as for intelligent beings, were we not arrogant to imagine that they would be so akin to us psychologically and culturally that we would find any common ground with them? The findings of the earliest extra-Solar expeditions seemed to confirm science in this abnegation of anthropomorphism.

Today the popular impression has swung to the opposite pole. We realize the galaxy is full of planets which, however exotic in detail, are as hospitable to us as ever Earth was. And we have all met beings who, no matter how unhuman their appearance, talk and act like one of our stereotypes. The Warrior, the Philosopher, the Merchant, the Old Space Ranger, we know in a hundred variant fleshly garments. We do business, quarrel, explore, and seek amusement with them as we might with any of our own breed. So is there not something fundamental in the pattern of Terrestrial biology and in Technic civilization itself?

No. As usual, the truth lies somewhere between the extremes. The vast majority of planets are in fact environments for man. But on this account we normally pass them by, and so they do not obtrude very much on our awareness. Of those which possess free oxygen and liquid water, more than half are useless, or deadly, to us, for one reason or another. Yet evolution is not a random process. Natural selection, operating within the constraints of physical law, gives it a certain direction. Furthermore, so huge is the galaxy that the random variations which do occur closely duplicate each other on millions of worlds. Thus we have no lack of New Earths.

Likewise with the psychology of intelligent species. Most sophonts indeed possess basic instincts which diverge more or less from man's. With those of radically alien motivations we have little contact. Those we encounter on a regular basis are

57

necessarily those whose bent is akin to ours; and again, given billions of planets, this bent is sure to be found among millions of races.

Of course, we should not be misled by superficial resemblances. The nonhuman remains nonhuman. He can only show us those facets of himself which we can understand. Thus he often seems to be a two dimensional, even comic personality. But remember, we have the corresponding effect on him. It is just as well that the average human does not know on how many planets he is the standard subject of the bawdy joke.

Even so, most races have at least as much contrast between individuals—not to mention cultures—as Homo Sapiens does. Hence there is a degree of overlap. Often a man gets along better with some nonhuman being than he does with many of his fellow-men. 'Sure,' said a prospector on Quetzalcoatl, speaking of his partner, 'he looks like a cross between a cabbage and a derrick. Sure, he belches H_2S and sleeps in a mud wallow, and his idea of fun is to spend six straight hours discussin' the whichness of the wherefore. But I can trust him—hell, I'd even leave him alone with my wife!'

—Noah Arkwright, *An Introduction to Sophontology*

Part 2 : A Sun Invisible

A Sun Invisible

The invaders had posted their fleet in standard patrol orbits. Otherwise they did nothing to camouflage themselves. It bespoke a confidence that chilled David Falkayn.

As his speedster neared Vanessa, he picked up ship after ship on his instruments. One passed so close that his viewscreens needed little magnification to show details. She was a giant, of Nova class, with only subtle outward indications that the hands which built her were not human. Her guns thrust across blackness and crowding constellations; sunlight blazed off her flanks; she was beautiful, arrogant, and terrifying.

Falkayn told himself he was not duly terrified. Himself wondered how big a liar he was.

His receiver buzzed, a call on the universal band. He flipped to Accept. The dial on the Doppler compensator indicated that the battleship was rapidly matching vectors with him. The image which looked out of the screen was—no, scarcely that of a Vanessan, but a member of the same species. It gabbled.

'Sorry, no spikka da——' Falkayn braked. Conquerors were apt to be touchy, and yonder chap sat aboard a vessel which could eat a continent with nuclear weapons and use his boat afterwards for a toothpick. 'I regret my ignorance of your various languages.'

The Kraok honked. Evidently he, she, or yx did not know Anglic. Well, the interspeech of the Polesotechnic League ... '*Loquerisne Latine?*'

The being reached for a vocalizer. Without such help, humans and Kraoka garbled each other's sounds rather badly. Adjusting it, the officer asked, '*Sprechen Sie Deutsch?*'

'Huh?' Falkayn's jaw hit his Adam's apple.

'*Ich haben die deutsche Sprache ein wenig gelehrt,*' said the Kraok with more pride than grammar, '*bei der grosse Kapitän.*'

Falkayn gripped tight to his pilot seat, and his sanity, and gaped.

Aside from being hostile, the creature was not an unpleasing sight. About two metres tall, the body resembled that of a slim tyrannosaur, if one can imagine tyrannosaurs with brown fur. From the back sprang a great, ribbed dorsal fin, partly folded but still shimmering iridescent. The arms were quite anthropoid, except for four-fingered hands where each digit had an extra joint. The head was round, with tufted ears, blunt muzzle, eyes smaller than a man's.

Clothing amounted to a brassard of authority, a pouch belt, and a sidearm. Falkayn could therefore search his memory and discover which of the three Kraokan sexes the officer belonged to: the so-called transmitter, which was fertilized by the male and in turn impregnated the female. *I should've guessed*, he thought, *even if the library on Garstang's didn't have much information on them. The males are short and meek and raise the young. The females are the most creative and make most of the decisions. The transmitters are the most belligerent.*

And right now are tracking me with guns. He felt altogether isolated. The throb and murmur of the boat, the odours of recycled air and his own sweat, his weight under the interior gee-field, were like an eggshell of life sensation around him. Outside lay starkness. The power of the League was distant by multiple parsecs, and these strangers had declared themselves its enemies.

'*Antworten Sie!*' demanded the Kraok.

Falkayn groped with half-forgotten bits of Yiddish that he had sometimes heard from Martin Schuster, during his apprenticeship. '*Ikh ... veyss ... nit keyn ... Deitch,*' he said, as slowly and clearly as possible. 'Get me ... *ah mentsch* ... uh, *zeit azay git.*' The other sat motionless. 'Damn it, you've got humans with you,' Falkayn said. 'I know the name of one. Utah Horn. Understand? Utah Horn.'

The Kraok switched him over to another, who squatted against a background of electronic apparatus. Unhuman tones whistled from an intercom. The new one turned to Falkayn.

'I know some Latin,' yx said. In spite of a vocalizer, the accent was thick enough to spread on pumpernickel. 'You identify.'

Falkayn wet his lips. 'I am the Polesotechnic League's factor on Garstang's,' he said. 'A messenger capsule brought me word about your, uh, advent. It said I had permission to come here.'

'So.' More whistles. 'Indeed. One boat, unarmed, we allow to make landing at Elan-Trrl. You make trouble, we kill.'

'Of course I won't,' Falkayn promised, *unless I get a chance*. 'I will proceed directly. Do you want my route plan?'

Yx did. The boat's pilot computer sent numbers to the battleship's. The track was approved. Maser beams flashed through space, alerting other vessels to keep an eye on the speedster. 'You go,' said the Kraok.

'But this Utah Horn——'

'Commander Horn see you when want to. Go.' The screen blanked and Falkayn went. Ohe acceleration strained his internal field compensators.

He gusted air from his lungs and stared outward. Hitherto, as he sped towards Thurman's Star, the view had been dominated by Beta Centauri, unwinking, almost intolerably brilliant across two-score light-years. But now the sun of Vanessa showed a visible disc. It wasn't that kind of type B supergiant: but nevertheless impressive, a white F_7, seething with prominences, shimmering with corona. If his shield screens should fail, its radiation would strike through the hull and destroy him.

Well, he gulped, *I wanted to be a dashing adventurer. So here I am, and mostly I want to dash.*

He stretched, opposed muscles to each other, worked out some of his tension. Then he felt hungry and went aft to build a sandwich; and when he had eaten and lit his pipe, a certain ebullience returned. For he was a bare twenty years old.

When he got his journeyman's papers, he was one of the youngest humans ever to do so. In large part, that was thanks to his role in the trouble on Ivanhoe. To set a similar record for a Master Merchant's certificate, he needed another exploit or two. Beljagor's message had made him whoop for glee.

Now it turned out that he was up against something more formidable than he had imagined. But he remained a scion of a baronial house in the Grand Duchy of Hermes. Mustn't let the side down, eh, what?

At a minimum, if he did nothing but convey word to Sector HQ about what had happened, that would bring him to the notice of the higher-ups. Maybe old Nick van Rijn himself would hear about this David Falkayn, who was so obviously being wasted in that dismal little outpost on Garstang's.

He practised a reckless grin. It looked better than last year. While his face remained uncurably snub-nosed, it had lost the chubbiness that used to distress him. And he was large and blond and rangy, he told himself, and had excellent taste in clothes and wine. Also women, he added, becoming more smug by the minute. If only he weren't the sole human on his assigned planet——! Well, perhaps this mysterious Horn person had brought along some spare females. . . .

Vanessa grew in the vision ports, a reddish globe mottled with green and blue, sparked with reflections off the small seas. Falkayn wondered what the inhabitants called it. Being colonists themselves, whose civilization had not fallen apart during the long hiatus in Kraokan space travel as had happened on other settlements, they doubtless had a single language. Why hadn't Thurman done the usual thing in such cases, and put the native name of his discovery into the catalogues?

Quite probably because men couldn't wrap their larynxes around it. Or maybe he just felt like dubbing the planet 'Vanessa'. Judas, what a radium-plated opportunity an explorer had! What girl could possibly resist an offer to name a whole world for her?

Another warship in sentry orbit became discernible. Falkayn stopped dreaming.

II

In the lost great days of the expansion, the Kraoka had never founded a city. The concept of so small a unit having an identity of its own—and composed of still lesser individual sub-units, each with *its* separateness—was too alien to them. However, they did give names to the interconnected warrens they built at various sites. Falkayn's bible (*terrestrial Pilot's Guide to the Beta Centauri Region*) informed him that Elan-Trrl, in any of several possible spellings, could be found in the middle northern latitudes, and was marked by a League radio beacon.

So crowded a microreel could say little about the planet. The only important hazards mentioned were ozone and ultraviolet. He got into a hooded coverall and donned a filter mask with goggles. The tiny spaceport swooped up at him. He landed and debarked.

For a moment he stood orienting himself, getting accustomed to strangeness. The sky overhead was cloudless, very pale blue, the sun too dazzling for him to look near. Colours seemed washed out in the cruel illumination. Beyond the port, hills rolled down to a lake from which irrigation canals seamed a landscape densely cultivated in bluish-green shrubs. Gnarled, feathery-leaved trees grew along the canal banks and high-prowed motor-boats glided on the water. The agricultural machines in the fields, and the occasional gravity craft that flitted overhead, must have been imported by League traders. On the horizon there bulked a dry brown mountain range.

Falkayn felt heavy, under the pull of one-point-two gees. A wind boomed around him, casting billows of heat. But in this parched air he wasn't grossly uncomfortable.

On the other side of the port, Elan-Trrl lifted bulbous towers. Their grey stone was blurred in outline, from millennia of weathering. He didn't see much traffic; mainly underground, he believed. His eyes went gratefully to the homelike steel-and-vitryl façades of the League compound at the edge of the space field. They wavered in the heat shimmers.

Two vessels rested near his. One was a stubby Holbert, evidently Beljagor's; the second, lean and armed, modelled after a Terrestrial chaser, must belong to the invaders. Several Kraoka stood guard in her shade. They must have been told to expect Falkayn, for they made no move towards him. Nor did they speak. As he walked to the compound, he felt their eyes bore at his back. His boots made a loud, lonely noise beneath the wind.

The door of the factor's quarters opened for him. The air in the lobby was no less hot and sere than outside, the light scarcely less harsh. But naturally the League would put someone from an F-type star here. Falkayn began to think more kindly about cool green Garstang's. And why hadn't this Beljagor unko come out to meet him?

An intercom said, 'Down the hall to your right,' in Latin and a gravelly bass.

Falkayn proceeded to the main office. Beljagor sat behind his desk, puffing a cigar. Above him hung the emblem of the Polesotechnic League, an early Caravel spaceship on a sunburst and the motto *All the Traffic Will Bear*. Computers, vocascribes, and other equipment were familiar, too. The boss was not. Falkayn had never met anyone from Jaleel before.

'So there you are,' Beljagor said. 'Took you long enough.'

Falkayn stopped and looked at him. The factor was somewhat anthropoid. That is, his sticky form sported two legs, two arms, one head, and no tail. But he was little over a metre tall; his feet each had three thick toes, his hands three mutually opposed fingers; the kilt which was his solitary garment revealed grey scales and yellow abdomen. His nose could best be likened to a tapir's snout, his ears to a sort of bat's wings. A bunch of carroty cilia sprouted from the top of his pate, a pair of fleshy chemosensor tendrils from above his eyes. Those eyes were as small as a Kraok's; animals which see into the ultraviolet and don't use the red end of man's spectrum have no need for large orbs.

As if for comparison, a Vanessan squatted on yxs—no, her this time—tail before the desk. Beljagor gestured with his cigar. 'This here is Quillipup, my chief liaison officer. And you are ... what is your silly name, now?'

'David Falkayn!' The newcomer could do nothing but snap a bit, when he was a mere journeyman face to face with a Master.

'Well, sit. Have a beer? You Earthtypes dehydrate easy.'

Falkayn decided Beljagor wasn't such a bad fellow after all. 'Thank you, sir.' He folded his lean frame into a lounger.

The Jaleelan ordered through his intercom. 'Have any trouble on your way?' he asked.

'No.'

'I didn't expect you would. You're not worth bothering with. Also, Horn wanted you to come, and he seems to rank high in their fleet.' Beljagor shrugged. 'Can't say I wanted you myself. An unlicked cub! If there'd been an experienced man anywhere nearby, we might have got something done.'

Falkayn swallowed another chunk of pride. 'Regrets, sir. But when the League has only been operating hereabouts for a few decades—I'm not sure what you have in mind. Your message just said the Thurmanian System had been invaded by a force of Kraoka who're ordering the League out of the whole Beta

Centauri region.'

'Well, somebody has to go warn HQ,' Beljagor grunted, 'and I won't myself. That is, I figure to stay here and stall, maybe even argue them into changing their minds. Your own post won't miss *you*.' He fumed in silence for a while. 'First, though, before you leave, I want you to try and make a few elementary observations. That's why I sent to Garstang's for help, instead of Roxlatl. Snarfen is probably ten times as able as you—he being a Master—but you are a human and there are humans in high positions among the Antoranites. Like Horn, who said he'd want to interview you, after I mentioned your origin. So maybe you can get a line on what's going on. Takes one member of your ridiculous race to understand another, I always say.'

Falkayn stuck grimly to the point. 'The Antoranites . . . sir?'

'The invaders call their base Antoran. They won't describe it beyond the name.'

Falkayn glanced at Quillipup. 'Don't you have some idea where they come from?' he asked.

'No,' said the Kraok into her vocalizer. 'It can be no world that the Race was known to have settled. But records are incomplete.'

'I don't understand how——'

'I shall explain. Ages before your species or Master Beljagor's were aught but savages, our great ancestors on Kraokanan——'

'Yes, I know about them.'

'Don't interrupt your superiors, cub,' Beljagor growled. 'Besides, I'm not sure you do know the history. And won't hurt you to hear it again, whether or not you've waded through a book or two.' His nose twitched in disdain. 'You're with Solar Spice & Liquors, right? They don't deal here. Nothing for them. As far as interstellar trade goes, Vanessa doesn't produce anything but drugs and fluorescents that aren't useful to your type of life. Me, I'm not only here as agent for General Motors of Jaleel, I often represent other companies from similar planets. So I have to know the situation inside out. Go on, Quillipup.'

'Now you are interrupting,' sulked the Vanessan.

'When I speak, it's not an interruption, it's an enlightenment. Go on, I said. But make it short. None of your damned singing chronicles, you hear?'

'The majesty of the Race cannot well be conveyed without

the Triumph Ballads.'

'Stuff the majesty of the Race! Carry on.'

'Oh, well, he probably could not appreciate the splendour anyway.'

Falkayn gritted his teeth. Where the hell was that promised beer?

'Thousands upon thousands of years ago, then,' Quillipup began, 'the Race mastered space flight and set forth to colonize among the stars. Long and mighty was that striving, and the tales of the hero-crews echo down the ages. As for example, Ungn——'

'Vector back,' ordered Beljagor, for Quillipup seemed about to burst into song.

Falkayn wondered if her bragging was due to an inferiority complex. The fact of the matter was that the Kraoka had never learned how to build a hyperdrive engine. Everything must be done at sunlight speeds: decades or centuries, from star to star. And then only the bright F-types, which are comparatively rare, were reasonable goals. Smaller suns, like Sol, were too cool and dim, too poor in the ultraviolet radiation on which a high-energy biochemistry depended. Bigger ones like Beta Centauri—indeed, any above F_5 in the main sequence—lacked planets. The Kraoka were lucky to have found fourteen new systems they could use.

'Try to imagine the ancestral achievement,' Quillipup urged. 'Not merely did they cross the unthinkable interstellar abysses, they often transformed the atmosphere and ecology of entire worlds, to make them habitable. Never has another species gained the skill in that art which they possessed.'

Well, naturally not, Falkayn thought. Modern spacefarers had no reason to be planetary engineers. If they didn't like a globe, they flitted off to look for another. Sublight travellers could not be so choosy.

He must admit that the Kraokan past had a certain grandeur. Men would hardly have mounted so vast a project for so long; they had more individual but less racial pride.

'When the Dark Ages descended,' Quillipup said, 'we remembered. Whatever else slipped from our grasp, we were yet able to look into the night sky and know what stars shone upon our kindred.'

According to what Falkayn had read, the collapse had been

gradual but inevitable. The sphere of operations simply became too big for expeditions so slow; it grew too costly, in time and labour and resources, to attain the next white sun. Thus exploration ended.

And likewise did trade between the colonies. It couldn't be made to pay. The Polesotechnic League exists merely because—given hyperdrive and gravity control—interstellar freight costs less for numberless planetary products than manufacture at home would cost. Though the ancient Kraoka had lacked a profit motive, they were not exempt from the laws of economics.

So they built no more star ships. In time, most of the colonies even quit interplanetary travel. Several fell into chaos and ultimate barbarism. Vanessa was luckier: civilization persisted, ossified and changeless, but on a fairly high technological level, for some three hundred centuries. Then Thurman came. And now the Kraoka again had news from their lost brothers and dreamed of reunifying the Race.

Which required money. A spaceship is not exactly cheap, and the League is no charitable organization. Let the Vanessans accumulate sufficient credit, and shipyards elsewhere in the galaxy would be glad to take their orders. But not before.

Falkayn grew aware that Quillipup was droning on about more immediately significant business.

'—neither chronicle nor tradition identifies a world that might be Antoran. Phonetic analysis of clandestinely recorded speech, and certain details of custom that have been observed, suggest that the planet was settled from Dzua. But Dzua was one of the first worlds on which civilization disintegrated, and no record remains of enterprises which might once have begun there. Antoran must, accordingly, be a fifteenth colony, forgotten at home and never mentioned to the rest of us.'

'Are you sure?' Falkayn ventured. 'I mean, could one of the known Kraokan planets not have——'

'Certainly not,' Beljagor said. 'I've been on all of them and I know their capabilities. A fleet like this one—and I was taken into space, shown how big a fleet it is and what it can do—can't be built without more industry than anybody could hide.'

'The invaders ... what have they said?'

'Not a clue-giving word, I told you. They don't belong to your blabbermouth species. Kraoka have too much tribal-identity instinct to break security.'

'They must at least have explained their reasons.'

'Oh, that. Yes. They're hell-bent to re-establish the old society, as an empire this time. And they want the League out of the entire region because they say we're a bunch of dominators, exploiters, corrupters of the pure tradition, and I don't know what stinking else.'

Falkayn stole a look at Quillipup. He couldn't read expressions on her face, but the dorsal fin—a body-cooling surface—was erecting itself and the tail switched. Vanessa had offered no resistance to the take-over. Quite probably Quillipup would not be a bit sorry if her present employers got booted out.

The human said carefully, 'Well, sir, in a way they're justified, aren't they? This is their home, not ours. We've done nothing for the Kraoka that we didn't make a fat profit on. And if they want to deal with us, they have to change a high, ancient culture——'

'Your idealism pierces me to the core; I won't say in what part of my anatomy,' Beljagor sneered. 'What matters is that the League stands to lose a megawhopping amount of money. All our facilities in the region are to be confiscated, you hear? So they'll get our trade with the cooler stars, too. And I don't think they'll stop there, either. Those humans who're with them, what do *they* want?'

'Well ... yes,' Falkayn conceded. There was no denying that his own species was among the most predatory in the universe. 'Your message mentioned somebody called Utah Horn. That does sound pretty, uh, Wild West and banditlike!'

'I'll notify him you're here,' Beljagor said. 'He wants to talk with a League official of his own race. Well, he'll have to settle for you. I wish I could hope you'll manage to worm something out of him.'

A server floated in with bottles. 'Here's the beer,' Beljagor announced. The machine opened two, Quillipup curtly declining a third. Her sinews were taut and her tail lashed the clawed feet.

'*Ad fortunam tuam*,' Beljagor said with no great sincerity, and tossed off half a litre.

Falkayn opened his mask at the mouth and did the same. Then he spouted the liquid back, choked, coughed, and fought not to vomit.

'Huh?' Beljagor stared. 'What in the nine pestulant hells——? Oh, I see. I forgot your breed can't stand Jaleelan proteins.' He slapped his thigh with a pistol noise. 'Haw, haw, haw!'

III

Humans being as ubiquitous as they are, nearly every League outpost on a nonterrestroid planet includes a suite conditioned and stocked for such visitors. Falkayn had been afraid that those Antoranite officers who were of his lineage would have taken the quarters over, leaving him to twiddle his thumbs in the cramped speedster. But they preferred their spaceships, he learned. Perhaps they were wary of booby traps. He was free to twiddle his thumbs in a series of rooms.

His phone chimed as Vanessa's nineteen-hour day was drawing to a close. A man in a form-fitting green uniform looked out of the screen. His features were hard, moustached, and so deeply tanned that at first Falkayn took him for an African. 'You are the one from the other Polesotechnic station?' he asked. He spoke coldly, with a guttural accent.

'Yes. David Falkayn. And you're Commander Horn?'

'No. Captain Blanck, in charge of security. Since Commander Horn is to have a conference with you, I am making safe arrangements.'

'I'm not quite sure what we are to confer about.'

Blanck cracked a smile. It seemed to hurt his face. 'Nothing very definite, Freeman Falkayn. We wish certain messages conveyed by you to the League. Otherwise, shall we say that it is mutually advantageous to get some personal impressions of each other, uncomplicated by inherent differences between species. Antoran will fight if need be, but would rather not. Commander Horn wishes to persuade you that we are no

69

monsters, nor engaged in an unreasonable cause. It is hoped that you in turn can convince your superiors.'

'Um-m-m . . . okay. Where and when?'

'I think best in your billet. We assume you are not so stupid as to attempt any breach of truce.'

'With a war fleet sitting right over my head? Don't worry!' Falkayn considered. 'How about dinner here? I've checked the supplies, and they're better than anything a spaceship is likely to have.'

Blanck agreed, set the time for an hour hence, and switched off. Falkayn got the kitchen servers busy. The fact that he was to dine with an enemy did not mean he couldn't dine well. Of course, a space cowboy like Utah Horn wouldn't know caviar from buckshot; but Falkayn was prepared to savour for two.

While he dressed, in a formal gold outfit, he lined up his thoughts. There didn't seem to be many humans with the invaders, but they all seemed to be key personnel. No doubt they were the ones who had originally shown the Antoranites how to build warcraft and were the experienced strategists and tacticians of the whole shebang. Horn was willing to come here because a fellow human taken aboard a ship might observe too much, critical little details which would have escaped Beljagor. But Falkayn could try to pump him. . . .

A tender landed from the orbiting flotilla. Dusk had fallen, and Falkayn could barely see that a single human walked towards his lodgings, accompanied by four Kraokan guards. Those took stations at the entrance.

A minute passed while his guest waited in the air lock for ozone to be converted; then Falkayn activated the inner door. The Antoranite had just hung up a filter mask. Falkayn lurched.

'What?' he yelled.

She couldn't be many years older than himself. The uniform was snug around a figure which would have stunned him even if he had not been celibate for months. Blue-black hair fell softly to her shoulders past enormous hazel eyes, tip-tilted nose, the most delightful mouth he had ever——

'But, but, but,' he said.

She turned Blanck's accent to music. 'Freeman Falkayn? I am Commander Horn.'

'*Utah* Horn?'

'Yes, that is correct, Jutta Horn of Neuheim. You are surprised?'

Falkayn nodded in a blackjacked fashion.

'You see, Neuheim's population being small, any who happen to have some ability must help. Besides, my father was the man who discovered the lost planet and began this whole crusade. The Kraoka, with their feeling for ancestry, revere me on that account; and moreover, they are used to thinking of females as leaders. So I am doubly useful: any orders transmitted by me are sure to be obeyed to the letter. You must have met women spacers before now.'

'Uh, it's only that, uh——' *I get it. When he dictated his letter to me, Beljagor was using a 'scribe adjusted for Anglic spelling. Quite understandable, when so few people speak German any more. He did use the masculine pronoun for her. But either he didn't happen to meet her personally, or he's too contemptuous of humans to bother noticing their sex.*

The loss is entirely his.

Falkayn collected himself, smiled his largest smile, and bowed his most sweeping bow. 'I wish I could be so pleasantly surprised every time,' he purred. 'Welcome, Commander. Do sit down. What would you like to drink?'

She looked doubtful. 'I am not sure if I ought.'

'Come, come. A dinner without an aperitif is like a—ahem! —a day without sunshine.' He had almost said, 'A bed without a girl,' but that might be rushing matters.

'*Ach*, I am not familiar with these things.'

'High time you became so, then.' Falkayn told the nearest server to bring old-fashioneds. He preferred a martini himself, by several light-years, but if her palate was uneducated she'd drink more of something sweet.

She settled primly on a chair. He saw that her waist communicator was energized, doubtless transmitting to the guards outside. If they heard anything suspicious, they would break in. Still, they wouldn't catch the nuances of what Falkayn was feverishly planning.

He sat down, too. She refused a cigarette. 'You must not have had a chance to be corrupted by civilization,' he laughed.

'No,' she agreed, deadpan. 'I was born and raised on Neuheim. My sole visits beyond the system, until now, were to unexplored stars in the course of training cruises.'

'What is this Neuheim?'

'Our planet. A part of the Antoranite System.'

'Eh? You mean Antoran is a star?'

Jutta Horn bit her lip. 'I did not know you had the opposite impression.'

In spite of her nearness, or maybe because of being stimulated thereby, Falkayn's mind leaped. 'Ah-ha!' he grinned. 'This tells me something. We took for granted that the Antoranites were from a single planet and their human allies simply adventurers. Earthmen don't call themselves Solarians. But Earthmen and Martians do collectively. Ergo, there's more than one inhabited planet going around Antoran. Your Neuheim; and how many Kraokan worlds?'

'No matter!' she clipped.

He waved his hand. 'I'm sorry if I've disturbed you. Here are our cocktails. Let's drink to a better understanding between us.'

She sipped, hesitantly at first, then with frank enjoyment. 'You are more friendly than I had expected,' she said.

'How could I be otherwise towards you, my lady?' She blushed and fluttered her lashes, yet obviously she was not playing coquette. He eased off; never embarrass your target. 'We're discussing our differences like two civilized people, trying to reach a compromise. Aren't we?'

'What authority have you to sign treaties?' She might never have been in civilization, but she had been taught how it worked.

'None,' Falkayn said. 'As the man on the spot, though, I can make recommendations that will have considerable weight.'

'You look so young to be so important,' she murmured.

'Oh, well,' said Falkayn modestly, 'I've knocked around a bit, you know. Had the chance to do this and that. Let's talk about you.'

She took his pronoun for plural and started off on what must be a prepared lecture.

Antoran did indeed have planets which the Kraoka of Dzua had once colonized. Though the settlers perforce gave up star travel, they had maintained interplanetary commerce down the millennia, keeping more technology than Vanessa did.

Forty-odd years ago, Robert Horn of Nova Germania was being chased by a League cruiser. He laid a course to throw the pursuer off his trail—the old star-dodge manoeuvre—and thus passed so near Antoran that he detected radio emissions. Later he slipped back to investigate and discovered the planets.

'Yes, he was an outlaw,' his daughter said defiantly. 'He was a leader in the Landholders' Revolt ... so good, so effective, that afterwards they dared not give him amnesty.'

Falkayn had heard vaguely about the matter. Something to do with a conspiracy among the Nova Germania's first families, descendants of the original pioneers, to get back the power that a new constitution had taken away from them. And, yes, the League was involved; the republican government offered better trading concessions than the Landholders had granted in their day. No wonder that this girl was busily doing the League all the dirt she could.

He smiled and refilled her glass. 'I can sympathize,' he said. 'Being from Hermes, you see. Aristocracy's far and away my favourite system.'

Her eyes widened. 'You are *adel*—nobly born?'

'Younger son,' Falkayn said, modest again. He did not add that he'd been shipped to Earth for his education because he kept kicking over the traces which an aristocrat was expected to carry. 'Do go on. You fascinate me.'

'The Antoranite System includes one planet which the Kraoka had modified for habitability, but which was too far out, too cold and dark, to be really worth their while. For humans it is better. That is my world, Neuheim.'

Hm, Falkayn thought. This implied at least one planet further inward which did provide a good Kraokan environment. Very possibly more than one; a war fleet as big as Beljagor claimed he had seen can't be built in a hurry without a lot of population and resources. But this in turn implied a large sun with a wide biothermal zone. Which didn't make sense! Every F-type star in this region had been visited by League surveyors; likewise the G-types; and there definitely was no such system as——

'My father returned in secret to Nova Germania,' Jutta Horn said. 'He got recruits there and elsewhere. The whole world of Neuheim was given them in exchange for their help.'

I feel pretty sure they planted the idea of conquest in the first place, Falkayn reflected. *Yeh, I can guess how Kraoka might fall for the concept of a reunified Vaterland. And given enough anti-League propaganda, they might well come to believe that the only way to get unification is to expel us first.*

'So Germania engineers showed the Antoranites how to make hyperdrive ships,' he said; 'and Germanian officers trained the crews; and Germanian secret agents kept track of events out-system—my, you've been busy.'

She nodded. Two drinks blurred her tone a little. 'That is true. Everything comes second to the crusade. Afterwards we can relax. How I look forward!'

'Why not start right away?' Falkayn asked. 'Why fight the League? We've no objection to the Kraoka building a star marine at their own expense, nor to any social arrangements you've made on Neuheim.'

'After the way the League meddled in the past?' she challenged.

'Yes, granted, we do, now and then, when our interests are threatened. But still, Jutta'—there, he'd established a first-name relationship—'the Polesotechnic League is not a state, not even a government. It's nothing but a mutual-benefit association of interstellar merchants, who're probably more wolfish towards each other than towards anybody outside.'

'Power is the one basis of negotiation,' she said, turning Clausewitzian. 'When we and our allies have secured this region, then perhaps we will allow you to operate here again ... under our rules. Otherwise you could too easily impose your will on us, if we did not happen to desire the same things as you.'

'The League isn't going to take this lying down,' he warned.

'I think the League had better do so,' she retorted. 'We are here, in the region, with interior lines of communication. We can strike from space, anywhere. A League war fleet must come across many parsecs. It will find its bases demolished. And it will not know where our home planets are!'

Falkayn backed off in haste. He didn't want her in that mood. 'You certainly have a tremendous advantage,' he said. 'The League can muster forces greater by orders of magnitude —surely you realize that—but the League may well decide that the cost of defeating you would be greater than any possible gain in doing so.'

'Thus my father calculated before he died. Merchants, who lust for nothing but money, can be cowed. *Adelsvolk* are

74

different. They live for an ideal, not for economics.'

I wish to hell you'd had a chance to stick that pretty nose out of your smug, ingrown little kingdom and see what working aristocrats are like, Falkayn thought. Aloud: 'Well, now, Jutta, I can't quite agree. Remember, I'm both a merchant and a nobleman's son. The psychologies aren't so unlike. A peer has to be a politician, with everything that that entails, or he's no good. And a merchant has to be an idealist.'

'What?' She blinked in startlement. 'How?'

'Why, you don't think we work for money alone, do you? If that were the object, we'd stay safe and snug at home. No, it's adventure, new horizons, life's conquest of inanimate nature— the universe itself, the grandest enemy of all.'

She frowned, but she was softened. 'I do not understand, quite.'

'Suppose I give you a few examples——'

IV

Dinner was served in the roof turret, which had a view like being outdoors. By night Vanessa took on beauty. Both moons were aloft, small and swift, turning the land to a fantasy of dim silver and moving shadows. The lake gleamed, the native towers looked like giant blossoms. Overhead the sky was splendid with stars, Beta Centauri the king jewel, its blue radiance matching the moons'.

And glowpanels caressed Jutta's sun-browned cheeks with their own light; and Beethoven's Seventh lifted softly from a speaker; and bubbles danced in the champagne glasses. Dinner had made its stately progression from hors d'oeuvres and consommé through fish, roast, and salad, to petits fours and now cheeses. Falkayn had kept the magnum flask busy. Not that either party was drunk—Jutta, alas, had so far kept her wits patriotically about her—but they both felt more than cheerful.

75

'Tell me other things,' she urged. 'You have had such a wonderful existence, David. Like the hero of an ancient saga—but this is now, which makes it twice as good.'

'Let me think,' he said, giving her a refill. 'Maybe the time I cracked up on a rogue planet?'

'A what?'

'Free planet, sunless. More of them floating around in space than there are stars. The smaller the body, you see, the likelier it was to form when the galaxy coalesced. Normally you find them in groups . . . to be honest, you don't normally find them, because space is big and they are little and dark. But by sheer chance, on the way from Tau Ceti to 70 Ophiuchi, I——'

The adventure had, in fact, happened to somebody else. So had most of the stories Falkayn had been relating. But he saw no reason to spoil a good yarn with pedantry.

Besides, she continued to sip, in an absentminded and unsuspecting way, while he talked.

'—and finally I replenished my air by boiling and processing frozen gases. And was I glad to leave!'

'I should think so.' She shivered. 'Space is bleak. Lovely, but bleak. I like planets better.' She gazed outward. 'The night here is different from home. I don't know which I like best, Neuheim or Vanessa. After dark, I mean,' she added, with a slightly wobbling laugh. 'None of the Kraokan worlds are pleasant by day.'

'None whatsoever? You must have seen quite a variety, with three of them for neighbours.'

'Five,' she corrected. Her hand went to her mouth, 'Lieber Gott! I didn't mean to tell.'

He chuckled, though inwardly he thrummed with a new excitement. Judas! Five planets—six, counting Neuheim—in the thermal zone where water was liquid . . . around one star! 'It doesn't make any practical difference,' he said, 'when you've evidently found some way to make your whole system invisible. I'd like to know more about you, that's all, and I can't unless you tell me something about your home.' He reached across the table and patted her hand. 'That's what gave you your dreams, your hopes—your charm, if I may say so. Neuheim must be a paradise.'

'No, it is a hard world for humans,' she answered earnestly. 'In my own lifetime, we have had to move entire villages towards the poles as the planet swung closer to the sun. Even the Kraoka have their troubles for similar reasons.' She pulled free of his touch. 'But I am talking of what I shouldn't.'

'Very well, let's keep to harmless things,' he said. 'You mentioned that the nights were different at home. In what way?'

'Oh ... different constellations, of course. Not greatly, but enough to notice. And then, because of the auroras, we never see the stars so clearly as here, from any location. I *must* not say more. You are far too observing, Davy. Tell me, instead, about your Hermes.' She smiled irresistibly. 'I would like to know where your own dreams come from.'

Nothing loth, Falkayn spoke of mountains, virgin wilderness, plains darkened by horned herds, surf-bathing at Thunderstrands—'What does that mean, Davy?'

'Why, bathing in the surf. You know, the waves caused by tidal action.' He decided to disarm her suspicions with a joke. 'Now, my poor innocent, you've given yourself away again. You imply Neuheim doesn't have tides.'

'No harm in that,' she said. 'True, we have not any moon. The oceans are like huge, still lakes.'

'Doesn't the sun——' He checked himself.

'Not so far away as it is, a tiny point of fire, I can't get used to the disc here.' Abruptly Jutta set down her glass. 'Listen,' she said, 'you are either very young and sweet or you are clever as Satan.'

'Why not both?'

'I cannot take the chance.' She rose. 'Best I leave now. I made a mistake to come.'

'What?' He scrambled to his own feet. 'But the evening's hardly begun. I thought we'd go back to the living room and relax with some more music.' The *Liebestod*, for instance.

'No.' Distress and determination chased each other across her face. 'I enjoy myself too much. I forget to guard my tongue. Take to the League this word from us. Before they can marshal against us, we will have the Kraokan stars, and more. But if the League will be reasonable, *jo*, perhaps we can discuss trade treaties.' Her eyes dropped. She flushed. 'I would like if you could return.'

God damn all politics! Falkayn groaned. He got nowhere trying to change her mind, and must finally see her to the door.

There he kissed her hand ... and before he could build on that beginning, she had whispered good night, and was outside.

He poured himself a stiff whisky, lit his pipe, and flung himself into a lounger. None were an adequate substitute.

Rats! he brooded. *Giant mutant rats! She'll have me hustled off the planet right away, tomorrow dawn, before I can use any information I might have gathered.*

Well, at least there'll be girls at Sector HQ. And maybe, eventually, I'll find myself back here.

As a journeyman assistant; and Jutta will be at the social apex of an interstellar empire. She wouldn't snub me on that account, but what chance would we ever have to get together?

He puffed hard and scowled at a repro of a Hokusai portrait, an old man, which hung opposite him. The old man smiled back till Falkayn wanted to punch him in the nose.

The long-range significance of the Neuheimer scheme was far nastier than several begacredits' loss to the merchant princes, Falkayn saw. Suppose it did succeed. Suppose the mighty Polesotechnic League was defied and defeated, and the Kraokan Empire was established. Well, the Kraoka by themselves might or might not be content to stop at that point and settle down to peaceful relationships with everybody else. In any event; they were no direct threat to the human race; they didn't want the same kind of real estate.

But the Neuheimer humans—— Already they spoke of themselves as crusaders. Consider the past history of Homo self-styled Sapiens and imagine what so spectacular a success would do to a bunch of ideologically motivated militarists! Oh, the process would be slow; they'd have to increase their numbers, and enlarge their industrial base, and get control of every man-useful planet in this neighbourhood. But eventually; for power, and glory, and upset of the hated merchants, and advancement of a Way of Life—war.

The time to squelch them was now. A good healthy licking would discredit the Landholders; peace, mercantilism, and co-operation with others (or, at least, simple cut-throat economic competition) would become fashionable on Neuheim; and, incidentally, a journeyman who played a significant part in that outcome could expect early certification as a Master Merchant.

Whereas a mere bearer of bad tidings——

'All right,' Falkayn muttered. 'Step One in the squelching

process : Find their damned planetary system !'

They couldn't hope to keep its location secret forever. Just long enough to secure a grip on this region; and given the destructive power of a space fleet, that needn't be very long. While it remained hidden, though, the source of their strength was quite efficiently protected. Hence their entire effort could go into purely offensive operations, which gave them a military capability far out of proportion to their actual force.

Nonetheless, if the League should decide to fight, the League would win. No question about that. In the course of the war, the secret was bound to be discovered, one way or another. And then—nuclear bombardment from space—*No!*

The Landholders were gambling that the League, rather than start an expensive battle for a prize that would certainly be ruined in the course of the fighting, would vote to cut its losses and come to terms. Antoran being hidden, the bet looked fairly good. But no matter how favourable the odds, only fanatics played with entire living worlds for stakes. Poor Jutta! What foul company she was mixed up in. How he'd like to introduce her to some decent people.

Okay, then, where was the silly star?

Someplace not far off. Jutta had betrayed nothing by admitting that the constellations at home were almost like the constellations here. The ancient Kraoka could not have travelled any enormous way, as interstellar distances go. Also, the home base must be in this territory so that its fleet could exploit the advantage of interior communications.

And Antoran must be large and bright, no later in the main sequence than, say G_0. Yet ... every possible sun was already eliminated by information the League had long possessed.

Unless—wait a minute—could it be hidden by a thick nebulosity?

No. There'd still be radio indications. And Jutta had spoken of seeing stars from her home.

Aurora. Hm. She'd mentioned the necessity for certain villagers to migrate towards the poles, as her planet got too near its primary. Which meant their original settlements were a good bit further towards the equator. Even so, auroras had been conspicuous : everywhere you went, she'd said. This, again, suggested a highly energetic sun.

Funny, about the eccentric orbit. More than one planet in

the system, too, with the same problem. Unheard of. You'd almost think that——

Falkayn sat bolt upright. His pipe dropped from his jaws to his lap. 'Holy . . . hyper . . . Judas,' he gasped.

Thereafter he thought most furiously. He did not come back to himself until the coals from his pipe set fire to his trousers.

V

The door to Beljagor's place, offices-cum-residence, barely had time to get out of Falkayn's way. But as he entered the lobby, he skidded to a stop. In a small room opening on this, two Kraoka were talking. One was armed and brassarded, an invader. The other was Quillipup. They froze.

'Greetings,' said the liaison agent after a pause. 'What brings you here?'

'I want to see your boss,' Falkayn answered.

'I believe he is asleep,' Quillipup said.

'Too bad.' Falkayn started down the hall.

'Stop!' Quillipup bounded after him. 'I told you he is asleep.'

'And I told you it's a pity he has to be wakened,' Falkayn rapped.

Quillipup regarded him. Her dorsal fin rose. The Antoranite glided close behind, hand not far from blaster.

'What have you to say which is so urgent?' Quillipup asked slowly.

Falkayn gave her eyeball for eyeball and responded, 'What's so urgent for you, that it can't wait till Beljagor has risen?'

Silence, under the icy white light. Falkayn grew aware of blood pounding in his ears. His skin prickled. That energy gun looked too businesslike for his taste. But Quillipup turned on her heel, without a word, and led her companion back to the office. Falkayn let out a hard-held breath and continued on his way.

He hadn't been told where in the building the factor lived, but the layout of places like this was pretty standardized. The suite door was locked. He buzzed. Nothing happened. He buzzed again.

The scanner must have a screen in the bedroom, because the voice from the annunciator rasped, 'You! Do you suppose I'd get up for a pestilential human?'

'Yes,' Falkayn said. 'Urgent.'

'Urgent that you jump off the nearest cliff, right. And a bad night to you.' The speaker clicked off.

That adjective 'urgent' was being overworked, Falkayn decided. He leaned on the buzzer.

'Stop your infernal racket!' howled Beljagor.

'Sure, when you let me in,' Falkayn said.

Click.

Falkayn whistled 'The Blue Danube' to pass the time while he leaned on the buzzer.

The door flew open. Beljagor bounced forth. Falkayn was interested to note that the Jaleelan slept in pyjamas, bright purple ones. 'You insolent whelp!' the factor bawled. 'Get out of here!'

'Yes, sir,' Falkayn said. 'You come, too.'

'What?'

'I have to show you something in my space boat.'

Beljagor's eyes turned red. His tendrils stood erect. He drank air until his small round form seemed ready to explode.

'Please, sir,' Falkayn begged. 'You've got to. It's terribly important.'

Beljagor cursed and swung a fist.

Falkayn sidestepped the blow, picked up the Master Merchant by collar and trousers, and bore him kicking and yelling down the hall. 'I told you you had to come,' the journeyman said patiently.

The two Kraoka in the lobby had left, and those on sentry-go at the warship made no move to interfere. Maybe, behind furry poker faces, they enjoyed the sight. Falkayn had left the gangway ramp extruded from his speedster but had put a recognition lock on the entrance. It opened for him. He carried Beljagor inside, set him down, and waited for the storm to break.

The Jaleelan spoke no word, only looked at him. His snout

81

quivered a little.

'Okay,' Falkayn sighed. 'You don't accept my apologies. You'll have my certificate revoked. You'll strangle me with my own guts. Anything else?'

'I suppose you have an explanation,' Beljagor said like fingernails going quite slowly over a blackboard.

'Yes, sir. The business won't wait. And I didn't dare speak any-place but here. Your Quillipup is acting far too friendly with the self-appointed liberators. Be no trick for her to bug your quarters.'

What ozone had come in with them—less than by day— must have been processed into oxygen by now. Falkayn slipped off his filter mask. Beljagor mumbled something about Earth-type atmosphere being good for naught except breaking wind. Otherwise, though, the factor had cooled off astonishingly fast. 'Talk, cub,' he ordered.

'You see,' Falkayn said, 'I know where Antoran is.'

'Heh?' Beljagor jumped several centimetres in the pilot chair he occupied.

'They'd never let me go if they found out I know,' Falkayn continued. He leaned back against a bulkhead. His gaze drifted beyond the viewports. Both moons had set, and Beta Centauri ruled heaven. 'As is, you'll have to come, too.'

'What? Impossible! If you think I'll abandon the property of General Motors to a gang of pirates——'

'They'll doubtless send you packing before long in any event,' Falkayn said. 'Admit that. You just hate to surrender. But we've got to take the bull by the tail and look the situation squarely in the face.'

'What do you mean, you know where Antoran is?' Beljagor spluttered. 'Did you swallow something the Horn creature told you for a joke?'

'No, sir, she didn't intend to give me any information. Only, well, she was raised in an isolated, dedicated, Spartan society. She wasn't equipped to handle me.' Falkayn grinned. 'Figura-tively, I mean, not literally. Her fellows didn't allow for the effects of alcohol and smooth talk. Not used to such things themselves, I imagine. Could be they also counted on my being so over-bowled by her looks that I'd merely gawk and listen to her. They seem to be a very romantic bunch. Dangerous as hell, but romantic.'

'Well? Well? What did Horn say?'

'Little items. They gave the show away, though. Like, Antoran isn't a planet but a star. And just one star hereabouts can possibly fit the data.' Falkayn let Beljagor rumble for a moment before he pointed skyward and said, 'Beta Centauri.'

The factor did explode. He hopped around the cabin, flapping his arms and raving. Falkayn filed the choicer epithets in his memory for later use.

At last Beljagor was sufficiently calm to stand in one spot, raise a finger, and say, 'You unutterable imbecile, for your information, Beta is a type B blue giant. People knew before space flight began, giant suns don't have planets. Angular momentum per unit mass proved as much. After the hyperdrive came along, direct expeditions to any number of them clinched the matter. Even supposing, somehow, one did acquire satellites, those satellites never would get habitable. Giant stars burn hydrogen so fast their existence is measured in millions of years. Millions, you hear, not billions. Beta Centauri can hardly be ten million years old. More than half its stable lifetime is past. It'll go supernova and become a white dwarf. Life'd have no chance to evolve before the planets were destroyed. Not that there are any, I repeat. The reason for only the smaller suns having planets is understood. A big protostar, condensing from the interstellar medium, develops too intense a gravitational field for the secondary condensation process to take place outside it.

'I thought even humans learned so much elementary astrophysics in the first grade of school. I was wrong. Now you know.'

His voice rose to a scream. '*And for this you got me out of bed!*'

Falkayn moved to block the cabin exit. 'But I do know,' he said. 'Everybody does. The Antoranites have based their whole strategy on our preconception. They figure by the time we discover Beta Centauri is a freak case, they'll control the whole region.'

Beljagor hurled himself back into the pilot chair, folded his arms, and grated. 'Well, get the farce over with, since you must.'

'Here are the facts,' Falkayn said. He ticked them off. 'One, the Antoranite System was colonized by Kraoka, who couldn't and didn't settle on planets with suns as cool as Sol. Two, Antoran has six planets in the liquid-water zone. No matter how you arrange their orbits, that zone has to be mighty broad—which indicates a correspondingly luminous star. Three, the outermost of those six planets is too cold and weakly irradiated for Kraokan comfort, but suits humans fairly well. Yet it has brilliant auroras even in the temperate zones. For that, you need a sun which shoots out some terrifically energetic particles: again, a giant.

'Four, this human planet, Neuheim, is far out. The proof lies in three separate facts. (a) From Neuheim, the sun doesn't have a naked-eye disc. (b) There are no solar tides worth mentioning. (c) The year is long, I figure something like two Earth centuries. I know the year is long, because Jutta let slip that her people had to shift some towns poleward a while back. Orbital eccentricity was making the lower latitudes too hot, maybe also too much UV was penetrating the ozone layer in those parts and making poisonous concentrations of ozone at the surface, like here. Nevertheless, the original human settlement was forty years ago. In other words, Neuheim's radius vector changes at so leisurely a rate that it was worth sitting down in areas which the colonists knew would have to be abandoned later. I suppose they wanted to exploit local minerals.

'Okay. In spite of its enormous distance from the primary, Neuheim *is* habitable, if you don't mind getting a deep suntan. What kind of star can buck the inverse-square law on so grand a scale? What but a blue giant! And Beta Centauri is the only blue giant close by.'

He stopped, hoarse and in need of beer. Beljagor sat like a graven image, assuming that anybody would want to grave such an image, while the minutes stretched. A space boat whined overhead, an enemy craft on an unknown errand.

Finally, tonelessly, Beljagor asked, 'How could there be planets?'

'I've worked that out,' Falkayn replied. 'A freak, as I remarked before, perhaps the only case in the universe, but still possible. The star captured a mess of rogue planets.'

'Nonsense. Single bodies can't make captures.' But Beljagor didn't yell his objection.

'Granted. Here's what must have happened. Beta was condensing, with a massive nucleus already but maybe half its mass still spread over God knows how many astronomical units, as a nebular cloud. A cluster of rogue planets passed through. Beta's gravity field swung them around. But because of friction with the nebula, they didn't recede into space again. Energy loss, you see, converting hyperbolic orbits into elliptical ones. Could be that there was also a secondary centre of stellar condensation, which later spiralled into the main mass. Two bodies can certainly make captures. But I think friction alone would serve.

'The elliptical orbits were almighty eccentric, of course. Friction smoothed them out some. But Jutta admitted that to this day the planets have paths eccentric enough to cause weather trouble. Which is not the normal case either, you recall. Makes another clue for us.'

'Hm-m-m.' Beljagor tugged his nose and pondered.

'The planets would've exuded gases and water vapour in the early stages of their existence, through vulcanism, like any other substellar globes,' Falkayn ploughed on. 'The stuff froze in space. But Beta unfroze it.

'I don't know how the Kraoka of Dzua learned what the situation was. Maybe they simply didn't know that blue giants don't have planets. Or maybe they sent a telemetric probe for astrophysical research, and it informed them. Anyhow, they discovered Beta had five potentially good worlds plus one that was marginal for them. So they colonized. Sure, the planets were sterile, with poisonous atmospheres. But the ancient Kraoka were whizzes at environmental engineering. You can sketch for yourself what they did: seeded the air with photo-synthetic spores to convert it, released other forms of life to consume the primeval organic matter and form the basis of an ecology, etcetera. Under those conditions, microbes would multiply exponentially, and it'd take no more than a few centuries for a world to become habitable.'

Falkayn shrugged. 'Beta will blow up and destroy their work in five or ten million years,' he finished. 'But that's ample time for anyone, hey?'

'Yes,' Beljagor said low.

He raised his head, looked directly at the man, and said, 'If this be true, we've got to tell the League. A war fleet that went straight to Beta should catch the enemy by complete surprise. Once the home planets were hostages to us, obviously there'd be no fighting.'

'Uh-huh.' Falkayn suppressed a yawn. Weariness was beginning to overtake him.

'But this is only a hypothesis,' Beljagor said. 'Your evidence is all hearsay. Horn could've been putting you on. The League can't base a whole operation on an idea which may turn out wrong. That'd be ruinous. We need positive proof.'

'Right,' Falkayn nodded. 'So we'll both go, in our separate boats. You can easily make some excuse for having changed your mind about staying here. They won't suspect a thing if you throw a temper tantrum and storm off into space.'

Beljagor grew rigid. 'What are you saying? I'm the most patient, long-suffering entity in this cosmos.'

'Huh?'

'When I think of what I have to put up with, impertinence like yours, stupidity, greed, thievishness, lack of appreciation——' Beljagor's tone mounted to a dull roar. Falkayn smothered a second yawn.

'Well, such is my life,' said the factor as a coda. 'I'll think of something. What do you propose after we take off?'

'We'll start ostensibly for HQ,' Falkayn said. 'Once we're out of detector range, we'll head towards Beta. We'll stop at a safe distance. You wait. I'll run in close to the star and make observations. Then I'll come back to you and we really will skite for friendlier country.'

'Why the separate excursion?'

'I might get caught. In that case—if I haven't rejoined you by the agreed time—you can tell the League what we do know and suggest they investigate Beta themselves.'

'Hm. Ha. Correct. But why do you volunteer for the dangerous part? I doubt that you're competent.'

'Sir,' Falkayn said tiredly, 'I may be young, but I can handle instruments. This speedster is built for humans—you couldn't operate her efficiently—and she's better adapted to a quick job of spying than your craft. So I'm elected. Besides,' he added, 'if I get clobbered, I'm a mere journeyman, a human at that. You're a Master Merchant from Jaleel.'

His sarcasm went to waste. Beljagor sprang erect with tears starting from his porcine eyes. 'Right!' he cried, choked by emotion. 'How noble of you to admit it!' He wrung Falkayn's hand. 'Please don't think badly of me. I may be loud now and then—I may talk rough when my patience wears thin—but believe me, I've got no prejudice against your race. Humans have fine qualities. Why, some of my best friends are human!'

VI

Danger began about one light-year from goal: the distance within which the instantaneous space-time pulses emitted by a vessel in hyperdrive are detectable. Beljagor's boat lay outside that radius, her own detectors wide open. Not that there was any measurable chance of a speck like her being found by accident. Falkayn would have trouble enough making rendezvous, knowing her location. But if Beljagor observed the 'wake' of another ship, he would be careful not to start his own secondary engines until the stranger was safely remote again.

Falkayn had no like choice. At full quasi-speed, he drove straight for Beta Centauri.

The sun grew and grew before him. Under magnification, he could see the disc, seething with nuclear storms, raging with billion-kilometre prominences, hell-blue and terrible. Eleven times the mass of Sol; fourteen hundred times the luminosity; across a full hundred and ninety light-years, one of the brightest stars in Earth's sky. He tried to whistle a tune, but the sound was too small and scared.

Inward. Inward. Now he could start the cameras. Photographing the viewscreens, which compensated for aberration and Doppler effect, they pictured a stable background of constellations. Planets, though, registered as meteorite streaks—yes, here! Falkayn changed course and repeated his observations. Before long he had the triangulation data to feed his computer.

He'd only spotted a few of the captured worlds, not all of them possible habitations. What he had was sufficient, however, especially when one turned out to be approximately thirty-seven astronomical units from the sun, the right distance and the right diameter for Neuheim. And, uh-huh, his detectors showed hypervibrations criss-crossing local space, comings and goings among the stars.

One indication was too damn near for his liking, and getting nearer. A patrol craft must have sniffed his trail and be on her way to investigate. Well, she'd have to be fiendish fast to catch this little beauty of his!

She was.

As he fled spacewards, Falkayn watched the intensity readings creep higher. He scowled, puffed his pipe, and figured. He could rendezvous with Beljagor before he was overhauled, but then the Antoranite would be within a light-year of them, and get a fix on both.

Well, they could separate. . . .

A second needle flickered on the detector panel. Falkayn said bad words. Another ship was closing in. Extrapolating directions and rates of amplitude increase, he found that Number Two couldn't run him down—but could snag Beljagor's ambling Holbert.

So. The thing to do was switch off the secondaries and lie doggo, hidden by the sheer vastness of space. . . . Uh-uh. If those fellows knew their business, they'd identify the point where he stopped—at this range—within several million kilometres. They'd also go sublight, and home on the neutrino emission of his power plant. Or simply finger him with a radar sweep.

'Brother,' Falkayn told himself, 'you've had it, with pineapples.'

He looked into the glory which was space, sun after sun until suns grew so thick that they melted into the great argent flood of the Milky Way. He remembered how light is trapped in the leaves of a wind-tossed tree; and how good the beer had tasted in a funny little Swiss tavern; and how often he had laughed among friends; and how a woman felt; and he sensed an utter lack of ambition to be a hero.

Don't irritate them. Surrender. Otherwise they'll phase into your hyperjump frequency and put a warhead between your ears.

Beljagor could still report to the League, after the enemy had returned home. Of course, then he'd have no confirmation of

Beta Centauri's nature. Falkayn's not showing up was inadequate proof, when he could have come to grief in any number of ways. So the League must send spies of its own, who would also be detected. Using ultrafast ships, they'd get away, but the enemy would be alerted and would mount strong guard on his home country. If war then came, it would be more savage than one dared think about, whole planets might be incinerated, Jutta be blown to incandescent gas, Falkayn himself—Judas!

Why wasn't there faster-than-light radio, so he could beam a message to the factor before he must stop? Damn the laws of physics!

The boat hummed and quivered with driving energies. Falkayn was maddeningly aware of thirst, an itch between his shoulder blades, a need for a haircut. This was no time to be human. *Think, blast you.*

He couldn't. He prowled the cabin, smoked his tongue leathery, forced down a plateful of rations, and came back to gloom at the detectors. Until finally he said, 'To hell with this,' killed his last bottle of Scotch and went to sleep.

He awoke some hours later, and there was his solution. For a while he lay staring at the overhead, awed at his genius. But according to computation, he'd soon reach Beljagor. Which meant he was in detection range right now, and the Jaleelan was certainly cursing a Beta-coloured streak as he watched his own instruments. He'd not be asleep under these circumstances —not him.

'No time like the present,' Falkayn said, thus proving his originality had limits. He sprang from his bunk and started scribbling notes.

'Okay, chum.' He settled into the pilot chair.

Switch off the secondaries and go sublight. One minute later, switch them back on. Thirty seconds later, off again. One minute later, on again.

Polesotechnic pulse code. The needles of whichever detectors were tuned on him must be jumping back and forth, dash-dot-dash-dot. HYPOTHESIS CONFIRMED. F. repeat the cycle, to be sure Beljagor noticed. And again. Let him wonder if the F was anything but an initial. He'd get the rest of the idea, which was all that mattered. God willing, the Antoranites would not; this particular code was kept secret.

The engines began objecting to abuse. Falkayn whiffed

scorched insulation and heard an ominous whine in the power hum. He switched vectors, taking off at a sharp angle to his former path, and drove steadily.

Arithmetic showed that when Enemy Number One pulled alongside him, they'd be well over a light-year from Beljagor. So would Enemy Number Two, who was obligingly coming about also. Falkayn left the board on automatic, showered, dressed in his fanciest clothes, and fixed a leisurely breakfast.

Next he destroyed his photographs, registry, route papers, and certain parts of his log, and did an artistic job of forging substitutes. League vessels are equipped for a variety of emergencies.

The Antoranite hove close, a Comet class with wicked-looking guns. Her probe light flashed the command to halt. Falkayn obeyed. The other went sublight likewise, matched kinetic velocities, and lay at a cautious distance. The radio buzzed. Falkayn accepted.

A long-jawed human officer type with a chestful of ribbons glared from the screen. 'Hell,' Falkayn said. 'Do you speak Anglic or Latin?'

'*Ja*,' said the man. He picked the former. 'Yourself identify.'

'PL speedster *Greased Lightning* out of Tricorn for Hopewell, journeyman Sebastian Tombs aboard solo. And who might you be?'

'Neuheim warship *Graf Helmuth Karl Bernhard von Moltke*, Landholder Otto von Lichtenburg commanding, *Oberleutnant* Walter Schmitt speaking.'

'Neuheim? Where the devil is Neuheim? Never heard of it.'

'Vot iss your purpose? Vy haff you tried to escape?'

'My purpose,' Falkayn said, 'is a trip from my post on Tricorn to ask for some emergency supplies from the Polesotechnic station on Hopewell. We had a flood and it rather messed us up. As for why I ran from you, good Lord, when strangers start chasing a fellow, what do you expect him to do?'

'You assumed ve vas unfriendly,' Schmitt said, more in anger than in sorrow. 'Maybe you iss unfriendly to us, ha?'

'No, ha. If you consult your navigation tables, you'll find Beta Centauri is almost directly between Tricorn and Hopewell. And I was bound for Hopewell, instead of some closer post, because Hopewell is the nearest planet where I can be sure of getting the stuff we need. Zipping past Beta, I noticed a roughness in the engines.' It was there yet, thanks to his using them for a radio. 'To check the vector control, I changed course a few times, as you probably noticed. Then all at once, whoosh, here I detected a ship headed for me where no ship ought to be. Perhaps you were a harmless scientific expedition, anxious for a gabfest. But I wasn't about to chance it. Pirates do exist, you know. I skedaddled. My engines began spontaneously popping in and out of secondary. I got the Lauritzens fixed and tried a change of course, hoping you'd understand I didn't want company and leave me alone. No luck. So here we are.'

Falkayn donned an indignant look and pounded the pilot board. 'Seems like you're the one who has explaining to do,' he barked. 'What is this Neuheim comedy? Why are warships hanging around a blue giant? What's the idea, taking off after a harmless passer-by? The Polesotechnic League is going to hear about this!'

'Perhaps,' said Schmitt. 'Shtand by to be boarded.'

'Damnation, you have no right——'

'Ve haff several nuclear cannon zeroed on you. Giffs t'at a right?'

'It does,' Falkayn sighed.

He co-operated in linking air locks by a gangtube. Schmitt entered with a squad, who pointed their rifles at him, and demanded to see his papers.

Presently: 'Fery vell, Herr Tombs. Might be you are honest. I do not know. Ve haff our orders. It vill be necessary to intern you on Neuheim.'

'What?' Falkayn bellowed. He held his breath till he turned scarlet and his eyes popped. 'Do you realize who I am? I'm a certified member of the Polesotechnic League!'

'Too bad for you,' Schmitt said. 'Come along.' He grabbed Falkayn's wrist.

Falkayn yanked it back, drew himself straight, and blessed his father for teaching him the proper mannerisms. 'Sir,' he said, and liquid helium dripped from every word, 'if I am to be a prisoner, I protest the illegality but I must yield. Nevertheless, there is such a thing as the laws of war. Furthermore, I am heir apparent to the Barony of Dragonshaw, United Kingdom of New Asia and Radagach. You will treat me with the respect according to my station!'

Schmitt paled. He clicked his heels, bowed, and followed with a salute. '*Jawohl, mein Herr,*' he gasped. 'I beg for your most gracious pardon. If you had seen fit to tell me more earlier—Landholder von Lichtenberg vill be reqvesting t'e honour uff your presence at tea.'

VII

Schloss Graustein was not the worst place in the cosmos to be a prisoner. Though gaunt and draughty on its high ridge, it was surrounded by forests where the hunting was excellent. The food was heavy but edible, and the local beer superb. Landholder Graustein did his best to make the distinguished, if compulsory, guest feel at home. During long conversations and occasional guided tours of the planet, Falkayn spotted interesting commercial opportunities, once the region had been pacified.

Unless—— He didn't want to contemplate the alternative. And after some weeks, time began to hang as leaden as the knackwurst.

Thus Falkayn was quite happy when a servant knocked at the door of his suite and announced a visitor. But then she stepped through. He had never thought she would be an unwelcome sight.

'Jutta,' he whispered.

She closed the door behind her and regarded him for a still moment. Dark wood and granite panels framed her where she stood vivid under the flourolight. She was in mufti, and if he had thought her beautiful when uniformed, he must now multiply by an astronomical factor.

'So it is indeed you,' she said.

'P-p-please sit down,' he managed.

She remained standing. Her features were stony, her voice flat. 'Those idiots took for granted you were what you claimed, a merchant who simply chanced to pass by and saw too much. They never interrogated you in depth, never notified the fleet command. I only heard of you yesterday, in conversation with Landholder von Lichtenberg, after I came home on leave. The description——' Words trailed off.

Falkayn rallied his courage. 'A stratagem of war, my dear,' he said gently. 'Not a war that my side began, either.'

'What have you done?'

He told his pulse to decelerate, took out his pipe, and made a production of loading and kindling it. 'You can squirt me full of babble juice, so I might as well Tell All,' he smiled. 'I guessed the truth and went for a look to make certain.'

'That funny little being who left about the same time as you did . . . he knew?'

Falkayn nodded. 'He's reported to HQ long ago. If the League is half as realistic as I think, a battle fleet you can't hope to resist is on its way right now.'

She clenched one hand over another. Tears stood in her eyes. 'What follows?'

'They should head straight here. I expect them any day. You've nothing in the Beta System except a few patrollers; the rest of your navy is spread over a dozen stars, right? The League doesn't want to bombard planets, but in this case——'

She uttered anguish. He went quickly to her, took both those hands, and said, 'No, no. *Realpolitik*, remember? The object of war is not to destroy the enemy but to impose your will on him. Why should we kill people that we might sell things to? We'll simply take the Beta System prisoner and then bargain about its release.

'I don't make policy, but I can predict what'll happen. The League will demand you disband your armed forces, down to a normal defence level. And, naturally, we'll want to keep our trade concessions. But that's all. Now that some Kraoka have starships, they can go ahead and unify, as long as they do it peacefully. We'd hoped to sell them a cargo and passenger fleet, at a huge markup, but that hope isn't worth fighting for—you do have bargaining power yourselves, in your own capabilities for making trouble, you know. Neuheim can keep any social order it wants. Why not? If you try to maintain this wretched autarchy, you'll be depriving yourselves of so much that inside of ten years your people will throw out the Landholders and yell for us.'

He chucked her under the chin. 'I understand,' he said. 'It's tough when a dream dies. But why should you, your whole life, carry your father's grudges?'

She surrendered to tears. He consoled her, and a private hope began to grow in him.

Not that he was in the market for a wife. Judas! At his age? However——

Afterwards they found themselves on the balcony. Night had fallen, the auroral night where vast banners shook red and green across the sky, dimming the stars, and the mountain swooped down to a forest which breathed strange sweet odours back upwards. Wineglasses were in their hands, and she stood close to him.

'You can report who I am,' he said, 'and cause me to have an unpleasant time, maybe even be shot.' Pale in the shuddering light, her face lost its look of happiness and he heard the breath suck between her teeth. 'Your duty, according to the articles of war,' he continued. 'And it won't make one bit of difference, it'll be too late—except that the League protects its own and will take a stiff price for me.'

'What choice have I?' she pleaded.

He flashed a well-rehearsed grin. 'Why, to keep your lovely mouth shut, tell everybody you were mistaken and Sebastian Tombs has nothing to do with the Falkayn character. When peace comes—well, you're quite influential on this planet. You could do a lot to help your people adjust.'

'And become merchants?' she said, in a dying flare of scorn.

'I remarked once,' he said, 'that we aren't really so ignoble. We're after a profit, yes. But even a knight must eat, and *our* bread doesn't come from slaves or serfs or anyone who had to be killed. Look beyond those lights. They're fine, sure, but how about the stars on the other side?'

She caught his arm. He murmured, as best he could in Latin, *'Thy merchants chase the morning down the sea . . .'* and when she turned questioning to him he added, low in the dusk,

> *'Their topmasts gilt by sunset, though their sails be whipped to rags,*

Who raced the wind around the world go reeling home
    again,
With ivory, apes, and peacocks loaded, memories and
    brags,
To sell for this high profit: knowing fully they are Men!'

'Oh-h-h,' he heard.

And to think he'd resented his schoolmasters, when he was a kid on Hermes, making him read Flecker and Sanders in the original.

'I will not tell anyone,' she said.

And: 'May I stay here for a while?'

Falkayn was downright regretful a week later, when the League fleet arrived to rescue him.

Did I ever meet Noah Arkwright? Did *I* ever meet *Noah Arkwright*? Just pull up a chair and tune up an ear. No, better not that chair. We keep it in case the Gratch should pay us a call. Glowberry wood, the tree concentrates uranium salts, so less'n you're wearing lead diapers ...

Sure, we'd heard of what skyhoot Noah Arkwright wanted to do. Space pilots flit the jaw, even this far out the spokes. We wanted no more snatch at his notion than any other men whose brain weren't precessing. Figured the Yonder could wait another couple hundred years; got more terry incog already than we can eat, hey? But when he bunged down his canster here, he never jingled a word about it. He had a business proposition to make, he said, and would those of us who had a dinar or two to orbit be interested?

Sounded right sane, he did: though with that voice I compute he could've gotten jewellery prices for what he'd call dioxide of ekacarbon. See you, nigh any planet small enough for a man to dig on has got to have its Victory Heads—Golcondas, Mesabis, Rands, if you want to go back to Old Earth—anyhow, its really rich mineral deposits. The snub always was, a planet's one gorgo of a big place. Even with sonics and spectros, you'll sniff around a new one till entropy overhauls you before you have a white dwarf chance of making the real find. But he said he had a new hyperwangle that'd spot from satellite altitude. He needed capital to proceed, and they were too stuffnoggin on Earth to close him a circuit, so why not us?

Oh, we didn't arc over. Not that we saw anything kinked in his not telling us how the dreelsprail worked; out here, secrets are property. But we made him demonstrate, over on Despair. Next planet spaceward, hardly visited at all before, being as useless a little glob as ever was sponged off God's thumbnail. Dis if his meters didn't swing a cory over what developed into the biggest rhenium strike since Ignatz.

Well, you know how it is with minerals. The rich deposits have an edge over extraction methods, like from sea water, but not so much of an edge that you can count your profits from one in exponentials. Still, if we had a way to find any number of 'em, quick and cheap, in nearby systems—— We stood in line to capitalize his company. And me, I was so tough and smart I rammed my way to the head of the line!

I do think, though, his way of talking did it. He could pull Jupiter from Sol with, oh, just one of his rambles through xenology or analytics or Shakespeare or history or hypertheory or anything. Happen I've still got a tape, like I notice you making now. You cogno yours stays private, for your personal journal, right? I wouldn't admit the truth about this to another human. Not to any being, if I wasn't an ångström drunk. But listen, here's Noah Arkwright.

'—isn't merely that society in the large goes through its repetitions. In fact, I rather doubt the cliché that we are living in some kind of neo-Elizabethan age. There are certain analogies, no more. Now a *life* has cycles. Within a given context, the kinds of event that can happen to you are of a finite number. The permutations change, the elements remain the same.

'Consider today's most romantic figure, the merchant adventurer. Everyone, especially himself, thinks he leads a gorgeously variegated existence. And yet, how different can one episode be from the next? He deals with a curious planetary environment, natives whose inwardness he must try to understand, crafty rivals, women tempting or belligerent, a few classes of dangers, the eternal problem of making his enterprise pay off—what more, ever? What I would like to do is less spectacular on the surface. But it would mean a breaking of the circle: an altogether new order of experience. Were you not so obsessed with your vision of yourself as a bold pioneer, you would see what I mean.'

Yah. Now I do.

We didn't see we'd been blued till we put the articles of partnership through a sematic computer. He must have used symbolic logic to write them, under all the rainbow language. The one isolated fusing thing he was legally committed to do was conduct explorations on our behalf. He could go anywhere, do anything, for any reason he liked. So of course he used our money to outfit his damned expedition! He'd found that rhenium beforehand. He didn't want to wait five years for the returns to quantum in; might not've been enough anyway.

So he dozzled up that potburning machine of his and—— On Earth they call that swindle the Gypsy Blessing.

Oh, in time we got some sort of profit out of Despair, though not half what we should've dragged on so big an investment. And he tried to repay us in selfcharge if not in cash. But—the output of the whole works is—here I am, with a whole star cluster named after me, and there's not a fellow human being in the universe that I can tell why!

—Recorded in the diary of Urwain
the Wide-Faring

The Trouble Twisters

Poker is not a very good three-handed game, so the crew of the trade pioneer ship *Muddlin'. Through* had programmed her computer to play with them. It bought chips with IOU's. Being adjusted to an exactly average level of competence, it just about balanced winnings and losses in the course of a mission. This freed the crew to go after each other's blood.

'Two cards,' said its mechanical voice. David Falkayn dealt them on to a scanner plate that he had rigged at one end of the saloon table. An arm projecting from a modified waldo box shoved the discards aside. Down in their armoured tank, at the middle of the ship, think cells assessed the new odds.

'One,' said Chee Lan.

'None for me, thank you,' rumbled Adzel.

Falkayn gave himself three and picked up his hand. He'd improved: a pair of treys to match his kings. Adzel might well stand pat on nothing better, and Chee had probably tried to complete a flush; the first round of betting, opened by the machine, had been unenthusiastic. But Muddlehead itself, now——

The steel arm dropped a blue chip into the pot.

'*Damn!*' shrieked Chee. Her tail bottled out to twice its normal size, the silky-white fur stood erect over her whole small body, and she threw her cards down so hard that the tabletop ought to have rung. 'Pestilence upon you! I hate your cryogenic guts!'

Imperturbably, Adzel doubled the bet. Falkayn sighed and folded. Chee's fury ebbed as fast as it had come. She settled down on her elevated stool and began washing, cat-fashion. Falkayn reached for a cigarette.

Muddlehead raised back. Adzel's dragon countenance wasn't able to change expression, except for the rubbery lips, but his huge scaly form, sprawled across the cabin, grew tense. He studied his cards again.

A bell tone interrupted him. That part of the computer which was always on watch had observed something unusual.

'I'll go,' Falkayn said. He rose and went quickly down the forward passageway: a tall and muscled young man, yellow-haired, blue-eyed, snub-nosed, and high of cheekbone. Even here, light years from the nearest fellow·human, he wore lounging pyjamas that would not have been out of place in Tycho Lodge. He told himself that he was obliged to maintain standards—younger son of a baronial house on Hermes, currently a representative of the Polesotechnic League, and all that sort of thing—but the fact was that he had not quite outgrown a certain vanity.

At the mid-section scanner turret, he punched controls. No oddities appeared in the screen. What the devil had the observer units noticed? So much computer capacity was engaged in the game that the ship herself couldn't tell him. Maybe he'd better—He shifted the cigarette in his mouth and increased the magnification.

Westward in a deep purplish sky, the sun stood at eternal late afternoon. It was a K_0 dwarf, barely one-tenth as luminous as man's home star, furnace-red. But at a mere third of an astronomical unit from Ikrananka, it showed nearly three and a half times the angular diameter and gave about as much irradiation. Through the dull light and thin air, a few other stars were visible. Spica, little more than three parsecs away, shone like a white jewel. Otherwise the heavens held nothing but a flock of leathery-winged flying beasties and, above the northern heights, the yellow cloud of a dust storm.

Halfway up a hill, *Muddlin' Through* commanded a wide overlook of the Chakora. That former sea bottom stretched ruddy-green and indigo shadowed, densely planted with low succulent crops. Here and there on it Falkayn could see clusters of buildings, woven in patterns from gaily coloured fibres, each surrounding a stone tower: the thorps and defensive keeps of agricultural families. Wherever a spring seeped forth, the vegetation became intensely verdant and gold. And there thickets of long stalks, like plumed bamboo, the closest this world had ever come to trees, swayed in the wind.

The hill itself was craggy, eroded, with little except scrub growing between the boulders. On its top loomed the ramparts of Haijakata. At the foot was a tower guarding the town's well, accessible from above through a tunnel. Nearby, a dirt road from the east twisted to enter the gates. Falkayn didn't see any natives abroad.

No, wait. Dust smoked on that highway, three or four kilometres off but rapidly nearing. Somebody was bound here in an awful hurry.

Falkayn adjusted the scanner. The scene leaped at him.

Half a dozen Ikranankans were urging their zandaras on. The big, brown-furred, thick-tailed bipeds rose in soaring arcs, touched earth, instantly gathered their leg muscles, and sprang again. The riders shook lances and sabres aloft. Their open beaks showed that they screamed.

A breeze blew aside the dust and Falkayn saw what they were pursuing. He just avoided swallowing his cigarette.

'No,' he heard himself feebly say. 'Such things don't happen. I swear they don't.'

His paralysis broke. He whirled and ran back aft. At a mere sixty-five per cent of Terrestrial gravity, he moved like a scared comet. He burst into the saloon, skidded to a halt, and roared, 'Emergency!'

Chee Lan hopped across the table and switched the computer back to normal function. Adzel thrust a final chip into the pot and turned over his cards. He had a straight. 'What is the matter?' Chee asked, glacially self-possessed as always when trouble showed.

'A . . . a woman,' Falkayn panted. 'Being chased.'

'By whom?'

'Not me, dammit. But listen, it's so! Bunch of native cavalry after a human female. Her zandara looks tired. They'll catch her before she gets here, and Lord knows what they'll do.'

While Falkayn was blurting, Adzel looked at Muddlehead's hand. Full house. He sighed philosophically and shoved the pot over. Rising, he said, 'Best we go remonstrate with them. Chee, stand by.'

The Cynthian nodded and pattered off to the bridge. Adzel followed Falkayn to the lower exit. His cloven hooves clanged on the deck. At the locker, the man slipped on a gun belt and stuck a radio transceiver into a pocket of the coat he grabbed. They valved through.

To avoid delays when going out, they maintained interior air pressure at local norm, about three-fourths of Earth sea level. But they preferred more warmth and moisture. Swift, dry, and chill, the wind struck savagely at Falkayn's mucous membranes. His eyes needed a moment to adapt. Adzel picked him up in two great horny hands and set him on his own back, just behind the centauroid torso. The Wodenite had had one of the sharp plates which jutted from his head, along his spine to the end of his tail, removed for that purpose. He started downhill in a smooth gallop. His musky odour blew back around Falkayn.

'One supposes that another ship has come,' he said, his basso as placid as if they were still dealing cards. 'By accident?'

'Must be.' Falkayn squinted ahead. 'She's dressed funny, though. Could she have run afoul of barbarian raiders? We do keep getting hints of war in the Sundhadarta mountains.'

He could barely make out the highest peaks of that range, glooming above the eastern horizon. On his left marched the tawny cliffs which had once been a continental shelf. To right lay only the ever-green fields of the Chakora. Behind him reared Haijakata hill, and his ship like a shining spearhead. But the view here had grown deadly familiar. He wasn't sorry for a bit of action. No danger to speak of: that gang would probably head for home and mother the minute they saw Adzel.

Muscles rippled between his thighs. The cloven air shrilled and nipped his ears. Hoofbeats drummed. And now, ahead, he could clearly see the girl and her pursuers. Harsh nonhuman yelps reached him.

She waved and spurred her flagging zandara to a last rush. The Ikranankans shouted to each other. Falkayn caught a few words—why, they spoke the Katandaran language——

One of them halted his beast and unslipped a crossbow from his saddle. It was a slender weapon. His arms had merely half a man's strength to cock it. But the darts it threw were needle sharp and travelled far in this gravity. He fired. The missile zipped within centimetres of her loosened auburn braids. He cried an order while he fitted another dart. Two more riders unlimbered their own bows.

'Judas on Pluto!' Falkayn gasped. 'They mean to kill her!'

Every sense he had surged to full alertness. He looked through red-tinged dust and ruby light as if he were face to face with the closest autochthon.

The being stood some one hundred and fifty centimetres tall. In body he resembled a barrel-chested, wasp-waisted man with unduly long, thin limbs. Sleek brown fur covered him; he was warm-blooded and omnivorous, and his mate brought forth her young alive; but for all that, he was no mammal. Atop a slender neck, his bowling-ball head sported a black ruff, pale eyes, donkeylike ears, and a corvine beak that might have been moulded in amber. His padded feet were bare so the three long toes on each could grip stirrups. Otherwise he wore tight cross-gaitered pants, a leather cuirass with iron shoulder pieces and a zigzag insignia on the breast, and a wide belt from which there hung dagger and sabre. Three sharp-nailed fingers and a thumb cranked the bow taut. His right hand lifted the stock.

Falkayn snatched forth his blaster and fired upward. It was a warning; also, the beam dazzled native eyes and spoiled their aim. The girl cheered.

The squad at her back scattered. They were all accoutred more or less alike. The kinship symbol they shared was not familiar to Falkayn. Their leader screeched a command. They rallied and charged on. A dart buzzed near the man. Another broke on Adzel's scales.

'Why—why—they have decided to kill us, too,' the Wodenite stammered. 'They must have been prepared for the sight of us.'

'*Get going!*' Falkayn howled.

He was born and bred an aristocrat on a planet where they still needed soldiers. Boyhood training took over in him. Gone mental steady, he narrowed his fire beam for maximum range and dropped one zandra in its tracks.

Adzel opened up. His ton of mass accelerated to a sprint of one hundred and fifty KPH. Wind whipped blindly in Falkayn's eyes. But he wasn't needed any more. Adzel had got in among the Ikranankans. He simply bowled over the first animal and rider. Two others spun through the air in a bow wave. His tail struck to one side, and that flattened a fourth. The last two bolted off across the fields.

Adzel braked himself and trotted back. A couple of the opposition were hotfooting it elsewhere, the other casualties seemed barely able to move. 'Oh, dear,' he said. 'I do hope we did not injure them seriously.'

Falkayn shrugged. 'A race of giants could afford to be gentler than men. Let's get back to the ship,' he said.

The girl had stopped further down the road. As they neared her, his lips shaped a whistle.

Perhaps she was a little too muscular for his taste. But what a figure! Tall, full, long-legged, and straight-backed ... and her outfit showed delightfully much of it, what with half-length boots, fur kilt hiked up for riding, doublet appropriately curved over a sleeveless blouse, and a short blue cloak. She was armed with cutlery similar to the natives', had a painted shield hung by her saddle and a flat helmet over her rusty coils of hair. Her skin was very white. The features had an almost Hellenic clearness, with big grey eyes and wide mouth to soften them.

'What *ho*!' Falkayn murmured. 'And where are you from, lass?'

She wiped sweat off her brow and breathed hard, which was pleasant to see. Adzel continued lumbering down the road. She clucked to her zandara. It walked alongside, too exhausted to be skittish of his enormousness.

'You ... are ... are in truth from Beyond-the-World?' she asked. Her husky Anglic held an accent he had never met before.

'Yes. I suppose so.' Falkayn pointed to the ship.

She traced a sign. '*Algat* is good!' The word was local, meaning approximately 'magic'.

Recovering some composure, she peered after her enemies. They had restored order, but weren't giving chase. Even as she watched, one of them on an unharmed animal started off, hell for leather, towards the far side of the hill. The rest followed slowly.

She reached out to touch Falkayn's hand, as if to make sure he was real. 'Only rumours drifted usward,' she said low. 'We heard a strange Ershokh had arrived in a flying chariot, and the Emperor forbade anyone to come near. But the story could've grown in telling. You are truly from Beyond-the-World? Even from Earth?'

'I said yes,' he answered. 'But what are you talking about? What do you mean. Ershokh?'

'Humans. Did you not know? They call us Ershoka in Katandara.' She considered him, and it was as if a mask slid over her. With a slowness and caution he did not understand, she ventured. 'Ever since our ancestors came, over four hundred years ago.'

'Four hundred?' Falkayn's jaw hit his Adam's apple. 'But the hyperdrive wasn't invented then!'

'Obviously she means Ikranankan years,' said Adzel, who was hard to surprise. 'Let me see, with a revolution period of seventy-two standard days ... yes, that makes about seventy-five Terrestrial years.'

'But—I say, how the deuce——'

'They were bound elsewhere, to ... what is the word? ... to be colonists,' the girl said. 'Robbers captured them and left them here, the whole five hundred.'

Falkayn tried to make his mind stop whirling. Vaguely he heard Adzel say, 'Ah, yes, doubtless a squadron from the Pirate Suns, venturing so far from their bases in the hope of just such valuable booty as a large ship. They were not interested in ransom. But it was meritorious of them to find a habitable planet and maroon rather than kill their prisoners.' He patted her shoulder. 'Do not fret, small female. The Polesotechnic League has long since taught the Pirate Sun dwellers the error of their ways.'

Falkayn decided that any comforting should be done by him. 'Well,' he beamed. 'What a sensation this will make! As soon as we tell Earth, they'll send transportation for you.'

Still she watched him, strangely and disappointingly careful. A damsel lately in distress ought not to act that way. 'You are an Ersho—I mean an Earthman?'

'Actually I'm a citizen of the Grand Duchy of Hermes, and my shipmates are from other planets. But we operate out of Earth. David Falkayn's my name.'

'I am Stepha Carls, a lieutenant in the household troops of——' She broke off. 'No matter now.'

'Why were those klongs chasing you?'

She smiled a little. 'One thing at a time, I beg. So much to tell each other, truth?' But then she did drop her reserve. Her eyes widened, her smile went up to about fifty megawatts, she clapped her hands and cried: 'Oh, this is purest wonder! A man from Earth—my own rescuer!'

Well, now, Falkayn thought, a bit stunned, *that's more like it.* He dropped his questions and simply admired the scenery. After all, he'd been away from mankind for a good many weeks.

At the ship they tethered the zandara to a landing jack. Falkayn bowed Stepha up the ramp to the lock. Chee Lan came springing to meet them. 'What a darling pet!' the girl exclaimed. Chee bristled. In some respects she was not unlike Master Beljagor. 'You try to kitchy-koo me, young lady, and you'll be lucky to get your fingers back.' She swung on her fellows. 'What in the name of nine times nine to the ninety-ninth devils is going on?'

'Didn't you watch the fight?' Falkayn said. Under Stepha's eyes, he preened himself. 'I thought we did a rather good job on those bandits.'

'What bandits?' Chee snapped. 'From here I could see them go right into town. If you ask me—if you have the wit to ask me, you pair of vacuum-headed louts—you've clobbered a squad of Imperial soldiers—the same Emperor's that we came here to deal with!'

II

They hied themselves to the saloon. Going into town might lead to being shot at. Let Gujgengi come and ask for an explanation. Besides, they had a lot of mutual explaining to get out of the way first.

Falkayn poured Scotch for himself and Stepha. Adzel took a four-litre bucket of coffee. His Buddhistic principles did not preclude drinking, but no ship on an extended mission could carry enough liquor to do him much good. Chee Lan, who was not affected by alcohol, kindled a mildly narcotic cigarette in an interminable ivory holder. They were all in bad need of soothing.

The girl squinted and scowled simultaneously at her glass— she wasn't used to Earth illumination—raised it to her lips, and tossed it off. 'Whoo-oo-oo!' she spluttered. Falkayn pounded her back. Between coughs and wheezes, her oaths made him blush. 'I thought you were being niggard,' she said weakly.

'I suppose you would have lost most of your technology in three generations, at that,' Adzel said. 'Five hundred people, children included, have insufficient knowledge between them to maintain a modern civilization, and a colony ship would not have carried a full microlibrary.'

Stepha wiped her eyes and looked at him. 'I always thought Great Granther was an awful liar,' she said. 'But reckon he must really have seen some things as a youngling. Where are you from?'

He was certainly an impressive sight. Counting the tail, his quadrupedal body was a good four and a half metres long, and the torso had arms, chest, and shoulders to match. Blue-grey scales shimmered overall, save where scutes protected the belly and plates the back; those were umber. The crocodilian head sat on a metre of neck, with bony ears and shelves over the eyes. But those eyes were large, brown, and wistful, and the skull bulged backwards to hold a considerable brain.

'Earth,' he said. 'That is, Zatlakh, which means "earth" in my language. Humans dubbed it Woden. That was before they ran out of Terrestrial names for planets. Nowadays, for the most part, one uses whatever term is found in the language of what seems the most advanced local culture: as, for instance, "Ikrananka" here.'

'Wouldn't *you* be good in combat?' Stepha mused. One hand dropped to her dagger.

Adzel winced. 'Please. We are most peaceful. We are only so large and armoured because Woden breeds giant animals. The sun is type F_5, you see, in the Regulus sector. It puts out so much energy that, in spite of a surface gravity equal to two and a half times Earth's, life can grow massive and——'

'Shut your gas jet, you blithering barbarian,' Chee Lan cut in. 'We've work on hand.'

Adzel came near losing his temper. 'My friend,' he growled, 'it is most discourteous to denigrate other cultures. Granted that my own people are simple hunters, nevertheless we would dare set our arts against anyone's. And when I got a scholarship to study planetology on Earth, I earned extra money by singing Fafnir in the San Francisco Opera.'

'Also by parading at Chinese New Year's,' said Chee poisonously.

Falkayn struck the table with his fist. 'That'll do for both of you,' he rapped.

'But where in truth is the, ah, lady from?' Stepha asked.

'The second planet of O_2 Eridani A,' Falkayn said. 'Cynthia, its human discoverers named it, after the captain's wife.'

'I have heard that she was not exactly his wife,' Chee murmured.

Falkayn blushed again and stole a glance at Stepha. But she didn't look embarrassed; and considering those cusswords she'd ripped out—— 'They'd reached about an Alexandrine level of technology on one continent, at the time,' he said, 'and had invented the scientific method. But they didn't have cities. A nation was equal to a trade route. So they've fitted very well into League activities.' He realized that now he was blithering, and stopped short.

Chee tapped the ash from her cigarette with one delicate six-digited hand. She herself was a mere ninety centimetres tall when she stood fully erect. Mostly she crouched on muscular legs and equally long arms, her magnificent brush curled over the back. Her head was big in proportion, round, with a short black-nosed muzzle, neat little ears, and cat whiskers. Save for a dark mask around the huge luminous-golden eyes, she was entirely covered by white Angora fur. Her thin voice turned brisk: 'Let us begin by reviewing your situation, Freelady Carls. No, pardon me, Lieutenant Carls, isn't it? I assume your ancestors were marooned in this general area.'

'Yes,' Stepha nodded. She picked her words with renewed care. 'They soon made touch with the natives, sometimes violent, sometimes not. The violence taught them humans have more strength and endurance than Ikranankans. And here is always war. Better, easier, to be the best soldiers than sweat in fields and mines, not so? Ever since, every Ershokh has grown into the—body?—the corps. Those who can't fight are quartermasters and such.'

Falkayn observed a scar on her arm. *Poor kid*, he thought in pity. *This is all wrong. She should be dancing and flirting on Earth, with me, for instance. A girl is too sweet and gentle a creature in her heart to*——

Stepha's eyes glittered. 'I heard old people tell of wars in Beyond-the-World,' she said eagerly. 'Could we hire out?'

'What? Well—er——'

'I'm good. You should have seen me at the Battle of the Yanjeh. Ha! They charged our line. One zandara spitted itself on my pike, ran right up.' Stepha jumped to her feet, drew her sabre and whizzed it through the air. 'I took the rider's head off with one sweep. It bounced. I turned and split the fellow beside him from gullet to guts. A dismounted trooper attacked on my left. I gave him my shield boss, crunch, right in the beak. Then——'

'Please!' roared Adzel, and covered his ears.

'We do have to find out the situation,' Falkayn added hastily. 'Are you or are you not an enemy of the Emperor in Katandara?'

Stepha checked her vehemence, sat down again, and held out her glass for a refill. Once more she was speaking with great caution. 'The Ershoka hired out to the first Jadhadi, when the old Empire fell apart. They helped set him on the Beast in Katandara, and rebuild the Empire and expand it, and since then they've been the household troops of each Emperor and the core of his army. Of late, some of them were the capturers of Rangakora, in Sundhadarta to the east on the edge of the Twilight. And that's a most important place to hold. Not alone does it command the chief pass through the mountains, but the water thereabouts makes that country the richest in the Chakora.'

'To chaos with your pus-bleeding geopolitics!' Chee interrupted. 'Why were you being chased by Imperial soldiers?'

'Um-m-m ... I am not sure.' Stepha sipped for a moment's silence. 'Best might be if you tell me of yourselves first. Then maybe between us we can find why the third Jadhadi has you off here instead of in Katandara. Or do you know?'

Adzel shook his ponderous head. 'We do not,' he answered. 'Indeed, we were unaware of being quarantined. We did have intimations. It seemed curious that we have not yet been invited to the capital, and that so few came to visit us among local dwellers. When we took the flitter out for a spin, we observed military encampments at some distance. Then Gujgengi requested that we refrain from flying. He said the unfamiliar sight produced too much consternation. I hesitate to accuse anyone of prevaricating, but the reason did seem rather tenuous.'

'You are truth-told walled away, by Imperial order,' Stepha said grimly. 'Haijakata has been forbidden to any outsiders, and no one may leave these parts. It hurts trade, but——' Falkayn was about to ask why she had violated the man, when she continued: 'Tell me, though. How come you to be here, in this piddling little corner of nowhere? Why did you come to Ikrananka at all?'

'She's stalling,' Cheé hissed to Falkayn in League Latin.

'I know,' he answered likewise. 'But can you blame her? Here we are, total strangers, and the last contact her people had with galactic civilization was that piracy. We've got to be kind, show her we really mean well.'

Cheé threw up her hands. 'Oh, cosmos!' she groaned. 'You and your damned mating instinct!'

Falkayn turned his back on her. 'Pardon us,' he said in Anglic. 'We, uh, had something personal to discuss.'

Stepha smiled, patted his hand, and leaned quite close to breathe, 'I do understand, David.... So pretty a name, David. And you from Beyond-the-World! I'm strangling to hear everything about you.'

'Well, uh, that is,' stuttered Falkayn, 'we're trade pioneers. Something new.' He hoped his grin was modest rather than silly. 'I, er, helped work out the idea myself.' With due regard for preserving the basic secret, he explained.

Nicholas van Rijn left his desk and waddled across to the transparency that made one entire wall of his office. From this height, he could overlook a sweep of slim city towers, green parkscape, Sunda Straits flashing under Earth's lordly sky. For a while he stood puffing his cigar, until, without turning round, he said:

'*Ja*, by damn, I think you has here the bacteria of a good project with much profit. And you is a right man to carry it away. I have watched you like a hog, ever since I hear what you did on Ivanhoe when you was a, you pardon the expression, teenager. Now you got your Master's certificate in the League, uh-huh, you can be good working for the Solar Spice & Liquors Company. And I need good men, poor old fat lonely me. You bring home the bacon and eggs scrambled with turmeric, I see you get rich.'

'Yes, sir,' Falkayn mumbled.

'You come speak of how you like to help open new places, for new stuffs to sell here and natives to buy from us what have not yet heard what the market prices are. Hokay. Only I think you got more possibilities, boy. I been thinking a lot, me these long, long nights when I toss and turn, getting no sleep with my worries.'

Falkayn refrained from telling van Rijn that everybody knew the cause of the merchant's current insomnia was blonde and curvy. 'What do you mean, sir?' he asked.

Van Rijn faced about, tugged his goatee, and studied him out of beady eyes set close to the great hook nose. 'I tell you confidential,' he said at length. 'You not violate my confidence, ha? I got so few friends. You break my old grey heart and I personal wring your neck. Understand? Fine, fine. I like a boy what has got good understandings.

'My notion is, here the League finds new planets, and everybody jumps in with both feets and is one cut-throat scramble. You thought you might go in at this. But no, no, you is too fine, too sensitive. I can see that. Also, you is not yet one of the famous space captains, and nobody spies to see where you is bound next. So . . . for Solar Spice & Liquors, you go find us our private planets!' He advanced and dug a thumb into Falkayn's ribs. The younger man staggered. 'How you like that, ha?'

'But—but—that is——'

Van Rijn tapped two litres of beer from his cooler, clinked glasses, and explained.

The galaxy, even this tiny fragment of one spiral arm which we have somewhat explored, is inconceivably huge. In the course of visiting and perhaps colonizing worlds of obvious interest to them, space travellers have leapfrogged past literally millions of others. Many are not even catalogued. Without a special effort, they are unlikely to become known for millennia. Yet from statistics we can predict that thousands of them are potentially valuable, as markets and sources of new exotic goods. Rather than continue to exploit the discovered planets, why not find new ones . . . and keep the fact quiet as long as possible?

A sector would be chosen, out where the traffic is still thin: Spica, for instance. A base would be established. Small, cheap automated craft would be dispatched by the hundreds. Whenever they found a world that, from their standardized observations of surface conditions, seemed promising, they would report back. The trade pioneer crew would go for a closer look. If they struck pay dirt, they would collect basic information, lay the groundwork for commercial agreements, and notify van Rijn.

'Three in a ship, I think, is enough,' he said. 'Better be enough, what wages and commissions your pest-bedamned Brotherhood charges! You, the Master merchant, trained in culture comparisons and swogglehorning. A planetologist and a xenobiologist. They should be nonhumans. Different talents, you see, also not so much nerve-scratching when cooped together. Nicer to have a lovingly girl along, I know, but when you get back again, ha, ha!—you make up good. Or even before. You got just invited to my next little orgy, boy, if you take the job.'

'So you knew there was a civilization here with metal,' Stepha nodded. 'Of course your robots—jeroo, to think I never believed Great Granther when he talked about robots!—they didn't see us few Ershoka. But what did they tell you was worth coming here for?'

'An Earthlike planet is always worth investigating,' Falkayn said.

'What? This is like Earth? Great Granther——'

'Any planet where men can live without special apparatus is Earthlike. They're not too common, you see. The physical conditions, the biochemistry, the ecology ... never mind. Irkananka has plenty of differences from Earth or Hermes, true.'

(Mass, 0·394 Terrestrial, density 0·815, diameter 0·783. But though its sun is feeble, it orbits close. To be sure, then tidal action has forced one hemisphere constantly to face the primary. But this slow rotation in turn means a weak magnetic field, hence comparatively little interaction with stellar charged particles, which are not emitted very strongly from a red dwarf anyway. Thus it keeps a reasonable atmosphere. Granted, most of the water has been carried to the cold side and frozen, making the warm side largely desert. But this took time, during which life based on proteins in water solution could evolve and adapt. Indeed, the chemistry remains startlingly like home.)

'What is there to get here?'

'Lots. The robots brought back pictures and samples. At least two new intoxicants, several antibiotics, potential spices, some spectacular furs, and doubtless much else. Also a well-developed civilization to gather the stuff for us, in exchange for trade goods that they're far enough advanced to appreciate.'

Chee smacked her lips. 'The commissions to be got!'

Stepha sighed. 'I wish you'd speak Anglic. But I'll take your word for true. Why did you land at Haijakata? You must have known Katandara is the biggest city.'

'It's complicated enough being a visitor from space, without getting swarmed over from the start,' Falkayn replied. 'We've been learning the local language, customs, the whole setup, in this backwater. It goes pretty quick, with modern mnemonic techniques. And the Emperor sent Gujgengi as a special teacher, once he heard of us. We were going to the capital before now; but as soon as we announced that, the professor started finding excuses for delay. That was three or four weeks back.'

'I wonder how much we really have learned,' Chee muttered.

'What are weeks?' Stepha asked.

'Forget it,' Chee said. 'See here, female, you have involved us in trouble that may cost us our whole market.'

'What a stupid!' the girl barked impatiently. 'Conquer them.'

'A highly immoral procedure,' Adzel scolded. 'Also it is against policy: as much, I confess, because of being economically unfeasible as for any other reason.'

'Will you get to the point, you yattertongues?' Chee screamed. 'Why were those soldiers after you?'

The alarm bell toned. The computer said, 'A party is approaching from the town.'

III

Falkayn decided he had better be courteous and meet the Imperial envoy-instructor at the air lock. He kept his blaster conspicuously on one hip.

Waiting, he could look up to the walls on the hillcrest. They were of dry-laid stone; water was too precious to use in mortar. Their battlements, and the gaunt towers at their corners, enclosed a few score woven houses. Haijakata was a mere trading centre for the local farmers and for caravans passing through. A rather small garrison was maintained. The northern highlights had been cleared of those barbarian raiders who haunted most deserts. Gujgengi admitted, so Falkayn suspected the troops were quartered here mainly as a precaution against revolt. What little he had found out of Ikranankan history sounded turbulent.

Which is still another worry, he fretted. *Old Nick isn't going to invest in expensive facilities unless there's a reasonably stable social order to keep the trade routes open. And the Katandaran Empire looks like the only suitable area on the whole planet. No trading post on Ikrananka, no commissions for me. What a jolly, carefree, swashbuckling life we explorers lead!*

His gaze shifted to the oncoming party. There were a couple of dozen soldiers, in leather breastplates, armed to the teeth they didn't have with swords, knives, crossbows, and big ugly halberds. All wore the curlicue insigne of the Tirut phratry; everyone in the garrison did. At their head stalked Gujgengi. He was tall for an Ikranankan, skinny, his blue-black fur grizzled, a pair of gold-rimmed spectacles perched precariously on his beak. A scarlet robe swept to his feet, emblazoned with the crest of the Deodakh, the Imperial, phratry. At his tasselled belt hung a long snickersnee. Falkayn had not yet seen any native male without a weapon.

The human made the knee bend with arms crossed on breast that did duty here for a salaam. 'To the most noble Gujgengi and his relatives, greeting,' he intoned ritually. He'd never be able to pronounce this guttural language right. His speaking apparatus was not designed for it. And his grammar was still ramshackle. But by now he was reasonably fluent.

Gujgengi did not use the formula, 'Peace between our kindred,' but rather, 'Let us talk,' which implied there was a serious matter on hand that he *hoped* could be settled without bloodshed. And he made signs against evil, which he hadn't done of late.

'Honour my house,' Falkayn invited, since the native tongue had no word for ship and 'wagon' was ridiculous.

Gujgengi left his followers posted and stiffly climbed the

ramp. 'I do wish you would put in decent lighting,' he complained. Since he saw no wavelength shorter than yellow, though his visual spectrum included the near infra-red, the fluoros were dim to him; his horizontal-pupilled eyes had little dark adaptation, which was scarcely needed on the sunward hemisphere.

Falkayn guided him to the saloon. Gujgengi grumbled the whole way. This place was too hot, one might as well be in Subsolar country, and it stank and the air was wet and would Falkayn please quit breathing damp on him. Ikranankans didn't exhale water vapour. What their metabolism produced went straight back into the bloodstream.

At the end, he stopped in the doorway, stiffened, and adjusted his glasses. 'So you are in truth sheltering her!' he croaked.

Stepha reached for her sabre. 'Now, now, now,' said Adzel, laying irresistible fingers around her arm. 'Is that nice?'

'Be seated, most noble,' said Falkayn. 'Have a drink.'

Gujgengi accepted some Scotch with ill-concealed eagerness. Ikranankans were quite humanlike in that respect. 'I was given to understand you came in friendship,' he said. 'I trust this occurrence can be satisfactorily explained.'

'Why, sure,' Falkayn said, more heartily than he felt. 'We saw this female of my race being chased by strangers who, as far as we could tell, were raiders. Naturally we supposed she was from our homeland.'

Chee blew a smoke ring and added in her silkiest voice, 'The more so when you, most noble, had never seen fit to tell us there was an old human settlement here.'

'Ak-krrr,' Gujgengi hemmed. 'With so much else to teach you——'

'But surely you knew how interesting this one thing would be,' Chee pursued.

'—at your own request——'

'Really, most noble, we are shocked and grieved.'

'They merely form another phratry of soldiers——'

'Of considerable importance to the Empire, with which we were negotiating in good faith.'

'She broke the Emperor's express command——'

'What command? That we be isolated? Now that, most noble, is another deplorable discovery. We begin to wonder

117

how much faith has been kept with us. Perhaps we are not welcome here? We can withdraw, you know. We have no wish to force ourselves or our trade goods on anyone.'

'No, no, no!' Gujgengi had inspected samples of everything from synthetic fabrics to chemical firearms. He breathed harder each time he thought about them. 'It was only——'

'Though to be frank,' Chee said, 'the withdrawal cannot be permanent. Our people at home must be told about these Ershoka, and come to arrange for their transportation to a more suitable clime. The overlords of Earth will not be pleased to learn that Katandara was keeping these unfortunates in concealment. Were they, perhaps, being mistreated? I am afraid that a very grave view will be taken of this affair.'

Falkayn was too rocked back to enjoy the spectacle of Gujgengi's rout. He hadn't thought of the implications. Returning the Ershoka home—why, that'd blow the gaff clear to Andromeda! And he was supposed to keep his discoveries quiet!

Maybe—— No. He looked at Stepha, seated proud and cat-lithe on the edge of her chair, the light glowing in her tresses and grey eyes, down the white curves of her, and knew he couldn't betray her with his silence. Anyhow, it would be useless. Once traders started coming here, they'd also learn the facts, and some conscientious bastard was certain to blab.

Gujgengi lifted his tumbler in a hand gone shaky, tilted his head back, and poured deftly into his open bill. 'I ought to confer with the Emperor,' he said. 'I really ought to. But ... under the circumstances ... perhaps we can reach an understanding.'

'I do hope so,' said Adzel.

'The fact is,' Gujgengi confessed, 'shortly before you came, a—ak-krrr—a most unhappy situation arose. The Empire has been in the process of conquering Sundhadarta.' No mealy-mouthed phrases about 'pacification' in this language. 'The key to that whole region is Rangakora city. Being strongly fortified, it was hard to take, so the Emperor dispatched a contingent of his own crack troops, the Ershoka, to help in the storming, under High Guardsman—uk-k-k——'

'Bobert Thorn,' said Stepha curtly, supplying the labials.

'They succeeded——'

'You might thank her,' said Chee.

Gujgengi looked confused and needed another drink. 'They succeeded,' he managed to continue. 'But then, uk, Ohertorn decided this could be the nucleus of a kingdom for himself. He and his men ... well, they threw out our troops and took possession. There they have been ever since. We have, uk, not yet got them dislodged. Meanwhile the Ershoka still in the capital grow restless. And then you, of the same race, conceivably of the same phratry, appear! Do you wonder that the Emperor wished to, ak-krrr, proceed with, shall we say, circumspection?'

'Judas on a crutch!' said Falkayn indistinctly.

Stepha sat for a moment in a silence deepened by the rustle of air in ventilators, the impatient tap of Chee's cigarette holder on the table, and Gujgengi's asthmatic breathing. She scowled at the deck and tugged her chin. Abruptly she reached a decision, straightened, and said:

'Yes, truth, this has hurt the Ershoka in Katandara. They know they're under suspicion. Let the Emperor get too bloody suspicious, and he may even try to have 'em massacred. I don't think that'd be so wise of him—any bets who'd come out of the fracas alive?—but we don't want to rip the Empire apart. At the same time, we've got to look out for our own. So we heard rumours about these newcome strangers. Bound to happen, you know. Haijakatans would've carried the news around before the ban was laid on. Now and then, a planter may still sneak past the guard posts. We had to find out, in the Iron House, what these yarns meant. Else we'd be like blind men on a cliff trail. I reckoned to reach this place. My own idea, I truespeak you. None else knew. But a patrol eyeballed me.'

Gujgengi did not seize on the obvious opportunity to bluster about loyalty and subordination. Or maybe there was no such chance. More and more during the weeks Falkayn had got the impression that Ikranankans were loyal to their own blood kindred and anything else was a mere bond of convenience.

But wait!

Excited, he sprang up. Gujgengi reached for his sword, but the man only paced, back and forth, feet jarring on the deck, as he rattled out:

'Hey, this whole thing is a turn of magic for us.' No word for good luck. 'Your Emperor was wrong to suspect us. We're traders. Our interest lies in a secure realm that we can deal with. The weapons on this ship can blow down any wall ever built. We'll take Rangakora for him.'

'No!' Stepha shouted. She boiled to her own feet, sabre gleaming forth. 'You filthy——'

Falkayn let her run down, in Adzel's grasp, before he asked, 'Why, what's wrong? Aren't you on the Imperial side?'

'Before I let you kill a thousand Ershoka,' she said between her teeth, I'll——' and she was off again, in quite a long and anatomical catalogue of what she would do to David Falkayn.

'Oh, but honey chil',' he protested. 'You don't understand. I'm not going to kill anybody. Just knock down a wall or two, and over-awe the garrison.'

'Then Jadhadi's soldiers will take care of them,' she said bleakly.

'Uh-uh. We'll protect them. Make some arrangement.'

'See here,' Gujgengi objected, 'the Emperor's prerogatives——'

Falkayn told him where the Emperor could store his prerogatives, but in Latin. In Katandaran he said, 'An amnesty is our price for helping. With safeguards. I don't think it's too high. But that's for the Emperor to decide. We'll fly to him and discuss the matter.'

'Now, wait!' Gujgengi cried. 'You cannot——'

'Precisely how do you plan to stop us, sonny boy?' Chee leered.

Gujgengi fell back on argument. The Emperor would be displeased if his orders were flouted. There was no suitable place in Katandara for landing the ship. The populace was so uneasy that the sight could provoke a riot. Etcetera, etcetera.

'Best we compromise,' Adzel whispered. 'Arrogance breeds resistance.'

After considerable haggling, Gujgengi agreed that, under the circumstances, the flitter might go. It was small, could dart in before many people saw it and sit unseen in the palace gardens. And indeed a message to Katandara by land would take an awkwardly long time.

'As well, at that, to keep the ship here,' Chee remarked. 'A reserve, in case you have trouble.'

'In case *we* do?' Adzel pounced.

'You don't think I intend to go live in that dust pot of an atmosphere, do you? Not if I can help it. And I can play my tapes in peace while you and your cast-iron ear are gone.'

'If you intend to play what, for lack of a suitably malodorous word, is called Cynthian music, then I will most certainly not be here.'

'We'll take you home with us,' Falkayn offered Stepha.

She had held oddly aloof, watching with the mask back in place. Now she hesitated. 'You won't get into trouble, will you?' he asked.

'N-n-no,' she said in Anglic, which Gujgengi didn't speak. 'My barrack mates will have covered my disappearance, even if they didn't know the reason for it. Not hard to do, when these stupid Ikranankans think all Ershoka look alike. But we must be—I mean, we're confined to the city for the time being. I can't walk right in the gates, and if I arrived openly with you, I'd be watched.' She pondered. 'You land quick, right in front of the Iron House, and I can dash in. If they ask you why, afterwards, tell them you mistook it for the palace.'

'Why do you care if you're watched?'

'I don't like the idea.' She grasped his hands and leaned close. 'Please, David. You've been so good a friend till now.'

'Well——'

She waggled her eyelashes. 'I hope we can become still better friends.'

'All right, dammit!'

Arrangements were quickly made. Falkayn changed into a warm tunic, trousers, and boots, with a white cloak and a bejewelled cap tilted rakishly across his brow to add class. Two guns snugged at his waist, blaster and stunner. Into a breast pocket he slipped a transceiver; the planet had sufficient ionosphere for radio to reach between here and Katandara. He stuffed a bag with extra gear and gifts for the Emperor. Adzel took no more than a communicator hung about his neck.

'We'll call in regularly, Chee,' Falkayn said. 'If you don't hear from either of us for eight hours straight, haul gravs and come a-running.'

'I still don't know why you bother,' the Cynthian grumbled. 'That wretched female has already spoiled this whole mission.'

'The secrecy angle? We may solve that somehow. At worst, even with competitors swarming in, Old Nick will get some good out of a stable Empire. And, uh, in any event we can't let bloodshed go on.'

'Why not?' She gave up. 'Very well, be off. I'll continue our sessions with Gujgengi. The more information we have, the better.'

The Imperial agent had already gone back to town with his escort. But Haijakata's parapets were dark with natives clustered to see the take-off.

'Oh-h-h!' Stepha gasped and clutched Falkayn's arm. He resisted the temptation to do some aerial acrobatics and lined off for Katandara, a little north of west. The preliminary survey had made excellent maps, and Gujgengi had identified points of interest on them.

Kilometre after kilometre, the Chakora fled beneath them. They rode in a humming bubble over endless red-green fields, tiny thorps, once a strung-out caravan of laden four-footed karikuts guarded by warriors on zandara-back. 'Those must be Shekhej,' Stepha remarked. 'Their phratry does most of the hauling in these parts.'

Adzel, squeezing the trio together by his bulk (not that Falkayn minded), asked. 'Is every trade a family affair?'

'Why, yes,' Stepha said. 'You're born a Shekhej, you're a caravaneer. All Deodaka used to be hunters till they conquered Katandara; now they're officials. The Tiruts and others, like we Ershoka, are soldiers. The Rahinjis are scribes. And so it goes.'

'But suppose one is born with the wrong sort of talent?'

'Oh, each phratry has lots of different things to do. The main job is the most honourable one. But somebody has to keep house, keep accounts, keep farms if the group owns any—everything. You'd not trust that to outsiders, would you?

'Also, a youth at the age when he's to begin learning the phratry secrets, he can be adopted into a different one if he wants and if it'll take him. That's one reason we Ershoka are so apart. We couldn't marry with any Ikranankans'—Stepha giggled and made a vulgar joke—'so we have to stay in the corps. On t' other hand, for that same reason, we know we can trust our young. They've no place else to go. So we initiate them early.'

'I understand most phratries are very ancient.'

'Yes. Kingdoms come and go, none last more'n a few generations, but a bloodline is forever.'

Her words confirmed what Falkayn had already gathered. It bespoke an ingrained clannishness that worried him. If the attitude was instinctive, this was a poor world in which to set up operations. But if it could be altered—if the Ikranankans could be made to feel loyalty towards something larger than a cluster of families——

Katandara hove into view. The city lay no more than two hundred kilometres from Haijakata, which in turn was halfway to Rangakora. The Empire's great extent was west and south, through the fertile Chakora.

Winding from the north-east came the Yanjeh River, a silver gleam surrounded by a belt of vegetation that glowed against stark eastern hills and tawny western ranchlands. Where it ran down the former continental shelf and emptied into broad, muddy Lake Urshi, Katandara was built. That was an impressive city, which must house half a million. Whole civilizations had possessed it, one after the other, as Rome and Constantinople, Peking and Mexico City, had been possessed: each adding to walls and towers and buildings, until now the ramparts enclosed a sprawl built almost entirely in stone. Old were those stones, the hewn outlines crumbling, and old were the narrow streets that twisted between façades grey, square, and secretive. Only at the landward end, where the ground rose steeply, was there anything not scoured by millennia of desert sand—the works of the newest rulers, marble-veneered and dome-topped, roofed with copper and decorated with abstract mosaics. That section, like those of earlier overlords, had a wall of its own, to protect masters from people.

With a magnifying scanner, Stepha could point out details at such a distance that the flitter was yet unseen. Falkayn went into a dive. Air shrieked. The controls thrummed beneath his hands. At the last instant, he threw in reverse grav and came to a bone-jarring halt.

'Farewell, David . . . till we meet again.' Stepha leaned over and brushed her lips across his. Blood beat high in her face. He caught the sweet wild odour of her hair. Then she was out the lock.

The Ershoka were barracked in a single great building near the palace. It fronted on a cobbled square, along with the homes of the wealthy. Like them, it was built around a courtyard and turned a blank entry to the world. But some memory of Earth lingered in peaked iron roof, gable ends carved into monster heads, even the iron doors. A few Ikranankans gaped stupefied at the flitter. So did the sentries at the barrack entrance, big bearded men in chain mail, helmets gilt and plumed, cloaks that the wind flung about in rainbow stripes. But at once their weapons snapped up and they shouted.

Stepha sped towards them. Falkayn took off. He had a last glimpse of her being hustled inside.

'Now ho for Ol' Massa's,' he said. 'Let's hope he asks questions first and shoots later.'

IV

A gong rang outside the guest apartment. 'Come in,' said Falkayn. A servant in close-fitting livery parted the thick drapes which served for interior doors in this wood-poor country. He saluted and announced that the Emperor wished audience with the delegates of the 'Olesotechnic'gir. His manner was polite but unservile, and he used no special titles for the ruler, like His Majesty or His Potency or His Most Awe-Inspiring Refulgence. The system of hereditary jobs did not amount to a caste hierarchy; backed by his kin, a janitor was as proudly independent as a soldier or scribe.

'My associate has gone out,' Falkayn said, 'but I suppose I'll do.'

Do what? he wondered to himself. We've been cooling our motors for a week by my watch. Maybe one of those couriers that keep scurrying back and forth has put a firecracker in Jadhadi's pants, at last. Or maybe this time I can, when he isn't looking. Sure wish so. All right, I'll go, and I'll do, and I'll do.

He went to get a suitably fancy tunic for the occasion. The rooms lent him were spacious, except for low ceilings, and luxurious in their fashion. Too bad the fashion wasn't his. He liked hangings of gorgeous orange fur, especially when he estimated what such pelts would fetch on Earth. But the murals were not only in an alien artistic idiom; half the colours registered on him as mere black. The bare floor was always cold. And he couldn't fit himself comfortably on to the gaunt settees or into a shut-bed designed for an Ikranankan.

The third-storey balcony gave him a view of the palace gardens. They suggested an Old Japanese lapout: rocks, low subtly hued plants, the extravagance of a fountain—which played inside a glass column, to control evaporation. Little but roofs were visible above the estate walls. To the west, the sun shone dull and angry crimson through a dust veil. Another storm, Falkayn thought; more trouble for the ranchers out yonder.

A week inside an imperial palace could have been interesting, if the imperium had been human and reasonably decadent. Katandara was neither. In sheer despair, he had been improving his language by reading what was billed as the greatest epic in the world. It had more begats than the Bible. He made a face at the codex and thumbed his transceiver. 'Hullo, Adzel,' he said in Latin, 'how're you doing?'

'We are about to enter what I assume is a tavern,' the Wodenite's voice replied. 'At least, the legend says this is The House of Exquisite Pleasures and Ferocious Booze.'

'Oh, Lord, and I have to mind the store. Listen, the big red wheel has summoned me. Probably just for more quizzing and more postponement of any decision, but you never know. So maintain radio silence, huh?' As far as the galactics could tell, the Ikranankans were ignorant of this means of communication. It was as well to keep some aces in the hole.

Unless the Ershoka had told—— No, that seemed unlikely. Set down with nothing more than clothes and a few hand tools, caught up almost at once in this tumultuous culture, their ancestors had rapidly forgotten the arts of home. Why build guns or anything else that would prove an equalizer, even if you found time and skill to do so, when you lived by being twice as tough as the locals? Except for a few gadgets useful in every day life, the humans had introduced nothing, and their knowledge dwindled away into fable.

'Very well,' Adzel said. 'I will assure Captain Padrick it is harmless magic. I have to calm him anyway. Good luck.'

Falkayn returned to the main room and followed the servant down long corridors and sweeping ramps. A hum of activity surrounded him, footfalls, voices, rustling robes, and papers.

Ikranankans passed: gowned officials, hooded merchants, uniformed flunkies, planters in kilts, ranchers in chaps and spurred boots, visitors from afar, even a trader from the warm lands of Subsolar, shivering in a hairy cloak—the ebb and flow of life through this crown on the queen city. Cooking odours reminded Falkayn he was hungry. He had to admit regional cuisine was excellent, auguring well for van Rijn. If.

At the entrance to the throne room, four Ershoka stood guard, as gaudily outfitted as the men before the Iron House. They weren't at attention. That hadn't been invented here, and the humans had been smart enough not to suggest the idea. But they and their gleaming halberds scarcely moved. Flanking them were a dozen Tirut archers. Falkayn felt pretty sure those had been added since the troubles began in Rangakora. You couldn't blame Jadhadi for a soured attitude, when he could no longer trust his own *Sicherheitsdienst*.

Still, there was something downright paranoid about his wariness. Instead of jumping at Falkayn's offer to recover the stolen town, he'd interrogated for a week. Since he had nothing to lose by accepting, or at least hadn't given any such reasons, it must be due to exaggerated xenophobia. But what caused that, and what could be done about it?

Falkayn's attendant switched the drapes aside, and he passed through.

Jadhadi III waited on the Beast, a chimera in gilt bronze whose saddle he bestrode. Falkayn stopped at the required distance of seven paces (which, he suspected, gave the Ershoka by the throne time to intervene if he should make an assassin's lunge) and saluted. 'Where is your companion?' asked the Emperor sharply. He was middle-aged, his fur still sleekly redblack, his beginning paunch hidden under a scarlet robe. One hand clutched a jewelled sceptre which was also a businesslike spear.

'An officer of the household troops invited us on a tour of your city, most noble,' Falkayn explained. 'Not wishing to be both absent——'

'What officer?' Jadhadi leaned forward. The nearest of his Ershoka, a woman who would have made a better Valkyrie were she not battle-scarred, grey-haired, and built like a brick washtub, dropped hand to sword. The others in attendance, scribes, advisers, magicians, younger sons learning the business of government, edged closer. Their eyes glowed in the murky light.

'Why . . . Hugh Padrick, his name was, most noble.'

'Ak-krrr. Will they be back soon?'

'I don't know, most noble. Is there any haste?'

'No. Perhaps not. Yet I mislike it.' Jadhadi turned to a native guards officer. 'Have them found and returned.' To a scribe: 'Post a notice that all Ershoka are forbidden contact with the delegates of the 'Olesotechnic'gir.'

'Most noble!' The one other human not on sentry-go in the room—its length, between the polished malachite columns, was filled with alternate Ershoka and Otnakaji—stepped out from the courtiers. He was an old man, with beard and shoulder-length hair nearly white, but erect in his tunic. Falkayn had met him at other audiences: Harry Smit, senior of the phratry and its spokesman before the Emperor. 'I protest.'

The chamber grew suddenly very still. Shadows wove beneath the silver chandeliers, whose luminance shimmered on marble and fur and rich dark fabrics. Bitter incense smoked snakishly from braziers. The harpists at the far end of the chamber stopped their plangent chords, the ornate clock behind them seemed to tick louder.

Jadhadi stiffened in his saddle. The diamond eyes of the Beast glittered as hard as his own. 'What say you?' the Emperor rasped.

Smit stood soldierly in front of him and answered: 'Most noble, we Ershoka of your household also rage at Bobert Thorn's insubordination. He is no longer one of us, nor will we receive his followers among us again.' (The woman guard acquired a look at those words, even more harsh than the situation warranted.) 'Only let us march to Rangakora, and we will show you that the house of Ershokh stands by the house of Deodakh no less now than in the years of the first Jadhadi. But you trust us not. You keep us idle, you spy on our every step, you assign other phratries to join us in the duties that were ours since this palace was raised. This we have borne in patience, knowing you cannot be sure how strong the call of blood may be. Nonetheless, we chafe. They grumble in the Iron House. Insult them so openly, and I may not be able to restrain them.'

For a moment glances clashed. Then Jadhadi looked away,

127

towards his chief magician. 'What say you, Nagagir?' he asked sullenly.

That stopped Ikranankan in the habit emblemed with devices of power refrained from saying the obvious—that this room held fifty Ershoka who wouldn't stand for any rough treatment of their phratry chief. Instead, he croaked shrewdly, 'The matter seems slight, most noble. Very few guards will find their way to your distinguished guests. If they feel so strongly about it, what difference?'

'I was speaking in your own best interests,' Harry Smit added in a mild voice.

Falkayn thought he saw an opening. 'If we don't linger here, most noble, the issue hardly arises, does it?' he said. 'Take my offer, and we'll be off to Rangakora; refuse, and we'll go home. What about a decision?'

'Krrr-ek.' The Emperor gave in. 'Cancel those orders,' he said. To Falkayn: 'I cannot decide blindly. We know so little about you. Even with friendly intentions, you could somehow bring bad luck. That was what I summoned you for today. Explain your rites to Nagagir, that he can evaluate them.'

Oh no! Falkayn groaned to himself.

However, he found the session interesting. He'd wondered before about what seemed a total absence of religion but hadn't got around to querying Gujgengi. While he couldn't ask Nagagir to explain things point by point—might be as dangerous to reveal ignorance as to keep it—he gathered a certain amount of information indirectly. By claiming, sometimes falsely, not to understand various questions, he drew the magician out on the key items.

Only a moron or a tourist would generalize about an entire planet from a single culture. But you could usually figure that the most advanced people on a world had at least one of the more sophisticated theologies. And Katandara's was astoundingly crude. Falkayn wasn't sure whether to call that mishmash a religion or not. There weren't any gods: merely a normal order of things, an expected course of events, which had obtained ever since primordial Fire and Ice happened to get together and condense into the universe. But there were vaguely personified demons, powers, call them what you will; and they were forever trying to restore chaos. Their modus operandi was to cause disasters. They could only be held at bay through magic, ranging from a hundred everyday observances and taboos to the elaborate arcana which Nagagir and his college practiced.

And magicians weren't uniformly good, either. You never knew if somebody hadn't been corrupted and was lending his abilities to the service of Destruction.

The mythology sounded as paranoid as the rest of Ikranankan thought. Falkayn began to despair of getting a trade treaty okayed.

'Yes, indeed,' he fended, 'we of the Polesotechnic League are mighty wizards. We have studied deeply the laws of chance that govern the world. I'll be glad to teach you a most educational rite we call poker. And for keeping off bad luck, why, we can sell you talismans at unbelievably low prices, such as those precious herbs named four-leaved clovers.'

Nagagir, though, wanted details. Falkayn's magic could be less effective than the human believed; Destruction sometimes lured people thus to their doom. It could even be black magic; the most noble would understand that this possibility had to be checked.

Not being Martin Schuster, to upset a whole cult by introducing the Kabbalah. Falkayn must needs stall. 'I'll prepare an outline, most noble, which we can study together.' *Lord help me, he said to himself. Or, rather, Chee Lan help me. Not Adzel—a Buddhist convert isn't good for much in this connection except soothing noises—but I've seen Chee tell fortunes at parties. I'll call her and we'll work out something.* 'If you would make a similar outline of your own system for me, that would be valuable.'

Nagagir's beak dropped open. Jadhadi rose in his golden stirrups, poised his spear, and screeched, 'You pry into our secrets?'

'No, no, no!' Falkayn spread his hands and sweated. 'Not your classified information—I mean, not anything hidden from the uninitiated of the sorcerer phratries. Just the things that everybody knows, except a foreigner like me.'

Nagagir cooled off. 'That shall be done,' he said, 'albeit the writing will take time.'

'How long?'

Nagagir shrugged. Nobody else was much more helpful. While mechanical clocks had been around for some centuries, and the Ershoka had made improvements, Katandara used these simply to equalize work periods. Born to a world without nights or seasons, the people remained vague about any interval shorter than one of their seventy-two-day years. Matters were worse in the boon-docks where *Muddlin' Through* sat. There, the Ikranankans just worked at whatever needed doing till they felt ready to knock off. Doubtless their attitude made for a good digestion. But Falkayn's innards curdled.

'May I go, most noble?' he asked. Jadhadi said yes, and Falkayn left before he spat in most noble's eye.

'Have some dinner brought me,' he instructed the servant who guided him back, 'and writing materials, and a jug of booze. A large jug.'

'What kind of booze?'

'Ferocious, of course. Scat!' Falkayn dropped the curtain across his door.

An arm closed around his throat. 'Guk!' he said, and reached for his guns while he kicked back.

His heel struck a heavy calf-length boot. The mugger's free hand clamped on his right wrist. Falkayn was strong, but he couldn't unlimber a weapon with that drag on him, nor the one on his left hip when another brawny Ershokh clung to that arm. He struggled for air. A third human glided into view before him. He lashed out with a foot, hit a shield, and would have yelped in anguish had he been able. The shield pressed him back against the mugger. And behind it was the face of Stepha Carls. Her right hand pushed a soaked rag over his nostrils. The strangler eased off; reflex filled Falkayn's lungs; an acrid smell hit him like a blow and whirled him towards darkness.

V

Ordinarily, Hugh Padrick said, Old City wasn't the safest area in the world. Aside from being the home of phratries specializing in murder, theft, strong-arm robbery—plus less antisocial occupations like gambling and prostitution—it was a skulking place for the remnants of earlier cycles, who resented the Deodakh conquest. Ershoka went down there in groups. However, Adzel counted as a group by himself.

'But I don't want to provoke a conflict,' the Wodenite said.

'Hardly reckon you will,' Padrick grinned. In undress uniform, tunic, trousers, boots, cloak, sword, and knife, he was a big young man. His curly brown hair framed rugged features, where a new-looking beard grew beneath a Roman nose. His conversation had been interesting on the several occasions when he dropped in at the apartment. An Adzel, whose bump of curiosity was in proportion to the rest of him, couldn't resist the guardsman's offer of a conducted tour.

They strolled out the palace gates and across New City. The Wodenite drew stares but caused no sensation. News had got around about the Emperor's guests. And the educated class had some knowledge of astronomy.

'Did you humans teach them that?' Adzel asked when Padrick remarked on it.

'A little, I reckon,' the Ershokh replied. 'Though I'm told they already knew about the planets going around the sun and being worlds, even had a notion the stars are other suns.'

'How could they? In this perpetual daylight——'

'From the Rangakorans, I think. That's a city with more arts than most. And close enough to Twilight that their explorers could go clear into the Dark for charting stars.'

Adzel nodded. Atmospheric circulation must keep the far side reasonably warm. Even the antipodes of Subsolar would hardly get below minus fifty degrees or so. For the same reason, as well as the planet being smaller and the sun having a larger angular diameter, there was less edge effect here than on Earth. Neither the poles nor the border of Twilight differed radically in climate from the temperate zones.

Natives who ventured into the frozen lands would be handicapped by poor night vision. But after establishing fuel depots, they'd have fire on hand. Probably the original motive for such a base had been mining. Scientific curiosity came later.

'In fact,' Padrick murmured, 'Rangakora's a lot better town than this. More comfortable and more, uh, civilized. Sometimes I wish our ancestors had met the Rangakorans before they joined with a slew of barbarians invading a busted empire.' He clipped his mouth shut and glanced around to make sure he hadn't been overheard.

Beyond the inner wall, the ground fell abruptly. Buildings grew progressively older, weathered grey blocks crowding each other, shut doors marked with the symbols of long-dead civilizations. In market sections, females occupied booths, crying their husbands' wares, food, drink, cloth, pelts, handicrafts. In the workshops behind them, iron rang, potters' wheels whirred, pedal-driven looms whickered. But the shops themselves were locked away from public sight, lest a demon or a wicked magician find ways to cause an accident.

Traffic was brisk, raucous, aggressive in fighting its way through the narrow sand streets. Planters' carts, drawn by spans of karikuts, loaded with Chakoran produce, creaked past near-naked porters with burdens on their shaven heads, but yielded to swaggering Shekheji caravaneers. A flatbed wagon was guarded by none less than several Tiruts, for it carried stalks spliced and glued together to make timber, more costly than bronze. Awkward when they must walk rather than leap, a dozen zandaras bore Lachnakoni come to trade hides for city goods; the desert dwellers gripped their lances tight and peered warily from behind their veils. Noise surfed around, harsh Ikranankan babble, rumblings, groanings, footfalls, clangour, and dust and smoke swirled with a thousand sharp smells.

No one disputed Adzel's right of way. Indeed, quite a few tried to climb straight up the nearest wall. A hundred beaked faces goggled fearfully off the verge of every flat roof. Padrick carried high a staff with the Deodakh flag, and of course *some* word about the strangers had penetrated this far. But the ordinary Katandaran didn't seem very reassured.

'Why is that one in the brown robe making signs at us, from yonder alley?' Adzel asked.

'He's a wizard. Taking your curse off the neighbourhood. Or so he hopes.' Padrick was hard to hear above the voice-roar that was rising towards a collective shriek.

'But I wouldn't curse anybody!'

'He doesn't know that. Anyhow, they reckon anything new is likely black-magical.'

An attitude which evidently prevailed in high society, too, Adzel reflected. That would help account for Jadhadi's reluctance to ally himself with the League envoys. *I must discuss this with David when I get back.*

Padrick spent some time showing points of interest: a statue five thousand Earth-years old, the palace of a former dynasty turned into a warehouse, a building whose doorway was an open beak ... museum stuff. Adzel paid more attention to the imposing houses of several great phratries, where the seniors lived and member families held council. Though they took part in the present government, these blood groups had not changed their headquarters to New City. Why should they? Empires, languages, civilizations, the march and countermarch of history, all were ephemeral. Only the phratry endured.

'The House of the Stone Axe,' Padrick pointed. 'Belongs to the Dattagirs. Their senior still carries that axe. Flint head; nobody knows when it was made, except must've been before metalworking.' He yawned. 'You getting bored? Let's go where we can find some life. Old City.'

'Won't they avoid me there, too?' Adzel asked. He hoped not. It pained him that mothers should snatch their cubs and run when he appeared—such cute, fuzzy little infants, he'd love to hold one for a while.

'Not so much,' Padrick said. 'Less scared of black magic, seeing as a lot of them are black magicians themselves.'

Down they went, past a ruined wall and into the casbah. The houses they found were more tall and narrow than those of later eras, shoulder to shoulder with overhanging balconies so that a bare strip of plum-coloured sky showed overhead and shadows were thick purple. Living in a more prosperous time, when the land was not quite as arid, the builders had cobbled their streets. Adzel's hooves rang loud on the stones, for this was a silent quarter, where cloaked dwellers passed on furtive errands and only the keening of a hidden harp resounded. Along the way, that toppled towards the sea bed, Adzel could look back to the red-tinged cliffs above the whole city; and down, to the remnants of wharves among the reeds where Lake

Urshi glimmered.

Padrick stopped. 'What say you of a drink?'

'Well, I like your brew——' Adzel broke off. The transceiver at his neck had come alive with Falkayn's voice.

'What the demons!' Padrick sprang back. His sword hissed from the scabbard. A pair of Ikranankans, squatting before a doorway across the lane, gathered their ragged capes around them and vanished inside.

Adzel waved a soothing hand and finished his Latin conversation with Falkayn. 'Don't be alarmed,' he said. 'A bit of our own magic, quite safe. A, ah, a spell against trouble, before entering a strange house.'

'That could be useful, I grant.' Padrick relaxed. 'Specially here-abouts.'

'Why do you come if you find danger?'

'Booze, gambling, maybe a fight. Gets dull in barracks. C'mon.'

'I, ah, believe I had better return to the palace.'

'What? When the fun's only beginning?' Padrick tugged Adzel's arm, though he might as well have tried to haul a mountain.

'Another time, perhaps. The magic advised me——'

Padrick donned a hurt expression. 'You're no friend of mine if you won't drink my liquor.'

'Forgive me,' Adzel capitulated. 'After your great kindness, I would not be discourteous.' And he was thirsty; and Falkayn hadn't intimated there was any hurry.

Padrick led the way through a half-rotted leather curtain. A wench sidled towards him with a croaked invitation, saw he was human, and withdrew. He chuckled. 'The stews are no use to an Ershokh, worse luck,' he remarked. 'Oh, well, things are free and easy in the Iron House.'

As the Wodenite entered, stillness fell on the crowded, smoky room. Knives slid forth at the wicker tables where the patrons sat. Torches guttering in sconces threw an uneasy light—dim and red to Adzel, bright to a native—on sleazy garments, avian faces, unwinking eyes. Padrick set down his flag and raised his hand. 'Peace between our kindred,' he called. 'You know me, Hugh of the Household, I've stood many a round. This is the Emperor's guest. He's big but gentle, and no demon's trailing him. Any demon 'ud be scared to.'

A drunk in a corner cackled laughter. That eased the atmosphere somewhat. The customers returned to their drinks, though they kept looking sideways and doubtless their mutterings were now chiefly about this dragonish alien. Padrick found a backless chair and Adzel coiled on the dirt floor across from him. The landlord gathered courage to ask what they wanted. When Padrick pointed to Adzel and said munificently, 'Fill him up,' the Ikranankan cocked his head, calculated probable capacity, and rubbed his hands.

The brandy, or gin or arrack or whatever you wanted to call a liquor distilled from extraterrestrial fruits, was no more potent than concentrated sulphuric acid. But it had a pleasant dry flavour. Adzel tossed off half a litre or so. 'I must not be greedy,' he said.

'Don't be shy. This is on me.' Padrick slapped a fat purse. 'We draw good pay, I must say that for him on the Beast.'

'I have been wondering. Surely not all the Ershoka live in the Iron House.'

'No, no. You serve there between getting your commission, if you do, and getting married. And it's phratry headquarters. But families take homes throughout New City, or they go to one of our ranches, or whatever they like. After marrying, women usually lay down their arms. Men go drill once a year and naturally join the colours in an important war.'

'How then did Bobert Thorn's contingent dare revolt? Their families at home were hostage to the Emperor.'

'Not so. If he touched a one of those left behind, we'd all rise, from Harry Smit on down to the youngest drummer boy, and set his head on a pike. But anyhow, a lot of the wives and kids went along. That's usual, if there's a siege or an extended campaign. Women make perfectly good camp guards, against these flimsy Ikranankans, and they're our quartermasters and——' Padrick finished listing their functions.

That wouldn't have been feasible, under such primitive conditions, if this were Earth. But few if any native germs affected humans. It made another reason why the Ershoka were prime soldiers. Before preventive medicine becomes known, disease thins armies more cruelly than battle.

'I sympathize with your plight,' Adzel said. 'It cannot be easy, when you are so close-knit, to be in conflict with your own relatives.'

135

'Who said we were?' Padrick bridled. 'That doddering Smit? The phratry bonds weren't so strong when he was growing up. He'd never get anyone my age to march against Thorn.' He drained his beaker and signalled for more. 'But seems the Iron House will obey its officers enough to stay neutral.'

To change a difficult subject, Adzel asked if he had seen Stepha Carls since her return. 'I sure to curses have!' Padrick said enthusiastically. 'What a girl!'

'A pleasant, if impulsive personality,' Adzel agreed.

'I wasn't talking about personality. Though truth, she's tough and smart as any man. Here's to Stepha!'

Beakers clunked together. Seeing the dragon so convivial, the house relaxed yet more. Presently an Ikranankan drinking buddy of Padrick's drifted over to his table and said hello. 'Siddown!' the Ershokh bawled. 'Have one on me.'

'I really should return,' Adzel said.

'Don't be stupid. And don't insult my good friend Rakshni. He'd like to make your 'quaintance.'

Adzel shrugged and accepted more booze. Others came to join the party. They started yarning, then they started arguing about the Rangakora situation—not very heatedly, since nobody in Old City cared what happened to the parvenu Emperor —and then they had a short brawl between three or four cutthroats that broke the last ice, and then they began toasting. They toasted their phratries and they toasted the wenches cuddling in among them and they toasted the memory of good King Argash and they toasted the Yanjeh River that kept Katandara alive and they toasted Lake Urshi that took charge of so many inconvenient corpses and they toasted Hugh Padrick often because he was buying and about then they lost track and the tetrahedral dice commenced to rattle and all in all they had quite a time. Booze was cheap and Padrick's purse was full. The party ended at last more because a majority had passed out on the floor than because he went broke.

'I ... mus' ... really must ... go back,' said Adzel. His legs seemed more flexible than he preferred, and his tail had made up its own mind to wag. That demolished most of the furniture, but the landlord didn't object. He had passed out, too.

'Uh, yeh, yeh, reckon so.' Padrick lurched erect. 'Duty calls.'

'In a shrill unpleasant voice,' Adzel said. 'My friend, you have uh—hic!—wrong concep'. If you were at one wi' the universe—now please don' fall inna common error iden'ifying Nirvana with annihilation, matterfack's t' be achieved in this life——' He was no zealot, but he felt this fine chap reeling beside him deserved at least to have an accurate understanding of Mahayana Buddhism. So he lectured the whole way back. Padrick sang songs. Natives scurried out of the way.

'—an' so,' Adzel droned, 'you see reincarnation not at all necesshry to the idea uh Karma——'

'Wait.' Padrick halted. Adzel bent his neck down to regard him. They were near the gates of New City.

'Why, whuzzuh mazzuh?'

'Remembered an errand.' The Ershokh was acting sober with unexpected swiftness. Had he really matched the others drink for drink? Adzel hadn't noticed. 'You go on.'

'But I uz jus' coming to the mos' in'eresting part.'

'Later, later.' Wind ran down the empty street, driving sand, and ruffled the bronze hair. No one else was in sight. Odd, thought Adzel hazily. The citizens had retreated from him before, but not to that extent. And there was no equivalent of night time; the same proportion were always awake.

'Well, thank you f'r a (whoops!) ver' inshuck—insturruck—insurrect—in-struc-tive 'shperience.' Adzel offered his hand. Padrick took it hurriedly, almost embarrassedly, and loped off. The sword jingled at his belt.

A strange place, this. Adzel's thoughts turned sentimentally back to Woden, the dear broad plains under the brilliant sun, where his hooves spurned kilometres ... and after the chase, the fellowship of the campfire, friends, children, females. ... But that was long behind him. His family having been close associates of the League factor, they had wanted him to get a modern education; and he'd got one, and now he was so changed that he would never feel at home among the hunters. The females he didn't miss, being sexually stimulated only by the odour of one in rutting season. But a certain sense of belonging, an innocence, was forever gone. He wiped his eyes and trotted on, weaving from side to side of the street.

'There he comes!'

Adzel jerked to a stop. The space before the New City wall was a broad plaza. It swarmed with soldiers. He had some trouble estimating how many, for they kept doubling when he looked at them, like amoebas; but a lot, and every one a native.

137

The gates were shut, with a line of catapults in front.

A cavalry troop bounded forward. 'Halt, you!' shouted the leader. His lance head flashed bloody in the red light.

'I awready halted,' said Adzel reasonably.

Though uneasy, the Imperial zandaras were well disciplined. They moved to encircle him. 'Most noble,' called the troop leader, in a rather nervous tone, 'let us talk. Trouble is afoot and the Emperor, ak-krrr, desires your presence.'

Adzel clapped a hand to his stomach—the scutes rang—and bowed. His neck kept on going till his snout hit the ground. That annoyed him, but he hung on to urbanity. 'Why, sure, any ol' thing t' oblizhe. Le's go.'

'Uk-k-k, as a matter of form only, most noble, the Emperor wishes you to, krrr-ek, wear these badges of dignity.' The officer waved forward a foot soldier, who obeyed without visible happiness. He carried a set of chains.

'What?' Adzel backed off. His mind wobbled.

'Hold, there!' the officer cried. 'Hold or we shoot!' The catapult crews swivelled their weapons about. One of those engines could drive a shell-headed shaft through even a Wodenite.

'Bu-bu-buh wha's wrong?' Adzel wailed.

'Everything. The demons must have broken all barriers. Your associate has vanished, with good score of Ershoka. When he learned this, the Emperor sensed treachery and had the Iron House surrounded. Those inside grew angry and would not surrender. They shot at our own people!' The officer ran clawlike fingers through his ruff. His cloak flapped in the wind, his zandara made a skittish leap. Crossbows cocked where lances were not couched; his troopers held their ring about the Wodenite.

'What?' Confound that liquor! And no anti-intoxicants on hand. Adzel thumbed the switch of his transceiver. 'David! Where are you? Whuh happen?'

Silence answered.

'David! 'Merzh'ncy! Help!'

'Now keep still,' the officer chattered. 'Hold out your wrists first. If you are blameless, you shall not be harmed.'

Adzel switched to the ship's wavelength. 'Chee! You there?'

'Of course I am there,' said the waspish voice. 'Where else would I be but where I am?'

Adzel recited a tantra or two under his breath. The beneficent influence cleared some of his private fog. He blurted out an explanation. 'I'll go 'long wi'm,' he said. 'Peaceful. You come in uh ship. They'll got . . . they will have to lemme go then, an' we'll look f' David.'

'At once,' said Chee.

A squad of magicians made frantic passes. Adzel turned to the officer. 'Yes, 'course I'll hic th' Emperor.' From the radio came an indistinct mumble. Chee must be talking with someone else. He extended his arms and opened his mouth. It was meant for a smile, but it showed an alarming array of fangs.

The officer pricked the chain-bearing infantryman with his lance. 'Go on,' he said. 'Do your duty.'

'You do it,' whimpered the other.

'What do I hear? Do you contradict an order?'

'Yes.' The infantryman backed away. His mounted comrades opened a sympathetic way for him.

'Oh, come now,' said Adzel. He wanted to see Jadhadi and get to the bottom of this affair as fast as possible. He sprang forward. The cavalry yelped and scuttled aside.

'But I on'y wanna help!' Adzel roared. He caught the soldier, removed the chains, and set him down again. The Ikranankan curled into a little ball.

Adzel hunkered on his tail and considered. The links had got fouled. 'How yuh 'spec' me to fasten these?' he asked pettishly. The more he tried to unsnarl the mess, the worse it got. The Imperial army watched in fascination.

A shout broke from the transceiver. 'Adzel! Get away! The unsanctified creature of unmentionable habits has caught me!'

There followed sounds of scuffling, a sharp blow, and nothing.

For a lunatic instant Adzel thought he was back on the ship playing Lord Love a Duck: seven card stud, low hole card wild. He had a trey in reserve, which with another trey on the board completed a royal flush, and he raised till his pay was hocked for the next six months, and then came the final draw and he got a deuce. The alcohol fumes blew out of him and he realized he wasn't actually in that situation. It merely felt that way.

The League trained its spacemen to react fast. He continued fumbling with the chains while his eyes flicked back and forth, assessing the terrain. Given a quick dash—yes, in yonder direction—and a certain amount of luck, he could make a break. But he mustn't hurt any of these poor misguided souls, if that could possibly be avoided.

He gathered his thews and leaped.

A cavalry trooper was in his way. He scooped the Ikranankan up, zandara and all, and threw him into the detachment of spearmen beyond. Their line of grounded pikes broke apart. He bounded through. Yells exploded around him, with a sleet of crossbow quarrels. A catapult shaft buzzed his ears. The mounted officer laid lance in rest and charged from the side. Adzel didn't see him in time. The steel point smote. It didn't go in but met the radio at the Wodenite's throat and smashed the case open. Adzel brushed past, still gathering speed. The zandara spun like a top, the rider went off in an arc.

A blank wall loomed ahead, four storeys high. Adzel hit it at full velocity. Momentum carried him upwards. He grabbed the verge and hauled himself over. The rough-surfaced stones gave sufficient grip. A catapult bolt struck by his flank, knocking out splinters of rock. Adzel crossed the roof, jumped to the next, dropped into an alley, and headed towards Old City.

No help for him there, of course, except that he'd be hard to track through that maze. He'd get to Lake Urshi. They had nothing to chase a swimmer but clumsy rafts that he could easily outdistance. Once on the far shore, he'd strike across the Chakora. No word could reach Haijakata ahead of him—— But damn the loss of his transceiver!

Well, Chee's would serve, after he'd bailed the little fluff-brain out of whatever trouble she'd got into. They'd raise ship, retrieve their flitter at the palace, and start looking for David. If David was alive. If they themselves stayed alive.

VI

Perhaps there was something to the Katandaran theory that supernatural beings were uniformly malevolent. If Chee Lan had been aboard the spacecraft when Adzel called—— But she herself, an uncompromising rationalist, would have said her luck, though bad, involved no great improbability. She had been spending almost half her time with Gujgengi. Both were anxious to learn as much as possible about each other's civilizations.

One new idea she introduced, not entirely to his liking, was that of regular appointments. Haijakata's lone clock kept such slapdash time that she presented him with a watch. After that, drums rolled and flags got replaced to signal a change of guard with some predictability; and she knew when to go uphill for another session.

The computer, which she had set to remind her, did so. 'You might be more respectful,' she grumbled, laying down her book. She had pretty well convinced her shipmates that the Cynthian volumes she had along were philosophical works (in fact, they were slushy love novels) but still she enjoyed the chance to read without inane interruptions.

'You did not programme me to be respectful,' said the mechanical voice.

'Remind me to. No, cancel that. Who cares about a machine's opinions?'

'No one,' said Muddlehead, which did not have rhetorical units.

Chee hopped off her bunk and made ready. Transceiver and taper in one hand, a ladylike needle gun at her waist, were all she needed. 'Standby orders as usual,' she said, and went out the lock.

Muddlehead hummed quietly to itself. Standby meant that, although the Katandaran language had been added to its memory bank, it would only obey commands—voice, radio, or code—from one of the crew. However, Chee had connected the external speaker, in case she ever wanted to ask from the outside what the sensors observed.

The entry valve locked behind her and she scampered down

the ramp. One hatch remained open immediately above the landing jacks, for an extra bolt-hole. There was no danger of natives wandering in and causing damage. Apart from their awe of the ship, the hatch merely led to the empty No. 4 hold, which no Ikranankan could harm, and *Muddlin' Through* wouldn't operate the door from it to 'tween-decks for anyone but a crew member. Chee prided herself on thinking ahead.

The crimson sun was whiter and brighter to her eyes than to Falkayn's or Adzel's. Nonetheless she found the landscape shadowy, swore when an unseen twig snagged the fur she had spent an hour grooming, and was glad to reach the highway. And the air drank moisture from her nose like Falkayn drinking after a cruise when the Scotch gave out; and the wind was as cold as van Rijn's heart; and it carried from the Chakora scents of vegetation akin to creosote and Gorgonzola. Oh, to be back on Ta-chih-chien-pi, Life home-under-Sky, again, in a tree-top house among forest perfumes! Why had she ever left?

Money, of course. Which she was currently not making, at a furious rate. She bottled her tail and hissed.

The sentries at the gate touched sword to beak in salute as her small form passed. After she was safely beyond, they fingered charms and whispered incantations. True, the newcomers had not caused any trouble so far, and in fact promised great benefits. But demons are notorious liars.

Chee would not have been surprised, or even offended, had she seen. More and more she was discovering how immensely conservative these Ikranankans were, how suspicious of everything new. That accounted for their being still prescientific, in spite of a fantastically long recorded history. She hadn't yet developed any explanation for the attitude itself.

She sprang lithely among the plaid-woven huts. A female sat outside one, putting food in the mouth of an infant. To that extent. Ikranankans were like Cynthians. Neither had mammary glands, the young being born equipped to eat solid food. (Cynthians use their lips to suck, not suckle.) But there the resemblance ended. An Ikranankan's wife was little, ruffless, drab, and subservient. A female Cynthian, who must carry her cub through the trees—though not strictly arboreal, among endless forests the race has made the branches a second environment—is bigger than her mate, and every bit as tough a carnivore. Matrilineal descent is the norm, polyandry occurs in numerous cultures, and the past has known some outright matriarchies. Chee supposed that was why her planet was so progressive.

She popped in the door of the large cabin where Gujengi had quartered himself. The envoy was seated at a table with his host, garrison commandant Lalnakh. They were playing some game that involved dropping coloured sticks on to a board divided in squares.

Chee soared to the table-top, nearly upsetting the frail wicker structure. 'What's that?' she asked.

Lalnakh scowled, Gujengi, more used to her unceremonious ways, said, 'It is called *akritel*,' and explained. The rules were rather complicated, but in essence the game amounted to betting on how the sticks would fall. 'Quite popular,' Gujengi added.

'Do you want to make your play or do you not?' Lalnakh snapped.

'Indeed, indeed. Give me time.' Gujengi adjusted his spectacles and pondered the distribution of rods that had already been dropped. The less likely a configuration he made, the more he would win; but if he failed to get a score within the range he declared, he would lose correspondingly. 'I do believe my luck is normal today,' he said, nodding at the stack of coins already before him. A galactic would have spoken of a run of good luck. 'I will try to——' He chose his sticks and made his declaration.

'You shouldn't guess,' Chee said. 'You should know.'

Lalnakh glared. 'What do you mean?'

'Not the actual outcome,' Chee said. 'But what the chances are. Whether the chance of winning is good enough to justify the bet you make.'

'How in Destruction can that be calculated?' Gujengi asked.

'Play, curse you!' Lalnakh said.

Gujengi rattled his sheaf of sticks and let them drop. He made his point.

'Arrr-k!' Lalnakh growled. 'That does for me.' He shoved his last coin across the table.

Gujengi counted. 'You appear to owe more,' he said.

Lalnakh made a vile remark and fished in the pouch below his doublet. He threw a dull-white disc into Gujengi's stack. 'Will you take that? Rangakoran work. I've carried it for a talisman. But the demons were too strong for it today.'

Gujgengi wiped his glasses and squinted. Chee had a look herself. The medallion bore a pleasing design, a wreath on the obverse and a mountainscape on the reverse. But part of the silver had rubbed off. 'Why, this is plated bronze,' she said.

'An art they have there, among others,' Gujgengi replied. 'They put the metal in a bath and—I know not what. Strong magic. I was there once on an embassy, and they had me grip two copper threads coming out of a box, and something *bit* me. They laughed.' He recollected his dignity. 'But at any rate, being so magical, objects like this are prized. That makes yet another reason why the conquest of Rangakora is desirable.'

'Which we could accomplish for you,' Chee pointed out. 'And, incidentally, we can sell you any amount of plated stuff ourselves.'

'Ak-krrr. Understand, most noble, I have no authority to make so, uk-k-k, momentous?—yes, so momentous a decision. I am simply the Emperor's representative.'

'You can make recommendations, can't you? Chee pursued. 'I know messengers go back and forth all the time.'

'Uk-k-k, indeed. Shall we continue our previous discussions?'

'I'm going,' Lalnakh said surlily.

That was when the transceiver spoke.

'Chee! You there?'

Adzel's voice, in badly slurred Anglic. Was the big slubber drunk? Chee hoped no Ershoka were present. Her skin prickled. 'Of course——' she began, more tartly than she felt.

Lalnakh sprang aside, yanking out his dagger. Gujgengi rose and made industrious signs against evil. His glasses slipped off his beak to interrupt him.

'What the plague is this?' Lalnakh demanded.

'Where are my spectacles?' Gujgengi complained from the floor. 'I cannot see my spectacles. Has a demon run away with them?'

'Protective magic,' said Chee quickly in Katandaran, while the radio muttered with noise of a large crowd. 'Nothing to fear.'

'Help me find my spectacles,' Gujgengi quacked. 'I need my spectacles.'

Lalnakh swore and retrieved them. Chee heard Adzel out. Her fur stood on end. But the self-possession of trouble came upon her, and her mind raced like a cryogenic calculator.

'At once,' she said, and looked at the Ikranankans. They stared back, stiff and hostile.

'I must go,' she said. 'My magic has warned me of trouble.'

'What kind of trouble?' Lalnakh rapped.

Gujgengi, more accustomed by now to outworld marvels, pointed a lean finger. 'That was the monster's voice,' he said. 'But he is in the capital!'

'Well, yes,' Chee said. Before she could improvise a story, Gujgengi went on:

'That must be a thing for speaking across distances. I had begun to suspect you possesed some such ability. Now, now, most noble, please do not insult me by denying the obvious. He has called you to his assistance, has he not?'

Chee could only nod. The Ikranankans trod closer, towering above her. She didn't want to be caught, later, in an outright lie; bad for future relations, which were ticklish enough already. 'The Ershoka have rebelled,' she said. 'They are barricaded in the, what you call it, the Iron House. Adzel wants me to come and overawe them.'

'No, you don't,' Lalnakh told her; and Gujgengi: 'I am distressed, most noble, but since your fellows arrived at the palace, I have been sent explicit orders that your conveyance is to remain in place.'

'Sandstorms and pestilence!' Chee exclaimed. 'Do you want a civil war? That's what you'll get, if the Ershoka aren't brought into line, and fast.' The racket from the radio grew louder. 'Use your judgment for a change. If we wanted Jadhadi's ruin, would I not sit here and let it happen?'

They paused. Lalnakh looked uncertain. Gujgengi scratched beneath his beak. 'A point,' he murmured. 'Yes, a distinct point.'

The set broke into a roar. Metal belled, voices howled, thuds and bumps shivered the speaker. A thin Ikranankan cry: 'Help, the beast is killing me!'

Lalnakh started. Sunlight slanting into the gloomy room touched his knife with red. 'Is that friendly?' the officer said, low in his throat.

Chee pulled her gun. 'Some misunderstanding,' she chattered. 'I true-speak that we are your friends, and I'll shoot anyone who calls me a liar.' Adzel's mild basso hiccuped forth, above

145

an iron rattle. 'Hear that? He isn't fighting, is he?'

'No,' Lalnakh said. 'Feeding.'

Chee poised on the table. 'I shall go,' she stated. 'I suggest you do not try to stop me.'

Gujgengi surprised her. She had taken him for a mere bumbling professor. He drew his sword and said quietly, 'I am a Deodakh. Did I fail to try, they would read my ghost out of the phratry.'

Chee hesitated. She didn't want to kill him. That would also louse up future negotiations. A disabling shot?

Her attention was distracted from Lalnakh. The officer's hand swept through an arc. His knife smashed into her weapon. The impact tore it from her hand. He threw himself over her. She had barely time to cry a warning, then she was on the floor, pinioned.

'Hak-k-k,' Lalnakh grated. 'Keep still, you!' He cuffed her so that her head rang, snatched off her transceiver and threw it aside.

'Now now,' Gujgengi chided. 'No violence, most noble, no violence until we learn whether violence is necessary. This is all most unfortunate.' He saluted Chee, where she lay in Lalnakh's grasp. Simultaneously, he crushed the radio under his foot. 'I shall dispatch a messenger at once. Until word comes, you shall be treated as honourably as circumstances allow.'

'Wait a bit!' Lalnakh said. 'I am the garrison chief.'

'But my dear friend, it may conceivably turn out that some accommodation can be reached.'

'I doubt it. These creatures are demons, or demon-possessed. But jail her any way you like, as long as I can inspect your security arrangements. What I am going to do is post a guard on that flying house. With catapults, in case the giant arrives, and orders to kill if he does.'

'Well,' said Gujgengi, 'that is not a bad idea.'

Falkayn didn't black out. Rather, consciousness fragmented, as if he were at a final stage of intoxication. His mind went off on a dozen different tracks, none involving will power.

Sagging against the wall as the Ershoka released him, he was dizzily aware of its hardness at his back; of how the floor pressed with a planet's mass on his boot soles; of air chill and dry in his nostrils, soughing in his lungs, and the bitter drug odour; of his heart slamming; of red light a-sheen on the naked floor, and the dusky sky in a window across its expanse, which seemed to be tilting; of the big blond man who had mugged him, and the equally big redhead who supported him; of the redhead's nose, whose shape had some cosmic and probably sinister significance—— He thought once that the Ikranankan stuff he'd breathed must have pharmaceutical possibilities; then he thought of his father's castle on Hermes and that he really must write home more often; but in half a second he was remembering a party at Ito Yamatsu's place in Tokyo Integrate; and this, by an obvious association, recalled several young women to him; which in turn led him to wonder——

'Give me a hand, Owen,' Stepha Carls muttered. 'His batman'll be back soon. Or anybody might chance by.'

She began to strip off Falkayn's clothes. The process could have been embarrassing if he weren't too muzzy to care, or fun if she'd been less impersonal. And, of course, if the blond warrior hadn't assisted. Falkayn did try to observe various curves as she handled him, but his brain wouldn't stay focused.

'All right.' Stepha jerked her thumb at a bundle on the floor. The yellow-haired man unrolled it, revealing Ershoka garb. The cloth was coarse, the pants reinforced with leather: a cavalry field outfit. She started to dress Falkayn. Her job wasn't easy, the way he lolled in redhead's arms.

The stupor was leaving, though. Almost, he tried to shout. But drilled-in caution, rather than wit, stopped him. Not a chance, yet. However, strength flowed back, the room no longer whirled, and presently they'd buckle on his dagger belt. . . .

Stepha did so. He could have whipped out the knife and

driven it into her back where she squatted before him. But that would be a dreadful waste. He lurched, sliding aside from the redhead. His hand brushed across the dagger haft, his fingers clamped, he drew and stabbed at the man's chest.

Ah! There was no blade, only a squared-off stub barely long enough to keep the thing in its sheath. The Ershokh took a bruise, no doubt; he recoiled with a whispered curse. Falkayn, still wobbly, staggered for the doorway. He opened his mouth to yell. The blond grabbed him arms and Stepha wet her rag. Tiger swift, she bounded forward and crammed it down his gape.

As he spun into pieces again, he saw her grin and heard her murmur genially, 'Nice try. You're a man of parts in more ways than one. But we reckoned you might be.'

She bent to take his guns. Light coursed along her braids. 'Hoy!' said the blond. 'Leave those.'

'But they're his weapons,' Stepha said. 'I told you what they can do.'

'We don't know what else they're good for, what black magic might be in 'em. Leave them be, I said.'

The redhead, rubbing his sore ribs, agreed. Stepha looked mutinous. But there was scarcely time to argue. She sighed and rose. 'Put the stuff in his cabinet, then, so they'll think he just stepped out, and let's go.'

With a man on either side supporting him by his elbows, Falkayn lurched into the hall. He was too loaded to remember what the fuss was about and obeyed their urging mechanically. In this residential part of the palace, few were abroad. On the downramp they passed his servant, returning with a jug of ferocious booze. The Ikranankan didn't recognize him in his new clothes. Nor did anyone in the more crowded passages below. One official asked a question. 'He got drunk and wandered off,' Stepha said. 'We're taking him to barracks.'

'Disgraceful!' said the bureaucrat. Confronted by three armed and touchy Ershoka who were sober, he did not comment more.

After some time Falkayn was so far recovered that he knew they'd come to a sally port in the north wall. Cityward, the view was blocked by a row of houses. Some twenty Ershoka, most of them men, waited impatiently in battle dress. Four Tiruts, the sentries, lay bound, gagged, and indignant. The humans slipped out.

The canyon of the Yanjeh lay west of town, marked by leafy sides and the loud clear rush of water. There, too, the upland highway entered. Here was sheer desert, which rose sharply in crags, cliffs, and talus slopes, ruddy with iron oxide and sun, to the heights. In such a wilderness, the Ershoka vanished quickly.

'Move, you!' The blond jerked Falkayn's arm. 'You're un-doped by now.'

'Uh-h-h, somewhat,' he admitted. Normality progressed with every stone-rattling stride. Not that that did him much good, hemmed in by these thugs.

After a while they found a gulch. A good fifty zandaras milled about in the care of two Ikranankan riders. Several were pack animals, most were mounts and remounts. The band swung into their saddles. Falkayn got on more gingerly. The natives headed back towards town.

Stepha took the lead. They climbed until they were above the cliffs, on dunes where nothing lived but a few bushes. At their backs, and northward, Yanjeh Belt shone green. The city gloomed below them, and beyond, the Chakora reached flat and murky to the horizon. But they pointed themselves east and broke into full gallop.

No, hardly the word! Falkayn's zandara took off with an acceleration that nearly tore him from his seat. He knew a sick moment of free fall, then the saddle and his lower jaw rose and hit him. He flopped to the right. The man alongside managed to reach over and keep him from going off. By then the zandara was once more aloft. Falkayn bounced backwards. He saved himself by grabbing the animal's neck. 'Hoy, you want to strangle your beast?' someone yelled.

'As ... a ... matter ... of ... fact ... yes,' Falkayn gusted between bounces.

Around him gleamed helmets, byrnies, spearheads, gaudy shields, and flying cloaks. Metal clattered, leather creaked, foot-falls drummed. Sweat and zandara musk filled the air. So did fine sand, whirled up in a cloud. Falkayn had a glimpse of Stepha, across the wild pack. The she-troll was laughing!

He gritted his teeth. (He had only meant to set them, but his mouth was full of sand.) If he was to survive this ride, he'd have to learn the technique.

Bit by bit, he puzzled it out. You rose slightly in the stirrups as the zandara came down, to take the shock with flexed knees. You swayed your body in rhythm with the pace. And, having thought yourself athletic, you discovered that this involved muscles you never knew you had, and that said muscles objected. His physical misery soon overwhelmed any speculation as to what this escapade meant.

A few times they stopped to rest and change steeds, and after some eternities to camp. That amounted to gulping down iron rations from the saddlebags, with a miserly drink of water from your canteens. Then you posted guards, got into your bedroll, and slept.

Falkayn didn't know how long he had been horizontal when Stepha roused him. 'Go 'way,' he mumbled, and burrowed back into the lovely dark. She grabbed a handful of hair and yanked. Eventually she dragged him to breakfast.

Their pace was easier now, though, and some of the aches worked themselves out of Falkayn. He began to notice things, the desert was getting hillier all the time, and a little more fertile, too. The sun behind him was lower, shadows stretched enormous in front, towards the Sundhadarta mountains, whose slate-blue bulk was slowly lifting over the world's edge. The Ershoka had relaxed, they joked and laughed and sang some rather bloodthirsty songs.

Near the end of the 'day', a lone rider with a few spare animals overtook them. Falkayn started. Hugh Padrick, by Satan! The Ershokh waved affably at him and rode to the head of the parade to confer with Stepha.

Those two were still talking when the second camp was made, on a hilltop among scattered vividly yellow bushes. The Ershoka didn't go to sleep at once but built small fires and lounged about in companionable groups. Falkayn let another man unsaddle his zandaras, hobble them, and then turn them out to graze. Himself, he sat down with the intention of sulking but got up fast.

A shadow in the long light fell across him. Stepha stood there. He must admit she was a handsome sight, big, full-bodied, queenly featured. More used to the chill than he, she'd stripped to blouse and kilt, which further lightened his mood.

'Come and join us,' she invited.

'Do I have a choice?' he said hoarsely.

The grey eyes were grave on his. She touched his hand in an

almost timid fashion. 'I'm sorry, David. No way to treat you. Not only after what you did for me. No, you deserve better'n this in your own right. But won't you let me explain?'

He followed her less grudgingly than he made out, to a fire where Padrick sat toasting some meat on a stick. 'Hullo,' the Ershokh said. A grin flashed white in his grimy beard. 'Hope you liked the ride so far.'

'What's become of Adzel?' Falkayn demanded.

'Dunno. Last I saw, he was headed for the palace, drunk's a brewmaster. Reckoned I'd better get out of town before the fun started, so I went back to Lake Urshi where I'd hid my animals and took off after you. Saw your dust a long ways off.' Padrick lifted a leather bottle. 'Took some booze.'

'Do you suppose I'll drink with you, after——'

'David,' Stepha pleaded. 'Hear us out. I don't think your big friend can have got into deep trouble. They'd not dare hurt him when the little one still has your flyer. Or Jadhadi may decide right away you were snatched, 'stead of leaving of your will.'

'I doubt that,' Falkayn said. 'A galactic might, but those Ikranankans see a conspiracy under every bed.'

'We've made trouble for our own mates, too, in the Iron House,' Stepha reminded him. 'Could come to blows between them and the beak faces, what with nerves being strung so tight on both sides.'

'That's a hell of a way to run a phratry,' Falkayn said.

'No! We're working for their good. Only listen to us.'

Stepha gestured at a saddle blanket spread over the ground. Falkayn yielded and lowered himself, reclining Roman fashion. The girl sat down beside him. Across the fire, Padrick chuckled tolerantly. 'Dinner coming soon,' he promised. 'How about that drink?'

'Oh, the devil, all right!' Falkayn glugged. The thermonuclear liquid scorched some of the aches from him and blunted his worry about Adzel.

'You're Bobert Thorn's people, aren't you?' he asked.

'We are now,' Stepha said. 'Me alone, at first. You see, Thorn sends out spies, Ikranankans, that is. If they must be conquered, the Rangakorans would mostly rather have Ershoka than Deodaka; we seem to get along better. So some of their units are fighting on our side, and then there are the merchants and—— Anyhow, it's not hard for one to sneak out and mingle with the besiegers, claiming to be a highland trader come to see if he can peddle anything. Or whatever.'

Rotten security, Falkayn reflected. How come, in a race that suspected everyone not an in-law of being an outlaw? . . . Well, yes, such clannishness would make for poor liaison between different kin-regiments. Which invited, if not espionage, at least the gathering of intelligence.

'Jadhadi's people also got wind of you,' Stepha said. 'I reckon he altered his top officers, and somebody blabbed.' Falkayn could imagine the process: a Tirut or Yandaji ordered by a Deodakh to have secrets from his own relatives, getting mad and spilling the beans on principle. 'Just dim, scary rumours seeped down to the ranks, you understand. But our spies heard them, too. We didn't know what they meant, and had to find out. Twilight was still over the area, so I got clear without being seen, rustled me a couple of zandaras, and headed off. A patrol near Haijakata did notice me, though. My spare mount took a quarrel. I bloody near did myself.' She laughed and rumpled Falkayn's hair. 'Thanks, David.'

'And, of course, when you sounded us out and learned we were on Jadhadi's side, you pretended to be likewise,' he nodded, mainly to rub his head against her palm. 'But why'd you take the risk of coming back to Katandara with us?'

'Had to do something, didn't I? You meant to break us. I didn't know what I could swing, but I did know there must be a lot of people who wished they'd been sent to Rangakora, too. And I knew nobody in the Iron House would give me away to the Ikranankans.' Stepha grinned mischievously. 'Oh, but old Harry Smit was mad! He wanted to court-martial me on the spot. But too many others wouldn't have it. He settled for confining me to barracks while he tried to figure out some answer to the whole mess. That was a mistake. I could sit there and talk, whenever he wasn't around. I could guess who to talk most with, too—old friends and lovers that I knew well.'

'Huh?' said Falkayn. Padrick looked smug.

'So we plotted,' Stepha said. 'We waited for a chance to act. Hugh hired a couple of his Old City buddies to buy animals and supplies and keep them stashed. We'd money enough between us, our gang. Then he went and got to know you. Plain, we'd never snatch you from Adzel. Would've been simpler if you'd gone out with Hugh. But when you let Adzel go first, we reckoned we'd better not lose more time. One by one, our people found excuses to stroll into town. Owen and Ross smuggled me out of the back. We headed for your apartment. Nasty shock when you weren't there! But you must've gone to an Imperial audience, so we waited and hoped. Glad we did.'

Falkayn took another comforting swig, rolled over on one elbow, and looked hard at the girl. 'What's the point of this fantastic stunt?' he demanded.

'To stop you from helping Jadhadi,' Padrick said. 'Maybe even get you to help us. We're your fellow humans, after all.'

'So are the Ershoka back in Katandara.'

'But we're doing this for them also,' Stepha insisted. 'Why should our phratry be hirelings, and have to live under law and custom never meant for them, when they could be masters of their own country?'

'A better country than back yonder, anyhow,' Padrick said.

'Bobert Thorn's thought,' Stepha agreed. 'He hoped the Ershoka would break from Jadhadi and come join him as soon as they learned what he'd done. Be tough, we know, cutting a way through the Imperial army. There'd be lives lost. But it could be done'—her voice rang forth—'and well worth the price!'

'You may have provoked matters so far by snatching me that the Ershoka won't have any choice,' Falkayn admitted bitterly. 'And for what? Didn't I tell you that you can all be returned to Earth?'

Stepha's eyes widened. Her hand went to her mouth. 'Oh I forgot!'

'Too late now,' Padrick laughed. 'Besides, take time to fetch your flyers, right, David? Meanwhile, what's to happen at Rangakora? And ... I'm not sure I'd want to leave. Earth ways may be too different, worse than Katandara.'

'Very well,' Falkayn said. 'You've succeeded this far. You've made trouble in the capital. You've prevented our ship taking action till my mates find out what's become of me. You may have driven a wedge between us and Jadhadi. But don't think we'll do your dirty work for you.'

'I wish you would, though,' Stepha murmured, and stroked his cheek.

'Now cut that out, girl! I come to curry Caesarism, not to raze it.'

'No matter,' said Padrick. 'Long's your, uh, ship keeps hands off'—Falkayn had a brief giddy vision of *Muddlin' Through* with hands—'we'll manage. And it'll sure do that while we've got you.'

'Unless she rescues me, knocking down your damned walls in the process.'

'They try,' said Padrick, 'and they'll find you in two pieces. We'll let 'em know that, if they do show up.' He didn't even have the decency to sound grim.

'It'll be such a pity,' Stepha cooed. 'We've hardly begun our friendship, David.'

'Meat's cooked,' said Padrick.

Falkayn resigned himself. He didn't mean to stay passive longer than he must. However, food drink, and a pretty woman constituted a situation which he could accept with an equanimity that would make Adzel proud of him. (*Adzel, you scaly old mutt, are you safe? Yes. You've got to be. All you need do is radio Chee for help.*) The conversation at dinner was amicable and animated. Padrick was a fine fellow after several drinks, and Stepha was a supernova. The only fault he could find, at length, was that they insisted on switching off the party to rest for the next stage. Dismal attitude.

His watch had been left behind with everything else, but as near as he could tell, the Ershoka had a well-developed time sense. The ancient cycles of Earth still governed them. An hour to get started, sixteen hours—with short breaks—to travel, an hour to make camp and relax, six hours' sleep, divided roughly between two changes of guard. Not that there was much to fear, in this wasteland.

But the country grew yet greener as the sun sank, until the Sundhadarta foothills were carpeted with mosslike growth, brooks rilled, and forests of plumed stalks swayed in the wind. Once clouds massed in the north, coloured hot gold. The mountains rose sheer to east, aglow in the level red light. Falkayn saw snow peaks and glaciers. Above them the sky was a royal purple deepening towards black, where fifty stars and a planet glimmered. They were at the edge of the Twilight Zone.

Not only did the atmosphere diffuse enough light to make a belt of dusk; Ikrananka had a rather eccentric orbit, and so librated. The gloaming swept back and forth across these lands, once in each seventy-two-day year. At present it had withdrawn, and the sun stood a little above the western piedmont. The slopes reflected so much heat, and so much infra-red got through at this altitude, that the region was actually warmer than Katandara. The precipitation of the cold season was melting, and rivers foamed down the cliffs. Falkayn understood now why Rangakora was coveted.

He estimated that the party had travelled about five Terrestrial days, covering some four hundred kilometres, when they turned south towards the eastern end of the Chakora. A shoulder thrust huge before them and they must climb, up towards the snow cone of Mount Gundra. Falkayn had got used to the saddle and let his zandara do the struggling while he admired the tremendous view and reminisced about his last session by the campfire. Padrick had gone off with some other girl, leaving him and Stepha alone. Well, not exactly alone; no privacy, with people scattered around; but still, he reflected, his captivity might turn out to have compensations. . . .

They rounded a precipice and Rangakora stood above them.

The city was built athwart a pass over the range, on a small plateau. A road of sorts wound heavenward from it, and on this side precipitously down towards the sea bottom. That glimmered misty, marshy, intensely green and gold. A river coursed near the wall. For the most part it was hidden by forest, but just above Rangakora it leaped over a sheer cliff and thundered in a waterfall crowned by rainbows. Falkayn caught his breath.

The Ershoka halted and drew together. Shields went on to arms, sabres into hands, crossbows were cocked, and lances couched. Falkayn realized with a gulp that now was no time to contemplate scenery.

The Plateau's verdure was scarred by feet. Campfires smoked around the city's rough walls, tents crowded, and banners flew. Tiny at this remove, Jadhadi's people sat in clumps before the prize from which they had been expelled.

'We'll make a rush,' Padrick said. The wind and the cataract boomed around his words. 'Thorn's folk'll see us and sally forth to fetch us in.'

Stepha brought her animal next to Falkayn's. 'I'd not want you to get ideas about bolting and surrendering to the others,' she smiled sweetly.

'Oh, hell,' said Falkayn, who already had them.

She looped a cord from her saddlebow to his zandara's bridle. Another girl tied his right ankle to the stirrup. He had often been told about the moral and psychological value of absolute commitment, but this seemed a bit extreme.

'Battle formation!' Padrick called. His sword flew clear. 'Charge!'

The beasts bounded forward. Drums beat staccato alarm from the Imperial outposts. A cavalry squadron marshalled themselves and started full tilt to intercept. Their lances flashed intolerably bright.

VIII

Being as prone to disorderly conduct as most races, the Ikranankans needed jails. Haijakata's was a one-room cabin near the market square. An interior grid of stout stalks, closely lashed together, protected the woven outside walls against any tenants. If a prisoner wanted light, he could draw back the door curtain; but the wooden-barred gate beyond would remain locked. Furniture amounted to a straw tick and some clay utensils. Chee had broken one of these and tried to cut her way out with a shard. It crumpled, showing that while her captors might be crazy, they were not stupid.

A click and rattle snapped her out of a rather enjoyable reverie. The gate creaked open, the curtain was pulled aside, relieving the purplish dusk, and Gujgengi's spectacles glittered. 'I was just thinking about you,' Chee said.

'Indeed?' The mandarin sounded flattered. 'May I ask what?'

'Oh, something humorous, but lingering, with either boiling oil or melted lead. What do you want?'

'I ... uk-k-k ... may I come in?' The curtain drew wider. Behind the gaunt, robed form, Chee saw a couple of armed and alert guards, and beyond them a few civilians haggling at the market booths. The quarantine had reduced trade to a minimum. 'I wish to ascertain if you are satisfactorily provided for.'

'Well, the roof keeps off the rain.'

'But I have told you that rainfall is unknown west of Sundhadarta.'

'Exactly.' Chee's glance fell wistful on the sabre at Gujgengi's side. Could she lure him in alone and snatch that—— No, he need only fend off an attack and holler. 'And why can't I have my cigarettes? That is, those fire-tubes you have seen me put in my mouth.'

'They are inside your house, most noble, and while the house does not appear to resent being guarded, it refuses to open for us. I asked.'

'Take me there, and I will give it orders.'

Gujgengi shook his head. 'No, I regret. That involves too many unknown powers you might unleash. When the present, ak-krrr, deplorable misunderstanding has been cleared up, yes, indeed, most noble. I have dispatched couriers post-haste to Katandara, and we should receive word before long.' Taking an invitation for granted, he stepped through. The soldiers closed the awkward padlock.

'Meanwhile poor Adzel arrives and gets himself killed by your hotheads,' Chee said. 'Pull that curtain, you dolt! I don't want those yokels gaping in at me.'

Gujgengi obeyed. 'Now I can scarcely see,' he complained.

'Is that my fault? Sit down. Yes, there's the bedding. Do you want some booze? They gave me a crockful.'

'Ek-k-k, well, I ought not.'

'Come on,' Chee urged. 'As long as we drink together, we are at least not deadly enemies.' She poured into a clay bowl.

Gujgengi tossed off the dose and accepted a refill. 'I do not perceive you drinking,' he said, in a heavy-footed attempt at humour. 'Do you plan to get me intoxicated, perhaps?'

Well, Chee thought with a sigh, *it was worth trying.*

Briefly, she grew rigid. The jolt passed, her mind hummed into overdrive, she relaxed her body and said, 'There isn't much else to do, is there?' She took the vessel and drank. Gujgengi couldn't see what a face she made. Pah!

'You malign us, you know,' she said. 'We have none but the friendliest intentions. However, if my comrade is killed when he arrives, expect revenge.'

'Krrr-ek, he will be only if he grows violent. Somewhat against Commandant Lalnakh's wish, I have posted criers who will shout warnings that he is to stay away. I trust hè will be sensible.'

'Then what do you plan to do about him? He has to eat,' Gujgengi winced. 'Here, have another drink,' Chee said.

'We, ak-krrr, we can try for some accommodation. Everything depends on what message I get from the capital.'

'But if Adzel has headed this way, he will be here well before that. Come on, drink and I'll recharge the bowl.'

'No, no, really, this is quite enough for an oldster like me.'

'I don't like to drink alone,' Chee urged.

'You have not taken much,' Gujgengi pointed out.

'I'm smaller than you.' Chee drained the vessel herself and glugged out some more from the crock. 'Though you would be astonished at my capacity,' she added.

Gujgengi leaned forward. 'Very well. As an earnest of my own wish for friendship, I will join you.' Chee could practically read his thought: *Get her drunk and she may reveal something.* She encouraged him with a slight hiccup.

He kept his own intake low, while she poured the stuff down at an ever mounting rate. Nonetheless, in the course of the next hour or so, his speech grew a little slurred.

He remained lucid, however, in contrast to Chee. He was not unsubtle about trying to trap her into an admission that Falkayn must have engineered the trouble in Katandara. When her denials grew belligerent, he abandoned that line. 'Let us discuss something else,' he said. 'Your capabilities, for example.'

'I'm'sh capable'sh you,' Chee said.

'Yes, yes, of course.'

'More sho.'

'Well, you have certainly revealed——'

'Prettier, too.'

'Uk-k-k, tastes vary, you know, tastes vary. But I must concede you an intrinsic——'

'So I'm not beautiful, huh?' Chee's whiskers dithered.

'On the contrary, most noble. Please, I beg you——'

'Sing real good, too. Lisshen.' Chee rose to her feet, bowl in hand, and staggered about waving her tail and caterwauling. Gujgengi folded his ears.

'*Ching, chang, guli, guli vassa,*

Ching, chang, guli, guli bum.'

'Most melodious! Most melodious! I fear I must be on my way.' Gujgengi stirred where he sat on the mattress.

'Don' go, ol' frien',' Chee pleaded. 'Don' lea' me 'lone.'

'I will be back. I——'

'Oops!' Chee reeled against him. The bowl swept across his glasses. They fell. Chee grabbed after them. She came down on top, with the bowl. There was a splintering.

'Help!' Gujgengi cried. 'My spectacles!'

'Sho shorry, sho shorry.' Chee fumbled around after the pieces.

The guards got in as fast as they could. Chee retreated. Gujgengi blinked in the sudden brightness. 'What's wrong, most noble?' asked a soldier. His sword was out.

'Li'l accshiden',' Chee babbled. 'Ver' shorry. I fix you up.'

'Stand back!' The sabre poked in her direction. The other guard stooped and collected the pieces.

'It was doubtless unintentional,' Gujgengi said, making signs against demons. 'I think you had best get some sleep now.'

'Fix you up. Got doctors, we do, fix your eyes sho you never need glasshes.' Chee was surprised at her own sincerity. The Imperial envoy wasn't such a bad sort, and doubtless he'd have a devil of a time getting replacements. Katandaran optometry must be a crude cut-and-try business.

'I have spares,' Gujgengi said. 'Conduct me to my residence.' He saluted Chee and shuffled out. She rolled over on her tick and closed her eyes.

'Too much light,' she complained. 'Draw 'at curtain.'

They obeyed, before locking the gate again. She waited a few minutes until she rose, though, and continued to emit realistic snores.

The liquor made her stomach uneasy. But it hadn't affected her mind. Ethanol is a normal product of Cynthian metabolism. And ... unseen in murk, by Gujgengi's weak eyes, she had palmed a couple of the largest fragments and slipped them under the mattress.

She ripped the ticking with her teeth, for rags to protect her hands, and got busy at the far end of the hut.

The glass wasn't very hard. As edges wore down, it sawed with ever less efficiency on the lashings of the framework. She could use pressure flaking to resharpen—a League academy gives a broad practical education—but only a few times before the chunks got too small to handle. 'Hell and damnation!' she shouted when one of them broke completely.

'What's that?' called a voice from outside.

'Z-z-z-z,' snored Chee.

A human would have sweated through that slow hour, but she was philosophical about the possibility of failing. Also, she needed less of an opening than a man would. Nonetheless, she barely finished before her tools wore to uselessness.

Now, arch your spine, pour through your arms and legs the strength they won leaping from branch to branch in the forests of home ... ugh! ... the canes bent aside, she squirmed through, they snapped back into position and she was caught against the outer wall. Its fabric was rough against her nose. Panting, shivering in the chill gloom, she attacked with teeth and nails. One by one, the fibres gave way.

Quick, through, before somebody noticed!

A rent appeared, ruddy sunlight and a windowless carpet wall across a deserted lane. Chee wriggled out and ran.

The city gates might or might not be watched too closely. But in either case, crossing that much distance, she'd draw half the town after her. Somebody could intercept her; or a crossbow could snap. She streaked around the jail and on to the plaza.

The natives screeched. A foodwife ducked behind her wares. A smith emerged from his shop, hammer in hand. Her guards took off after her. Ahead was a kiosk, at the centre of the square. Chee sprang through its entrance.

Rough-hewn steps wound downward into the hill. A dank draft blew in her face. The entrance disappeared from sight and she was in a tunnel, dug from earth and stone, lit at rare intervals by shelved lamps. She stopped to pinch the wicks of the first two. Though she must then slow, groping until she reached the next illuminated spot, the Ikranankans were more delayed. Their cries drifted to her, harsh and distorted by echoes. Not daring to meet the unknown in the dark, they'd have to go back for torches.

But that time she was out at the bottom of the hill. A short stone passage led to a room with a well in the middle. A female let go the windlass handle and jumped on to the coping with a scream. Chee ignored her. The gate here was open and unguarded when the town faced no immediate threat. She'd seen that before, at the time Gujgengi gave her party the grand tour. She bounded from the tower, forth into brush and sand.

A glance behind showed turmoil at Haijakata's portals. She also glimpsed *Muddlin' Through*, nose thrusting bright into the sky. For a moment she debated whether to try regaining the ship. Once aboard, she'd be invincible. Or a shouted command for the vessel to lift and come get her would suffice.

No. Spears and shields ringed in the hull. Catapults crouched skeletal before them. She'd never get within 'earshot' without being seen, nor finish a wigwag sentence before a quarrel pierced her. And Muddlehead hadn't been programmed to do anything without direct orders, no matter what the detectors observed.

Oh, well. Adzel could set that right. Chee started off. Before long she was loping parallel to the Haijakata road, hidden by the farm crops that lined it, all pursuit shaken.

The air was like mummy dust—thin mummy dust—and she grew thirstier by the minute. She managed to suppress most symptoms by concentrating on how best to refute a paper she'd seen in the *Journal of Xenobiology* before they left Earth. The author obviously had hash for brains and fried eggs for eyes.

Even so, eventually she had to get a drink and a rest. She slanted across the fields towards a canebrake that must mark a spring. There she glided cautiously, a shadow among shadows, until she peered out at the farmstead it enclosed.

Adzel was there. He stood with a pig-sized animal, from a pen of similar beasts, hooting in his arms, and said plaintively to the barred and shuttered central keep: 'But my good fellow, you must give me your name.'

'For you to work magic on?' said a hoarse male voice from within.

'No, I promise you. I only wish to give you a receipt. Or, at least, know whom to repay when I am able. I require food, but I do not intend to steal.'

A dart whined from an arrow slot. He sighed. 'Well, if you feel that way——'

Chee came forth. 'Where's some water?' she husked.

Adzel started. 'You! Dear friend, what in the universe has happened to you?'

'Don't "dear friend" me, you klong. Can't you see I'm about to dry up and blow away?'

Adzel tried to bristle. Having no hair, he failed. 'You might keep a civil tongue in your head. You would be astonished at how much less detested that can make you. Here I have been travelling day and night——'

'What, clear around the planet?' Chee gibed. Adzel surrendered and showed her the spring. The water was scant and muddy, but she drank with some understanding of what Falkayn meant by vintage champagne. Afterwards she sat and groomed herself. 'Let's catch up on our news,' she proposed.

Adzel butchered the animal while she talked. He had no tools for the job, but didn't need them either. In the end, he looked forlorn and said: 'Now what shall we do?'

'Call the ship, of course.'

'How?'

Chee noticed for the first time that his transceiver was also broken. They stared at each other.

Gujgengi adjusted his spare glasses. They didn't fit as well as the old ones had. The view was fuzzy to his eyes. *This might be preferable, though,* he thought. *The thing is so huge. And so full of sorcery. Yes, I do believe that under present circumstances I am quite satisfied not to see it too clearly.*

He gulped, mustered his whole courage, and tottered a step closer. At his back, the soldiers watched him with frightened expressions. That nerved him a trifle. *Must show them we Deodaka are uniformly fearless and so forth.* Though he would never have come except for Lalnakh. Really, the Commandant had behaved like a desert savage. One knew the Tiruts weren't quite one's equals—who was?—but one had at least taken them for a civilized phratry. Yet Lalnakh hàd stormed and raved so about the prisoner escaping that ... well, from a practical standpoint, too, it would not help Gujgengi's reputation. But chiefly for the honour of the bloodline, one must answer the Tirut's unbridled tirade with stiff dignity and an offer to go consult the flying house. Would the Commandant care to be along? No? Excellent. One did not say so immediately, for fear of provoking him into changing his mind, but when one returned, one might perhaps drop a hint or two that most noble Lalnakh had not *dared* come. Yes, one must maintain a proper moral superiority, even at the risk of one's life.

Gujgengi swallowed hard. 'Most noble,' he called. His voice sounded strange in his ears.

'Are you addressing me?' asked the flat tones from overhead.

'Ak-krrr, yes.' Gujgengi had already had demonstrated to him, before the present wretched contretemps, that the flying house (no, the word was *shi'*, with some unpronounceable consonant at the end, was it not?) could speak and think. Unless, to be sure, the strangers had deceived him, and there was really just someone else inside. If so, however, the someone had a peculiar personality, with little or no will of its own.

'Well?' said Gujgengi when the silence had stretched too far.

'I wait for you to proceed,' said the shi'.

'I wish, most noble, to ask your intentions.'

'I have not yet been told what to intend.'

'Until then you do nothing?'

'I store away whatever data I observe, in case these are required at a later time.'

Gujgengi let out a hard-held breath. He'd hoped for something like this. Greatly daring, he asked: 'Suppose you observed one of your crew in difficulties. What would you do?'

'What I was observed to do, within the limits of capability.'

'Nothing else? I mean, krrr-ek, would you take no action on your own initiative?'

'None, without verbal or code orders. Otherwise there are too many possibilities for error.'

Still more relieved, Gujgengi felt a sudden eagerness to explore. One had one's intellectual curiosity. And, of course, whatever was learned might conceivably find practical application. If the newly come Ershokh and his two eldritch companions were killed, well, the shi' would still be here. Gujgengi turned to the nearest officer. 'Withdraw all personnel a distance,' he said. 'I have secrets to discuss.'

The Tirut gave him a suspicious glance but obeyed. Gujgengi turned back to the shi'. 'You are not totally passive,' he pointed out. 'You answer me in some detail.'

'I am so constructed. A faculty of logical judgment is needed.'

'Ak-krr, do you not get, shall we say, bored sitting here?'

'I am not constructed to feel tedium. The rational faculty of me remains automatically active, analyzing data. When no fresh data are on hand, I rehearse the logical implications of the rules of poker.'

'What?'

'Poker is a game played aboard my hull.'

'I see. Uk-k-k, your responsiveness to me is most pleasing.'

'I have been instructed to be nonhostile to your people. "Instructed" is the closest word I can find in my Katandaran vocabulary. I have not been instructed not to reply to questions and statements. The corollary is that I should reply.'

Excitement coursed high in Gujgengi. 'Do you mean—do I understand you rightly, most noble—you will answer any question I ask?'

'No. Since I am instructed to serve the interests of my crew, and since the armed forces around me implies that this may have come into conflict with your interests, I will release no information which might enhance your strength.'

The calmness was chilling. And Gujgengi felt disappointed that the shi' was not going to tell him how to make blasters. Still, a shrewd interrogator might learn something. 'Would you advise me about harmless matters, then?'

The wind blew shrill, casting whirls of grit and tossing the bushes, while the hidden one considered. Finally: 'This is a problem at the very limits of my faculty of judgment. I can see no reason not to do so. At the same time, this expedition is for the purpose of gaining wealth. The best conclusion I can draw is that I should charge you for advice.'

'But, but how?'

'You may bring furs, drugs, and other valuables, and lay them in that open doorway you presumably see. What do you wish me to compute?'

Taken aback, Gujgengi stuttered. He had a potential fortune to make, he knew, if only he could think. . . . Wait. He remembered a remark Chee Lan had made in Lalnakh's house before her arrest. 'We play a game called *akritel*,' he said slowly. 'Can you tell me how to win at it?'

'Explain the rules.'

Gujgengi did so. 'Yes,' the shi' said, 'this is simple. There is no way to win every time without cheating. But by knowing the odds on various configurations that may be achieved, you can bet according to those odds and therefore be ahead in the long run, assuming your opponents do not. Evidently they do not, since you ask, and since Drunkard's Walk computations involve comparatively sophisticated mathematics. Bring writing materials and I will dictate a table of odds.'

Gujgengi restrained himself from too much eagerness. 'What do you want for this, most noble?'

'I cannot be entirely certain. Let me weigh what information I have, in order to estimate what the traffic will bear.' The shi' pondered awhile, then named what it said was a fair amount of trade goods. Gujgengi screamed that this would impoverish him. The shi' pointed out that in that case he need not buy the information. It did not wish to haggle. Doubtless there were others who would not find the fee excessive.

Gujgengi yielded. He'd have to borrow a sum to pay for that much stuff; still, with the market depressed by the quarantine, the cost wouldn't be unmanageable. Once he left this miserable hamlet and returned to Katandara, where they gambled for real stakes——

'Did you learn anything, most noble?' asked the officer as Gujgengi started uphill again.

'Yes,' he said. 'Most potent information. I will have to pay a substantial bribe, but this I will do out of my own pocket, in the interests of the Emperor. Ak-krr . . . see to it that no one else discourses with the shi'. The magic involved could easily get out of hand.'

'Indeed, most noble!' shuddered the officer.

IX

The heroes of adventure fiction can go through any harrowing experience and—without psychochemicals, usually without sleep, always without attending to bodily needs—are at once ready to be harrowed all over again. Real people are built otherwise. Even after a possible twelve hours in the sack, Falkayn felt tired and sore. He hadn't been hurt during that wild ride through the Katandaran lines, but bolts zipped nastily close, and Stepha sabred an enemy rider seconds before he reached the Hermetian. Then Bobert Thorn's people sallied, beat off the opposition, and brought the newcomers into Rangakora. Falkayn wasn't used to coming that near death. His nerves were still tied in knots.

It didn't help that Stepha was utterly cheerful as she showed him around the palace. But he must admit that the building fascinated him. Not only was it more light and airy than anything in Katandara, not only did it often startle him with beauty; it held the accumulated wealth of millennia less violent than further west. There were even interior doors such as he knew at home, of bronze cast in bas reliefs; reasonably clear glass windows; steam heating.

They left the electroplating shop, a royal monopoly operated in the palace, and strolled to a balcony. Falkayn was surprised at how far the grave philosophers had progressed: lead-acid batteries, copper wire, early experimentation with a sort of Leyden jar. He could understand why this was a more congenial society for humans than Katandara.

'Jeroo, there's Thorn himself, and the King,' Stepha exclaimed. She led Falkayn to the rail where they stood. His two guards trampled behind. They were friendly young chaps, but they never left him and their weapons were loose in the scabbards.

Thorn put down the brass telescope through which he had been looking and nodded. 'That camp gets sloppier every watch,' he said. 'They're demoralized, right enough.'

Falkayn glanced the same way. The palace was a single unit, many-windowed, several stories high. He was near the top. No wall surrounded it, simply a garden, and beyond that the city. Like Katandara, Rangakora was so old as to be almost entirely stone-built. But the houses here were a symphony of soft whites, yellows, and reds. Facing outward rather than inward, with peaked tile roofs and graceful lines, they reminded him somewhat of First Renaissance architecture on Earth. Traffic moved on comparatively wide, paved avenues, distance-dwarfed figures, a faint rumble of wheels and clatter of feet. Smoke drifted into a Tyrian sky where a few clouds wandered. Behind, the heights soared grey-blue to Mount Gundra, whose snowcap glowed gold with perpetual sunset. The falls tumbled on his right, white and green and misted with rainbows, querning their way down to a Chakora which here was brilliant with fertility.

His gaze stopped short, at the beseigers. Beyond the city ramparts, their tents and campfires dotted the plateau, their animals grazed in herds and metal flashed where the soldiers squatted. Jadhadi must have sent powerful reinforcements when he learned of the rebellion. 'I'd still not like to take them on, the way they outnumber your effectives,' he said.

Bobert Thorn laughed. He was a stocky, grizzle-bearded man with fierce blue eyes. Old battle scars and well-worn sabre stood out against his embroidered scarlet tunic and silky trousers. 'No hurry,' he said. 'We've ample supplies, more than they're able to strip off the country. Let 'em sit for a while. Maybe the rest of the Ershoka will arrive. If not, come next twilight, they'll be so hungry and diseased, and half blinded to boot, we can rout 'em. They know that themselves, too. They haven't much guts left.' He turned to the slim red-pelted young Ikranankan in saffron robe and gilt chaplet. 'King Ursala, this here's the man from Beyond-the-World I told you about.'

The monarch inclined his avian head. 'Greeting,' he said in a dialect not too thick to follow. 'I have been most anxious to meet you. Would the circumstances had been friendlier.'

'They might be yet,' Falkayn hinted.

'Not so, if your comrades carry out their threat to bring up under Katandara,' said Ursala. His mild tone softened the import.

Falkayn felt ashamed. 'Well, uh, there we were, strangers with no real knowledge. And what's so bad about joining the Empire? Nobody there seemed to be ill treated.'

Ursula tossed his ruff and answered haughtily: 'Rangakora was ancient when Katandara was a village. The Deodaka were desert barbarians a few generations ago. Their ways are not ours. We do not set phratry against phratry, nor decree that a son is necessarily born into his father's profession.'

'That so?' Falkayn was taken aback.

Stepha nodded. 'Phratries here're just family associations,' she said. 'Guilds cut right across them.'

'That's what I keep telling you, most noble,' said Thorn self-righteously. 'Once under the protection of the Ershoka——'

'Which we did not ask for,' Ursala interrupted.

'No, but if I hadn't decided to take over, Jadhadi's viceroy would be here now.'

'I suppose you are the best of a hard bargain,' sighed the King. 'The Irshari may have favoured us too long; we seem to have lost skill in war. But let us be honest. You will exact a price for your protection, in land, treasure, and power.'

'Of course,' said Thorn.

To break an uncomfortable silence, Falkayn asked who or what the Irshari might be. 'Why, the makers and rulers of the universe,' said Ursala. 'And you as superstitious in Beyond-the-World as they are in the Westlands?'

'Huh?' Falkayn clenched his fists. A shiver ran through him. He burst into questions.

The responses upset every preconception. Rangakora had a perfectly standard polytheistic religion, with gods that wanted sacrifices and flattery but were essentially benevolent. The only major figure of evil was he who had slain Zuriat the Bright, and Zuriat was reborn annually while the other gods kept the bad ones at bay.

But then the Ikranankans were not paranoid by instinct!

What, then, had made the western cultures think that the cosmos was hostile?

Falkayn's mind leaped: not at a conclusion, he felt sure, but at a solution that had been staring him in the face for weeks. Ikrananka's dayside *had no seasons*. There was no rhythm to life, only an endless struggle to survive in a slowly worsening environment. Any change in nature was a disaster, a sandstorm, a plague, a murrain, a drying well. No wonder the natives were suspicious of everything new, and so by extension of each other. No wonder that they only felt at ease with full initiated members of their own phratries. No wonder that civilizations were unstable and the barbarians free to come in so often. Those poor devils!

Rangakora, on the edge of the Twilight Zone, knew rain and snow and quickening, in the alternation of day and dusk. It knew, not just a few isolated stars, but constellations; after its people had ventured into the night land, it knew them well. In short, Falkayn thought, while the local citizens might be S.O.B.'s, they were Earth's kind of S.O.B.'s.

But then——

No. Rangakora was small and isolated. It simply hadn't the

capability of empire. And, with the factions and wild raiders of this planet, van Rijn would deal with nothing less than an empire. Turning coat and helping out this city might be a quixotic gesture, but the Polesotechnic League didn't go in for tilting at windmills. A liberated Rangakora would be gobbled up again as soon as the spaceship left; for there would be no further visits.

Yet its steadying influence could prove invaluable to out-world traders. Wasn't some compromise possible?

Falkayn glanced despairingly heavenward. When in hell was *Muddlin' Through* going to arrive? Surely Chee and Adzel would look first for him here. Unless something dreadful had happened to them.

He grew aware that Ursala had spoken to him and climbed out of his daze. 'Beg pardon, most noble?'

'We use no honorifics,' the King said. 'Only an enemy needs to be placated. I asked you to tell me about your home. It must be a marvellous place, and the Irshari know I could use some distraction.'

'Well—uh——'

'I'm interested, too,' said Thorn. 'After all, if we Ershoka are to leave Ikrananka, that throws everything off the wagon. We might as well pull out of Rangakora now.' He didn't look too happy about it.

Falkayn gulped. When the humans were evacuated to Earth, he himself would be a public hero, but van Rijn would take him off trade pioneering. No doubt he'd still have a job: a nice, safe position as third officer on some milk run, with a master's berth when he was fifty and compulsory retirement on a measured pension ten years later.

'Uh, the sun is more bright,' he said. 'You saw how our quarters were lit, Stepha.'

'Damn near blinded me,' the girl grumbled.

'You'd get used to that. You'd have to be careful at first anyway, going outdoors. The sun could burn your skin.'

'The plague you say!' exploded one of Falkayn's guards.

The Hermetian decided he was giving a poor impression. 'Only for a while,' he stumbled. 'Then you're safe. Your skin turns tough and brown.'

'What?' Stepha raised a hand to her own clear cheek. Her mouth fell open.

'It must be hot there,' said Ursala shrewdly.

'Not so much,' Falkayn said. 'Warmer than here, of course, in most places.'

'How can you stand it?' Thorn asked. 'I'm sweating right now.'

'Well, in really hot weather you can go indoors. We can make a building as warm or cool as we please.'

'D'you mean to say I'd have to just *sit*, till the weather made up its own confounded mind to change?' Thorn barked.

'I remember,' Stepha put in. 'The air you had was muggier'n a marsh. Earth like that?'

'Depends on where you are,' Falkayn said. 'And actually, we control the weather cycle pretty well on Earth.'

'Worse and worse,' Thorn complained. 'If I'm to sweat, I sure don't want to do it at somebody else's whim.' He brightened. 'Unless you can fight them when you don't like what they're up to?'

'Good Lord, no!' Falkayn said. 'Fighting is forbidden on Earth.'

Thorn slumped back against the rail and gaped at him. 'But what am I going to do then?'

'Uh ... well, you'll have to go back to school for a number of years. That's Earth years, about five times as long as Ikra-nankan. You'll have to learn, oh, mathematics and natural philosophy and history and—— Now that I think about it, the total is staggering. Don't worry, though. They'll find you work, once you've finished your studies.'

'What sort of work?'

'M-m-m, couldn't be too highly paid, I fear. Not even on a colony planet. The colonies aren't primitive, you realize, and you need a long education to handle the machines we use. I suppose you could become a'—Falkayn groped for native words—'a cook or a machine tender's helper or something.'

'Me, who ruled a city?' Thorn shook his head and mumbled to himself.

'You must have some fighting to do,' Stepha protested.

'Yes, unfortunately,' Falkayn said.

'Why "unfortunately"? You're a strange one.' Stepha turned to Thorn. 'Cheer up, Cap'n. We'll be soldiers. If Great Granther didn't lie, those places are stuffed with plunder.'

'Soldiers aren't allowed to plunder,' Falkayn said. They

looked positively shocked. 'And anyway, they also need more skill with machines than I think you can acquire at your present ages.'

'Balls ... of ... fire,' Thorn whispered.

'We've got to hold a phratry council about this,' said a guard in an alarmed voice.

Thorn straightened and took command of himself again. 'That wouldn't be easy right now,' he pointed out. 'We'll carry on as we were. When the siege is broken and we get back in touch with our people, we'll see what we want to do. Ursala, you and I were going to organize that liaison corps between our two forces.'

'Yes, I suppose we must,' said the King reluctantly. He dipped his head to Falkayn. 'Farewell. I trust we can talk later at length.' Thorn's good-bye was absent-minded; he was in a dark brown study. They wandered off.

Stepha leaned her elbows on the rail. She wore quite a brief tunic, and her hair was unbound. A breeze fluttered the bronze locks. Though her expression had gone bleak, Falkayn remembered certain remarks she had let drop earlier. His pulse accelerated. Might as well enjoy his imprisonment.

'I didn't mean to make Earth sound that bad,' he said. 'You'd like it. A girl so good-looking, with so exotic a background— you'd be a sensation.'

She continued to stare at the watchtowers. The scorn in her voice dismayed him. 'Sure, a novelty. For how long?'

'Well—— My dear, to me, you will always be a most delightful novelty.'

She didn't respond. 'What the deuce are you so gloomy about all of a sudden?' Falkayn asked.

Her lips compressed. 'What you said. When you rescued me, I reckoned you for a big piece of man. Should've seen right off, nothing to that fracas, when you'd a monster to ride and a, a *machine* in your hand! And unfair, maybe, to call you a rotten zandaraman. You never were trained to ride. But truth, you are no good in the saddle. Are you good for anything, without a machine to help?'

'At least one thing,' he tried to grin.

She shrugged. 'I'm not mad, David. Only dis'pointed. My fault, truth, for not seeing before now 'twas just your being different made you look so fine.'

My day, Falkayn groaned to himself.

'Reckon I'll go see if Hugh's off duty,' Stepha said. 'You can look 'round some more if you want.'

Falkayn rubbed his chin as he stared after her. Beginning bristles scratched back. Naturally, this would be the time when his last dose of antibeard enzyme started to wear off. Outside the ship, there probably wasn't a razor on all Ikrananka. He was in for days of itchiness, until the damned face fungus had properly sprouted.

The girl had not spoken without justification, he thought bitterly. He had indeed been more sinned against than sinning, this whole trip. If Chee Lan and Adzel had come to grief, the guilt was his; he was the captain. In another four months, if they hadn't reported back, the travel plan they'd left at base would be unsealed, and a rescue expedition dispatched. That might bail him out, assuming he was still alive. At the moment, he wasn't sure he wanted to be.

A shout spun him around. He stared over the rail and the city wall. Thunder seemed to crash through his head.

Adzel!

The Wodenite came around the bend of the lower road at full gallop. Scales gleamed along the rippling length of him; he roared louder than the waterfall. A shriek lifted from the enemy camp. Drums rolled from Rangakora's towers. Men and Ikranankans swarmed beweaponed to the parapets.

'Demons alive!' gasped at Falkayn's back. He glanced, and saw his two guards goggling ashen-fashed at the apparition. It flashed through him: a chance to escape. He slipped towards the door.

Stepha returned. She seized his arm and threw her weight against him. 'Look aware!' she yelled. The men broke from their paralysis, drew blade, and herded him back. He felt sick.

'What's going on?' he choked. 'Where's the spaceship?'

Now he could only watch. A Katandaran cavalry troop rallied and charged. Adzel didn't stop. He ploughed on through. Lances splintered against his armour, riders spilled and zandaras fled in panic. He might have been halted by catapult fire. But the field artillery had not been briefed on extraplanetary beings, nor on what to do when an actual, visible demon made straight for them. They abandoned their posts.

Terror spread like hydrogen. Within minutes, Jadhadi's army

was a howling, struggling mob, headed downhill for home. Adzel chased them awhile, to make sure they kept going. When the last infantry soldier had scuttled from view, the Wodenite came back, across a chaos of dropped weapons, plunging zandaras and karikuts, idle wagons, empty tents, smouldering fires. His tail wagged gleefully.

Up to the gates he trotted. Falkayn couldn't hear what he bellowed but could well imagine. The human's knees felt liquid. He struggled for air. No time seemed to pass before a messenger hastened out to say he was summoned. But the walk through hollow streets—Rangakora's civilian population had gone indoors to wail at the gods—and on to the parapet, took forever.

The wait calmed him somewhat, though. When he stood with Thorn, Ursala, Stepha, and a line of soldiers, looking down on his friend, he could again think. This close, he saw Chee's furry form on the great shoulders. At least they were both alive. Tears stung his eyes.

'David!' bawled Adzel. 'I hoped so much you'd be here. Why don't they let me in?'

'I'm a prisoner,' Falkayn called back in Latin.

'No, you don't,' said Thorn. 'Talk Anglic or Katandaran, that I can understand, or keep mouthshut.'

Because the spearheads bristling around looked so infernally sharp, Falkayn obeyed. It added to the general unpleasantness of life that everybody should learn how his ship was immobilized. And now he really was stuck here. His gullet lumped up.

Thorn said eagerly: 'Hoy, look, we've got common cause. Let's march on Haijakata together, get that flying thing of yours away from them, and then on to Katandara.'

Ursula's tone grew wintry. 'In other words, my city is to be ruled from there in spite of everything.'

'We've got to help our brethren,' Thorn said.

'I intercepted a courier on my way here,' Adzel told them. 'I am afraid I lost merit by frightening him, but we read his dispatches. The Ershoka who were in town but not in the Iron House assembled and attacked from the rear. Thus combined, their forces crumpled the siege lines and fought their way out of the city. They took over—what was the name now? a Chakoran village—and sent for outlying families to come and be safer. Jadhadi does not dare attack them with his available troops. He is calling for reinforcements from the various Imperial garrisons.'

Thorn tugged his beard. 'If I know my people,' he said, 'they'll march out before that can happen. And where would they march but to us?' His countenance blazed. 'By Destruction! We need but sit, and we'll get everything I wanted!'

'Besides,' Stepha warned, 'we couldn't trust Falkayn. Soon's he got back that flying machine of his, he could do what he felt like.' She gave the Hermetian a hostile look. 'Reckon you'd bite on us.'

'The one solitary thing I wish for is to get away from this planet,' he argued. 'Very far away.'

'But afterwards? Your stinking merchant's interest does lie with Katandara. And could well be others like you, coming later on. No, best we keep you, my buck.' She leaned over the battlements, cupped her hands, and shouted: 'Go away, you, or we'll throw your friend's head at you!'

Chee stood up between the spinal plates. Her thin voice barely reached them through the cataract's boom: 'If you do that, we'll pull your dungheap of a town down around your ears.'

'Now, wait, wait,' Ursala pleaded. 'Let us be reasonable.'

Thorn ran an eye along the faces crowding the wall. Sweat glistened and tongues moistened lips; beaks hung open and ruffs drooped. 'We can't well sally against him,' he said *sotto voce*. 'Our people are too scared right now, and besides, most zandaras would bolt. But we can keep him at his distance. When the whole phratry arrives—yes, that'll be too many. We can wait.'

'And keep me alive for a bargaining counter,' said Falkayn quickly.

'Sure, sure,' Stepha fleered.

Thorn issued an order. Engineers began to wind catapult skeins. Adzel heard the creaking and drew back out of range. 'Have courage, David!' he called. 'We shall not abandon you.'

Which was well meant but not so useful, Falkayn reflected in a grey mood. Thorn not only desired to keep Rangakora he had to, for the sake of his kinfolk. The Ershoka had been sufficiently infected by the chronic suspiciousness of Katandara that they'd never freely let Falkayn back in his ship. Rather, they'd make him a permanent hostage, against the arrival of other spacecraft. And once firmly established here, they'd doubtless try to overthrow the Deodakh hegemony. Might well succeed, too. The most Falkayn could hope for was that a rescue expedition could strike a bargain; in exchange for him, the League would stay off Ikrananka. The treaty would be observed, he knew; it didn't pay to trade with a hostile population. And when he learned this market must not merely be shared, but abandoned, van Rijn would bounce Falkayn clear to Luna.

What a fine bouillabaisse he'd got himself into!

His guards hustled him off towards the palace apartment which was his jail. Adzel collected what few draft animals had not broken loose from their tethers, for a food supply, and settled down to his one-dragon siege of the city.

X

Chee Lan had no trouble reaching the east wall unseen. The Katandarans hadn't been close enough to trample the shrubs, nor had the Rangakorans gone out to prune and weed. There was plenty of tall growth to hide her approach. Crouched at the foot, she looked up a sheer dark cliff; a cloud scudded through the purple sky above and made it seem toppling on her. Pungent tarry smells of vegetation filled her nose. The wind blew cold. From the opposite side she heard the cataract roar.

Here in the shadow it was hard to make out details. But slowly she picked a route. As usual, the stones were not dressed except where they fitted together, and the rains and frosts of several thousand years had pitted them. She could climb.

Her sinews tautened. She sprang, grabbed finger- and toe-holds, reached for the next and the next. Chill and rough, the surface scratched her belly. She was handicapped by her loot from the empty camp, two daggers at her waist and a rope coiled around her. Nonetheless, unemotionally, she climbed.

When her fingers grasped the edge of a crenel, she did hesitate a moment. Guards were posted at intervals here. But—— She pulled herself over, hunched down between the merlons, and peeped out. Some metres to left and right she saw the nearest watchers. One was human, one Ikranankan. Their cloaks fluttered as wildly as the banners atop the more distant towers. But they were looking straight outward.

Quick, now! Chee darted across the parapet. As expected— any competent military engineer would have designed things thus—several metres of empty paving stretched between the inside foot of the wall and the nearest houses. With commerce to the outer world suspended, no traffic moved on it. She didn't stop to worry about chance passers-by, but spidered herself down with reckless speed. The last few metres she dropped. Low gravity was helpful.

Once she had streaked into the nearest alley, she took a while to pant. No longer than she must, though. She could hear footfalls and croaking voices. Via a window frame, she got on to the roof of one house.

There she had a wide view. The bloated red sun slanted long rays over streets where gratifyingly few natives were abroad. Hours after Adzel's coming, they must still be too shaken to work. *Let's see . . . David's sure to be kept in the palace, which must be that pretentious object in the middle of town.* She plotted a path, roof to roof as much as possible, crossing the narrowest lanes when they were deserted, and started off.

Wariness cost time; but cheap at the price. The worst obstacle lay at the end. Four spacious avenues bordered the royal grounds, and they were far from deserted. Besides a trickle of workaday errands, they milled with anxious clusters of Ikranankans, very humanlike in seeking what comfort they could get from the near presence of their rulers. Chee spent a couple of hours behind a chimney, studying the scene, before a chance came by.

A heavy wagon was trundling down the street in front of her at the same time as an aged native in sweeping official robes was headed for the palace. Chee leaped down into the gut between this house and the next. She had counted on buildings being crowded. The karikuts clopped past, the wagon creaked and rumbled behind, its bulk screened her. She zipped underneath it and trotted along on all fours. At closest approach, she had about three metres to go to the Ikranankan gaffer. If she was noticed, the gardens were immediately beyond, with lots of hedges and bowers to skulk in. But she hoped that wouldn't be necessary.

It wasn't, since she crossed the open space in half a second flat. Twitching up the back of the old fellow's skirt, she dived beneath and let the cloth fall over her.

He stopped. 'What? What?' she heard, and turned with him, careful not to brush against his shins. 'Krrr-ek? What? Swear I felt ... no, no ... uk-k-k. ...' He shambled on. When she judged they were well into the grounds, Chee abandoned him for the nearest bush Through the leaves she saw him stop again, feel his garments, scratch his head, and depart mumbling.

So far, so good. The next stage could really get merry. Chee prowled the garden for some while, hiding as only a forester can hide when anyone passed near, until the permutations of perambulation again offered her an opportunity.

She had worked her way around to a side of the palace. A stand of pseudobamboo veiled her from it, with a hedge at right angles for extra cover, and nobody was in sight: except a native guard, scrunching down the gravel path in breastplate and greaves. He ought to know. Chee let him go by and pounced. A flying tackle brought him on his stomach with a distressing clatter. At once she was on his shoulders, left arm choking off his breath and right hand drawing a knife.

She laid the point against his throat and whispered cheerfully: 'One squeak out of you, my friend, and you're cold meat. I wouldn't like that either. You can't be very tasty.'

Slackening the pressure, she let him turn his head till he glimpsed her, and decided to pardon the gargle he emitted. It must be disturbing to be set on by a grey-masked demon, even a small one. 'Quick, now, if you want to live,' she ordered. 'Where is the prisoner Ershokh?'

'Ak-k-k—uk-k-k——'

'No stalling.' Chee pinked him. 'You know who I mean. The tall yellow-haired beardless person. Tell me or die!'

'He—he is in——' Words failed. The soldier made a gallant attempt to rise. Chee throttled him momentarily insensible. She had taken care, while at Haijakata, to get as good a knowledge of Ikranankan anatomy as was possible without dissection. And this was a comparatively feeble species.

When the soldier recovered, he was quite prepared to co-operate. Or anyhow, he was too terrified to invent a lie; Chee had done enough interrogation in her time to be certain of that. She got exact directions for finding the suite. Two Ershoka watched it, but outside a solid bronze door.

'Thank you,' she said, and applied pressure again. Cutting some lengths of rope and a strip of his cloak for a gag, she immobilized her informant and rolled him in among the plumed stalks. He was regaining consciousness as she left. 'You'll be found before too long, I'm sure,' she said. 'Probably before they water the garden.'

She slipped off. Now there was indeed need to hurry. And she couldn't. Entering the capitol of this damned nightless city un-noticed made everything that had gone before look like tiddlywinks. An open window gave access to a room she had seen was empty. But then it was to get from tapestry to settee to ornamental urn to statue, while aleph-null servants and guards and bureaucrats and trades-people and petitioners and sisters and cousins and aunts went back and forth through the long corridors; and take a ramp at the moment it was deserted, in the hope that no one would appear before she found her next hiding place; and on and on—— By the time she reached the balcony she wanted, whose slender columns touched the eaves, even her nerves were drawn close to breaking.

She shinnied up, swung herself over the roof edge, and crawled to a point directly above a window that must belong to Falkayn's apartment. Her prisoner had told her it was between the second and third north-side balconies. And two storeys down, with a wall too smooth for climbing. But she had plenty of rope left, and plenty of chimneys poked from the tiles. She made a loop around the nearest. After a glance to be sure no one was gawping from the ground, she slid.

Checked, she peered in the window. An arabesque grille of age-greened bronze would let her pass, but not a man. Why hadn't she thought to search the Katandaran litter for a hack-saw? She reached through and rapped on the glass behind. There was no response. With a remark that really shouldn't have come out of such fluffy white fur, she broke the pane with a dagger butt and crept inside. While she looked around, she pulled in the rope.

The rooms were well furnished, if you were an Ikranankan. For a man they were dark and cold, and Falkayn lay asleep curled up like a hawser. Chee padded to the bed, covered his mouth—humans were so ridiculously emotional—and shook him.

He started awake. 'Huh? Whuff, whoo, ugh!' Chee laid a finger on her muzzle. His eyes cleared, he nodded and she let him go.

'Chee!' he breathed shakenly. His hands closed around hers. 'How the devil?'

'I sneaked in, you idiot. Did you expect me to hire a band? Now let's figure some way to get you out.'

Falkayn gasped. 'You mean you don't know?'

'How should I?'

He rose to his feet, but without vigour. 'Me too,' he said.

Chee's courage sank. She slumped down on the floor.

With a rush of love, Falkayn stooped, lifted her, and cradled her in his arms. 'Just knowing you tried is enough,' he murmured.

Her tail switched. The vinegar returned to her voice. 'Not for me it isn't.' After a moment: 'All we need is an escape from here. Then we can wait in the outback for the relief expedition.'

Falkayn shook his head. 'Sorry, no. How'd we get in touch? They'd spot *Muddlin' Through*, sure, but as soon as we reached that area, we'd be filled with ironmongery, so Jadhadi could throw the blame for our disappearance on Thorn. He'd probably get away with it, too. Think how these natives would stick together in the face of an alien.'

Chee reflected a while. 'I could try to slip within voice range of our ship's detectors.'

'M-m-m.' Falkayn ran a hand through his hair. 'You know you'd never manage that, as witness the fact you didn't try in the first place. No cover worth itemizing.' Rage welled in him. 'Damn that chance that Adzel's transceiver got smashed! If we could have called the ship——'

And then his mind rocked. He stumbled back and sat down on the bed. Chee jumped clear and watched with round yellow eyes. The silence grew huge.

Until Falkayn smashed fist into palm and said, 'Judas on Mercury! Yes!'

The discipline of his boyhood came back. He'd been drugged and kidnapped and given one figurative belly kick after another, and been unable to do a thing about it, and that had shattered him. Now, as the idea took shape, he knew he was a man yet. The possibility that he would get killed mattered not a hoot in vacuum. Under the thrumming consciousness, his soul laughed for joy.

'Listen,' he said. 'You could get out of town again, even if I can't. But your chance of surviving very long, and Adzel's, wouldn't be worth much. Your chance of being rescued would be still smaller. If you're willing to throw the dice right now—go for broke—then——'

Chee did not argue with his plan. She pondered, made a few calculations in her head, and nodded. 'Let us.'

Falkayn started to put on his clothes but paused. 'Wouldn't you like a nap first?'

'No, I feel quite ready. Yourself?'

Falkayn grinned. His latest sleep had restored him. The blood tingled in his flesh. 'Ready to fight elephants, my friend.'

Dressed, he went to the door and pounded on it. 'Hey!' he shouted. 'Help! Emergency! Urgency! Top secret! Priority One! Handle with care! Open the door, you scratchbrains!'

A key clicked in the lock. The door swung wide. A large Ershokh stood in the entrance with drawn sword. His companion waited a discreet distance behind. 'Well?'

'I've got to see your boss,' Falkayn babbled. Anything to get within arm's length. He stepped closer, waving his hands. 'I've thought of something terrible.'

'What?' growled from the beard.

'This.' Falkayn snatched at the man's cloak, on either side of the brooch, with wrists crossed. He pulled his hands together. The backs of them closed on his victim's larynx. Simultaneously, Chee hurtled into the hall and over the clothes of the other guard.

Falkayn's man slashed downward with his sabre, but Falkayn's leg wasn't there any more. That knee had gone straight up. The soldier doubled in anguish. Then strangulation took him. Falkayn let him fall and bounded to the next Ershokh.

Chee swarmed on that one, and had so far kept him from uttering more than a few snorts and grunts, but she couldn't overpower him. Falkayn chopped with the blade of a hand. The guard collapsed.

He wasn't badly injured either, Falkayn saw with some relief. He stooped, to drag them both inside and don a uniform. But there had been too much ruckus. A female Ikranankan stuck her head out of an entrance further down the hall and began to scream. Well, you couldn't have everything. Falkayn grabbed a sabre and sped off. Chee loped beside him. The screams hit high C and piled on the decibels.

Down yonder ramp! A courtier was headed up. Falkayn stiff-armed him and continued. Several more were in the corridor below. He waved his sword. 'Blood and bones!' he yelled. 'Boo!' They cleared a path, falling over each other and clamouring.

And here was the electrical shop. Falkayn stormed in. Across workbenches crammed with quaintly designed apparatus, two scientists and several assistants gaped at him. 'Everybody out,' Falkayn said. When they didn't move fast enough, he paddled the Grand Chief Philosopher of Royal Rangakora with the flat of his blade. They got the message. He slammed the door and shot the bolt.

The uproar came through that heavy metal, louder by the minutes, voices, feet, weapon clatter, and alarm drums. He glanced around. The windows gave no access, but another door opened at the far end of the long room. He bolted that, too, and busied himself shoving furniture against it. If he piled everything there that wasn't nailed down and used Chee's rope to secure the mass further, he could probably make it impassable to anyone short of the army engineers. And they wouldn't likely be called, when the other approach looked easier.

He ended his task and returned, breathing hard. Chee had also been busy. She squatted on the floor amid an incredible clutter of batteries and assorted junk, coiling a wire into a helix while she frowned at a condenser jar. She could do no more than guess at capacitances, resistances, inductances, voltages, and amperages. However, the guess would be highly educated.

Both doors trembled under fists and boots. Falkayn watched the one he had not reinforced. He stretched, rocked a little on his feet, willed the tension out of his muscles. Behind him, Chee fiddled with a spark gap; he heard the slight frying noise.

A human voice bawled muffled: 'Clear the way! Clear the way! We'll break the obscenity thing down, if you'll get out of our obscenity way!' Chee didn't bother to look from her work.

The racket outside died. After a breathless moment, feet pounded and a weight smashed at the bronze. It rang and buckled. Again the ram struck. This time a sound of splintering was followed by hearty curses. Falkayn grinned. They must have used a balk of glued-together timber, which had proved less than satisfactory. He went to a gap where the door had been bent a little clear of the jamb and had a look. Several Ershoka could be seen, in full canonicals, fury alive on their faces. 'Peekaboo,' Falkayn said.

'Get a smith!' He thought he recognized Hugh Padrick's cry. 'You, there, get an obscenity smith. And hammers and cold chisels.'

That would do the job, but time would be needed. Falkayn returned to help Chee. 'Think we've got ample juice in those batteries?' he asked.

'Oh yes.' She kept eyes at the single workbench not manning the barricade, where she improvised a telegraph key out of scrap metal. 'Only four hundred kilometres or so, right? Even that slue-footed Adzel made it in a few standard days. What worries me is getting the right frequency.'

'Well, estimate as close as you can, and then use different values. You know, make a variable contact along a wire.'

'Of course I know! Didn't we plan this in your rooms? Stop yattering and get useful.'

'I'm more the handsome type,' said Falkayn. He wielded a pair of pliers awkwardly—they weren't meant for a human grasp—to hook the batteries in series. And a Leyden jar, though you really should call it a Rangakora jar. . . .

The door belled and shuddered. Falkayn kept half his mind in that direction. Probably somewhat less than an hour had passed since he crashed out. Not a hell of a lot of time to play Heinrich Hertz. But Chee had put on the last touches. She squatted before the ungainly sprawl of apparatus, tapped her key, and nodded. A spark sizzled across a gap. She went into a rattle of League code. Invisible, impalpable, the radio waves surged forth.

Now everything depended on her finding the waveband of the late lamented transceivers, somewhere among those she could blindly try. She hadn't long, either. The door would give way in another minute or two. Falkayn left her for his post.

The bolt sprang loose. The door sagged open. An Ershokh pushed in, sword a-shimmer.

Falkayn crossed blades. Steel chimed. As expected, the man was a sucker for scientific fencing. Falkayn could have killed him in thirty seconds. But he didn't want to. Besides, while he held this chap in the doorway, no others could get past. 'Having fun?' he called across the whirring edges. Rage snarled back at him.

Dit-dit-dah-dit. . . . Come to Rangakora. Land fifty metres outside the south gate. Dit-dah-dah. Clash, rattle, clang!

The Ershokh got his back to the jamb. Abruptly he sidled past the entrance, and another man was there. Falkayn held the first one by sheer energy while his foot lashed out in an epical savate kick. The second man yelped agony and lurched back into the arms of his fellows. Whirling, Falkayn deflected the blade of the first one with a quick beat and followed with a glide. His point sank into the forearm. He twisted deftly, ripping through tissue, and heard the enemy sabre clank on the floor.

Not stopping to pull his own weapon free, he turned and barely avoided the slash of a third warrior. He took one step forward and grabbed, karate-style. A tug—a rather dreadful snapping noise—the Ershokh went to his knees, grey-faced and broken-armed, and Falkayn had his blade. It rang on the next.

The Hermetian's eyes flicked from side to side. The man he had cut was hunched over. Blood spurted from his wound, an impossibly brilliant red. The other casualty sat slumped against the wall. Falkayn looked into the visage that confronted him (a downy-cheeked kid, as he'd been himself not so long ago) and said, 'If you'll hold off a bit, these busters can crawl out and get help.'

The boy cursed and hacked at him. He caught the sword with his own in a bind and held fast. 'Do you want your chum to bleed to death?' he asked. 'Relax. I won't bite you. I'm really quite peaceful as long as you feed me.'

He disengaged and poised on guard. The boy stared at him an instant, then backed off, into the crowd of humans and Ikranankans that eddied in the corridor behind him. Falkayn nudged the hurt men with a foot. 'Go on,' he said gently. They crept past him, into a descending hush.

Hugh Padrick trod to the forefront. His blade was out, but held low. His features worked. 'What're you about?' he rasped.

'Very terrible magic,' Falkayn told him. 'We'll save trouble all around if you surrender right now.'

Dit-dah-dah-dah!

'What do you want of us?' Padrick asked.

'Well, to start with, a long drink. After that we can talk.' Falkayn tried to moisten his lips, without great success. Damn this air! No wonder the natives didn't go in for rugs. Life would become one long series of static shocks. Maybe that was what had first got the Rangakorans interested in electricity.

'We might talk, yes.' Padrick's sabre drooped further. Then in a blinding split second it hewed at Falkayn's calf.

The Hermetian's trained body reacted before his mind had quite engaged gears. He leaped straight up, under two-thirds of a Terrestrial gee. The whetted metal hissed beneath his boot soles. He came down before it could withdraw. His weight tore the weapon from Padrick's grasp. 'Naughty!' he cried. His left fist rocketed forward. Padrick went on his bottom, nose a red ruin. Falkayn made a mental note that he be charged through that same nose for plastic surgery, if and when van Rijn's factors got around to offering such services.

An Ikranankan poked a spear at him. He batted it aside and took it away. That gained him a minute.

He got another while Padrick reeled erect and vanished in the mob. And still another passed while they stared and shuffled their feet. Then he heard Bobert Thorn trumpet, 'Clear the way! Crossbows!'—and knew that the end was on hand.

The crowd parted, right and left, out of his view. Half a dozen Ikranankan archers tramped into sight and took their stance before him, across the hall. But he put on the most daredevil grin in his repertory when Stepha ran ahead of them.

She stopped and regarded him with wonder. 'David,' she breathed. 'No other man in the world could've—— And I never knew.'

'You do now.' Since her dagger was sheathed, he risked chucking her under the chin. 'They teach us more where I've been than how to handle machines. Not that I'd mind a nice safe armoured vehicle.'

Tears blurred the grey eyes. 'You've got to give up, though,' she begged. 'What more can anyone do?'

'This,' he said, dropped his sabre and grabbed her. She yelled and fought back with considerable strength, but his was greater. He pinioned her in front of him and said to the archers, 'Go away, you ugly people.' The scent of her hair was warm in his nostrils.

Imperturbably, Chee continued to signal.

Stepha stopped squirming. He felt her stiffen in his grip. She said with an iron pride, 'No, go 'head and shoot.'

'You don't mean that!' he stammered.

'Sure do.' She gave him a forlorn smile. 'Think an Ershokh's less ready to die than you are?'

The archers took aim.

Falkayn shook his head. 'Well,' he said, and even achieved a laugh, 'when the stakes are high, people bluff.' A howl, a babble, distant but rising and nearing, didn't seem very important. 'Of course I wouldn't've used you for a shield. I'm an awful liar, and you have better uses.' He kissed her. She responded. Her hands moved over his back and around his neck.

Which was fun, and moreover gained a few extra seconds. . . .

'The demon, the demon!' Men and Ikranankans pelted by. A thunderclap was followed by the sound of falling masonry.

Stepha didn't join the stampede. But she pulled free, and the dagger flashed into her hand. 'What's that?' she cried.

Falkayn gusted the air from his lungs. His head swam. Somehow he kept his tone level. 'That,' he said, 'was our ship. She landed and took Adzel on for a pilot, and now he's aloft, losing merit but having a ball with a mild demonstration of strength.' He took her hand. 'Come on, let's go out where he can see us and get taken aboard. I'm overdue for a dry martini.'

XI

The conference was held on neutral ground, an autonomous Chakoran village between the regions claimed of old by Katandara and Rangakora. (Autonomy meant that it paid tribute to both of them.) Being careful to observe every possible formality and not hurt one party's feelings more than another's, Falkayn let its head preside at the opening ceremonies. They were interminable. His eyes must needs wander, around the reddish gloom of the council hut, over the patterns of the woven walls, across the local males who squatted with their spears as a sort of honour guard, and back to the large stone table at which the conference was benched. He wished he could be outside. A cheerful bustle and chatter drifted to him through the open door, where Adzel lay so patiently; the soldiers who had escorted their various chiefs here were fraternizing.

You couldn't say that for the chiefs themselves. King Ursala had finished droning through a long list of his grievances and desires, and now fidgeted while Emperor Jadhadi embarked on his own. Harry Smit glared at Bobert Thorn, who glared back. The Ershoka senior still blamed his phratry's troubles on the rebellion. His honour the mayor of his town rustled papers, doubtless preparing an introduction to the next harangue.

Well, Falkayn thought, *this was your idea, lad. And your turn has got to come sometime.*

When the spaceship hovered low above them and a giant's voice boomed forth, suggesting a general armistice and treaty-making, the factions had agreed. They didn't know they had a choice. Falkayn would never have fired on them, but he saw no reason to tell them that. No doubt Chee Lan, seated before the pilot board in the sky overhead, had more to do now with keeping matters orderly than Adzel's overwhelming presence. But why did they have to make these speeches? The issues were simple. Jadhadi wanted Rangakora and felt he could no longer trust the Ershoka. A large number of the Ershoka wanted Rangakora, too; the rest wished for the status quo ante, or a reasonable substitute, but didn't see how to get it; each group felt betrayed by the other. Ursala wanted all foreign devils out of his town, plus a whopping indemnity for damages suffered. And Falkayn wanted—well, he'd tell them. He lit his pipe and consoled himself with thoughts of Stepha, who awaited him in the village. Quite a girl, that, for recreation if not for a lifetime partner.

An hour passed.

'—the distinguished representative of the merchant adventurers from Beyond-the-World, Da'id 'Alk'ayn.'

His boredom evaporated. He rose to his feet in a tide of eagerness that he could barely mask with a smile and a casual drawl.

'Thank you, most noble,' he said. 'After listening to these magnificent orations, I won't even try to match them. I'll state my position in a few simple words.' That should win him universal gratitude!

'We came here in good faith,' he said, 'offering to sell you goods such as I have demonstrated at unbelievably reasonable prices. What happened? We were assaulted with murderous intent. I myself was imprisoned and humiliated. Our property was illegally sequestered. And frankly, most nobles, you can be plaguey thankful none of us was killed.' He touched his blaster. 'Remember, we do represent a great power, which has a fixed policy of avenging harm done to its people.' *When expedient,* he added, and saw how Jadhadi's ruff rose with terror and Smit's knuckles stood white on his fist.

'Relax, relax,' he urged. 'We're in no unfriendly mood. Besides, we want to trade, and you can't trade during a war. That's one reason I asked for this get-together. If the differences between us can be settled, why, that's to the League's advantage. And to yours, too. You do want what we have to sell, don't you?

'So.' He leaned forward, resting his fingertips on the table. 'I think a compromise is possible. Everybody will give up something, and get something, and as soon as trade starts you'll be so wealthy that what you lost today will make you laugh. Here's a rough outline of the general agreement I shall propose.

'First, Rangakora will be guaranteed complete independence, but drop claims to indemnification——'

'Most noble!' Jadhadi and Ursala sprang up and yelled into each other's beaks.

Falkayn waved them to silence. 'I yield for a question to King Ursala,' he said, or the equivalent thereof.

'Our casualties ... crops ruined ... dependent villages looted ... buildings destroyed——' Ursala stopped, collected himself, and said with more dignity: 'We were not the aggressors.'

'I know,' Falkayn said, 'and I sympathize. However, weren't you prepared to fight for your freedom? Which you now have. That should be worth something. Don't forget, the League will be a party to any treaty we arrive at here. If that treaty guarantees your independence, the League will back the guarantee.' *Not strictly true. Only Solar Spice & Liquors is to be involved. Oh, well, makes no practical difference.* He nodded at Jadhadi. 'By my standards, most noble, you should pay for the harm you did. I'm passing that in the interests of reconciliation.'

'But my borders,' the Emperor protested. 'I must have strong borders. Besides, I have a rightful claim to Rangakora. My great ancestor, the first Jadhadi——'

Falkayn heroically refrained from telling him what to do to his great ancestor and merely answered in his stiffest voice: 'Most noble, please consider yourself let off very lightly. You did endanger the lives of League agents. You cannot expect the League not to exact some penalty. Yielding Rangakora is mild indeed.' He glanced at his blaster, and Jadhadi shivered. 'As for your border defences,' Falkayn said, 'the League can help you there. Not to mention the fact that we will sell you firearms. You won't need your Ershoka any more.'

Jadhadi sat down. One could almost see the wheels turning in his head.

Falkayn looked at Thorn, who was sputtering. 'The loss of Rangakora is your penalty, too,' he said. 'Your followers did seize me, you know.'

'But what shall we do?' cried old Harry Smit. 'Where shall we go?'

'Earth?' Thorn growled. Falkayn had been laying it on thick of late, how alien Earth was to these castaways. They weren't interested in repatriation any more. He didn't feel guilty about that. They would in fact be happier here, where they had been born. And if they were staying of their own free choice, van Rijn's traders could be trusted to keep silence. In the course of the next generation or two—the secret wouldn't last longer in any event—their children and grandchildren could gradually be integrated into galactic civilization, much as Adzel had been.

'No, if you don't want to,' Falkayn said. 'But what has your occupation been? Soldiering. Some of you keep farms, ranches, or town houses. No reason why you can't continue to do so; foreigners have often owned property in another country. Because what you should do is establish a nation in your own right. Not in any particular territory. Everything hereabouts is already claimed. But you can be an itinerant people. There are precedents, like nomads and gypsies on ancient Earth. Or, more to the point, there are those nations on Cynthia which are trade routes rather than areas. My friend Chee Lan can explain the details of organization to you. As for work—well, you are warriors, and the planet is full of barbarians, and once the League gets started here there are going to be more caravans to protect than fighters to protect them. You can command high prices for your service. You'll get rich.'

He beamed at the assembly. 'In fact, we'll all get rich.'

'Missionaries,' said Adzel into the pensive silence.

'Uh, yes, I'd forgotten,' Falkayn said. 'I don't imagine anyone will object if the ships bring an occasional teacher? We would like to explain our beliefs to you.'

The point looked so minor that no one argued. Yet it would bring more changes in the long run than machinery or medicine. The Katandarans would surely leap at Buddhism, which was infinitely more comfortable than their own demonology. Together with what scientific knowledge trickled down to them, the religion would wean them from their hostility complex. Result: a stable culture with which Nicholas van Rijn could do business.

Falkayn spread his hands. 'That's the gist of my suggestions,' he finished. 'What I propose is what an Earthman once called an equality of dissatisfaction. After which the League traders will bring more satisfaction to you than you can now imagine.'

Thorn bit his lip. He wouldn't easily abandon his dream of kingship. 'Suppose we refuse?' he said.

'Well,' Falkayn reminded him, 'the League has been offended. We must insist on some retribution. My demands are nominal. Aren't they?'

He had them, he knew. The carrot of trade and the stick of war; they didn't know the war threat was pure bluff. They'd make the settlement he wanted.

But of course they'd do so with endless bargaining, recrimination, quibbles over details, speeches—oh, God, the speeches! Falkayn stepped back. 'I realize this is a lot to swallow at once,' he said. 'Why don't we recess? After everyone's had time to think, and had a good sleep, we can talk to more purpose.'

Mainly, he wanted to get back to Stepha. He'd promised her a jaunt in the spaceship; and Adzel and Chee could jolly well wait right here. When the assembly agreed to break, Falkayn was the first one out of the door.

Metal hummed. The viewpoint blazed with stars in an infinite night. That red spark which was Ikrananka's sun dwindled swiftly towards invisibility.

Staring yonder, Falkayn sighed. 'A whole world,' he mused. 'So many lives and hopes. Seems wrong for us to turn them over to somebody else.'

'I know why you would go back,' Chee Lan clipped. 'But Adzel and I have no such reason. We've a long way to Earth——'

Falkayn brightened. He had analogous motives for looking forward to journey's end

'—so move your lazy legs,' Chee said.

Falkayn accompanied her to the saloon. Adzel was already there, arranging chips in neat stacks. 'You know,' Falkayn remarked as he sat down, 'we're a new breed. Not troubleshooters. Trouble twisters. I suspect our whole career is going to be a sequence of ghastly situations that somehow we twist around to our advantage.'

'Shut up and shuffle,' Chee said. 'First jack deals.'

A pair of uninteresting hands went by, and then Falkayn got a flush. He bet. Adzel folded. Chee saw him. The computer raised. Falkayn raised back. Chee quit and the computer raised again. This went on for some time before the draw. Muddlehead must have a good hand, Falkayn knew, but considering its style of play, a flush was worth staying on. He stood pat. The computer asked for one card.

Judas in a nova burst! The damned machine must have got

four of a kind! Falkayn tossed down his own. 'Never mind,' he said. 'Take it.'

Somewhat later, Chee had a similar experience, still more expensive. She made remarks that ionized the air.

Adzel's turn came when the other two beings dropped out. Back and forth the raises went, between dragon and computer, until he finally got nervous and called.

'You win,' said the mechanical voice. Adzel dropped his full house, along with his jaw.

'*What?*' Chee screamed. Her tail stood vertical and bottled. 'You were bluffing?'

'Yes,' said Muddlehead.

'But, no, wait, you play on IOU's and we limit you,' Falkayn rattled. 'You can't bluff!'

'If you will inspect the No. 4 hold,' said Muddlehead, 'you will find a considerable amount of furs, jewels, and spices. While the value cannot be set exactly until the market involved has stabilized, it is obviously large. I got them in exchange for calculating probability tables for the native Gujgengi, and am now prepared to purchase chips in the normal manner.'

'But, but, but you're a machine!'

'I am not programmed to predict how a court would adjudicate title to those articles,' said Muddlehead. 'However, my understanding is that in commercially and individualistically oriented civilization, any legitimate earnings belong to the earner.'

'Good Lord,' said Falkayn weakly, 'I think you're right.'

'You're not a person!' Chee shouted. 'Not even in fact, let alone the law!'

'I acquired those goods in pursuit of the objective you have programmed into me,' Muddlehead replied, 'namely, to play poker. Logic indicates that I can play better poker when properly staked.'

Adzel sighed. 'That's right, too,' he conceded. 'If we want the ship to give us an honest game, we have to take the syllogistic consequences. Otherwise the programming would become impossibly complicated. Besides ... sportsmanship, you know.'

Chee riffled the deck. 'All right,' she said grimly. 'I'll win your stake the hard way.'

Of course she didn't. Nobody did. With that much wealth at

its disposal, Muddlehead could afford to play big. It didn't rake in their entire commissions for Operation Ikrananka in the course of the Earthward voyage, but it made a substantial dent in them.